AIRS ABOVE THE GROUND

The "airs above the ground" are the beautiful leaps and dancing steps made by the white Lipizzan stallions of the Spanish Riding School in Vienna. Vanessa March had always wanted to see them, but little did she realise what part they were to play in the whirlwind of events that started when she left London that calm day.

"Mary Stewart's writing is magical, with every word and phrase carefully chosen for beauty and sound and shape. She also writes a story of breathless excitement whose characters are of blood and bone, heart and mind."—

Los Angeles Times

**Also by the same author,
and available in Coronet Books:**

Airs Above the Ground

Mary Stewart

CORONET BOOKS
Hodder and Stoughton

Copyright © 1965 by Mary Stewart
First printed 1965 by Hodder and Stoughton Ltd

Coronet edition 1967
Thirteenth impression 1985

_____

Set, printed and bound in Great Britain for
Hodder and Stoughton Paperbacks, a
division of Hodder and Stoughton Ltd.,
Mill Road, Dunton Green, Sevenoaks,
Kent (Editorial Office: 47 Bedford
Square, London, WC1 3DP) by
Cox & Wyman Ltd., Reading

ISBN 0 340 02458 5

For my Father
FREDERICK A. RAINBOW

AUTHOR'S NOTE

Since there is only one Spanish Riding School,
any story that I wished to invent about the
white Lipizzan stallions of Vienna must
necessarily involve it. I must put it on record
here that this is not a true story. I am grateful to
the Director of the Spanish Riding School,
Colonel Alois Podhajsky, for generously
allowing me to involve his School—and even
himself—in this story. I should also like to
express my gratitude to Dr H. Lehrner, Director
of the Austrian National Stud at Piber, for his
helpfulness and kindness to me on my visit
there. Finally, and by no means least, my thanks
are due to Mr and Mrs Georg Prachner, of
Kärntnerstrasse, Vienna, not only for the
unstinting help they gave me, but also for the
pains they took to make my visits to Vienna so
rewarding.

M.S.

Chapter One

Nor take her tea without a stratagem.
                    Edward Young: *Love of Fame*

Carmel Lacy is the silliest woman I know, which is saying a good deal. The only reason that I was having tea with her in Harrods on that wet Thursday afternoon was that when she rang me up she had been so insistent that it had been impossible to get out of; and besides, I was so depressed anyway that even tea with Carmel Lacy was preferable to sitting alone at home in a room that still seemed to be echoing with that last quarrel with Lewis. That I had been entirely in the right, and that Lewis had been insufferably, immovably, furiously in the wrong was no particular satisfaction, since he was now in Stockholm, and I was still here in London, when by rights we should have been lying on a beach together in the Italian sunshine, enjoying the first summer holiday we had been able to plan together since our honeymoon two years ago. The fact that it had rained almost without ceasing ever since he had gone hadn't done anything to mitigate his offence; and when, on looking up 'Other People's Weather' in the *Guardian* each morning, I found Stockholm enjoying a permanent state of sunshine, and temperatures somewhere in the seventies, I was easily able to ignore the reports of a wet, thundery August in Southern Italy, and concentrate steadily on Lewis's sins and my own grievances.

"What are you scowling about?" asked Carmel Lacy.

"Was I? I'm sorry. I suppose I'm just depressed with the weather and everything. I certainly didn't mean to glower at you! Do go on. Did you decide to buy it in the end?"

"I haven't made up my mind. It's always so terribly difficult to decide . . ." Her voice trailed away uncertainly as she contemplated the plate of cakes, her hand poised between a meringue and an éclair. "But you know what they're like

9

nowadays, they won't keep things for you. If I wait much longer they'll simply sell it, and when that happens, one realises one's really wanted it like mad all along."

And if you wait much longer, I thought, as she selected the éclair, it won't fit you any more. But I didn't think it unkindly; plumpness suits Carmel Lacy, who is one of those blonde, pretty women whose looks depend on the fair, soft colouring which seems to go on indestructibly into middle age, and to find a whole new range of charm when the fair hair turns white.

Carmel—whose hair was still a rather determined shade of gold—had been my mother's contemporary at school. Her kind of prettiness had been fashionable then, and her good-tempered softness had made her popular; her nickname, according to my mother, had been Caramel, which seemed appropriate. She had not been a close friend of mother's at school, but the two girls were thrown together in the holidays by the nearness of their families, and by professional connections between them. Carmel's father had owned and trained racehorses, while my grandfather, who was a veterinary surgeon, had been, so to speak, surgeon in attendance. Soon after the girls left school their ways parted: my mother married her father's young partner and stayed in Cheshire; but Carmel left home for London, where she married 'successfully', that is, she acquired a wealthy London banker whose dark, florid good looks told you exactly the kind of man he would be in his forties, safely ensconced in the Jaguar belt with three carefully spaced children away at carefully chosen schools. But the marriage had not worked out. Carmel, to all appearances the kind of soft maternal creature who, you would have sworn, would make the ideal wife and mother, combined with this a possessiveness so clinging that it had threatened to drown her family like warm treacle. The eldest girl had gone first, off into the blue with a casually defiant announcement that she had got a job in Canada. The second daughter had torn herself loose at nineteen, and followed her Air Force husband to Malta without a backward look. The husband had gone next, leaving a positive embarrassment of riches in the way of evidence for the divorce. Which left the youngest child, Timothy, whom I vaguely remembered meeting around his grandfather's stables during school holidays; a slight, darting, quicksilver boy with a habit of sulky silences, readily forgivable in any child exposed to the full blast of his mother's devotion.

She was moaning comfortably over him now, having disposed (as far as I had been able to follow her) of her dressmaker, her doctor, her current escort, her father, my mother, two more cream cakes and for some reason which I cannot now remember, the Postmaster General . . .

". . . And as a matter of fact, I don't know what to do. He's being so difficult. He knows just how to get on my nerves. Doctor Schwapp was saying only yesterday—"

"Timmy's being difficult?"

"Well, of course. Not that his father wasn't just the same, in fact his father started the whole thing. You'd really think he'd have the decency to keep out of Timmy's life now, wouldn't you, after what he did?"

"Is he coming back into Timmy's life?"

"My dear, that's the whole point. It's all just come out, and that's why I'm so upset. He's been writing to Timmy, quite regularly, imagine, and now apparently he wants him to go and see him."

I said, feeling my way: "He's abroad, isn't he, your—Tim's father?"

"Graham? Yes, he's living in Vienna. We don't write." said Carmel with what was, for her, remarkable brevity.

"And has he seen anything of Timothy since the divorce?" I added awkwardly: "I didn't know what the arrangements were at the time, Aunt Carmel."

She said with an irritation momentarily more genuine than any feeling she had shown up to now: "For goodness' sake don't call me that, it makes me feel a hundred! What do you mean, you don't know what the arrangements were? Everybody knew. You can't tell me your mother didn't tell you *every single detail* at the time."

I said, more coldly than I had meant to: "I wasn't at home, if you remember: I was still in Edinburgh."

"Well, Graham got access, if that's what you mean by 'arrangements'. But he went abroad straight away, and Timmy's never seen him since. I never even knew they were writing... And now this!" Her voice had risen, her blue eyes stared, but I still thought that she sounded aggrieved rather than distressed.

"I tell you, Timmy just burst it on me the other day, boys are so thoughtless, and after all I've been to him, father and mother both, all the poor boy has . . . And all without a word to me! Would you believe such a thing, Vanessa? *Would* you?"

I hesitated, then said more gently: "I'm sorry, but it seems quite natural to me. After all, Timothy hasn't quarrelled with his father, and it seems a pity to keep them apart. I mean, they're bound to want to see each other now and again, and you mustn't think you mean any the less to him because he sometimes feels the need of his father. I—it's none of my business, Carmel, and I'm sorry if I sound a bit pompous, but you did ask me."

"But not to tell me! So underhand! That he should have secrets from me, his mother . . . !" Her voice throbbed. "I feel it, Vanessa, I feel it *here*." She groped for where her heart presumably lay, somewhere behind the ample curve of her left breast, failed to locate it, and abandoning the gesture, poured herself another cup of tea. "You know what it says in the Bible about a thankless child? 'Sharper than a something's paw it is,' or something like that . . .? Well, I can tell you as a mother, that's *exactly* how it feels! Sharper than the whatever-it-is . . . But of course, I can't *expect* you to understand!"

The more than conscious drama which was creeping into Carmel's conversation had dispelled any pity which I might have been feeling for her, and centred it firmly on Timothy. And I was wondering more than ever just where I came in. She had surely not telephoned me so urgently just because she needed an audience; she had her own devoted Bridge set with whom, doubtless, all this had already been gone over; moreover, she had managed to make it clear already that she didn't expect either sympathy or understanding from anyone of my generation.

"I'm sorry, I'm not being unsympathetic, I am trying to understand; but I can't help seeing Timothy's side of it too. He's probably just wild to get a holiday abroad, and this is a marvellous chance. Most boys of his age would grab at any chance to go to Austria. Lord, if I'd had a relative abroad when I was that age, I'd have been plaguing the life out of them to invite me away! If his father really does want to see him—"

"Graham's even sent him the money, and without a *word* to me. You see? As if it wasn't hard enough to hold them, without him *encouraging* them to leave the nest."

I managed not to wince at the phrase. "Well, why not just be sweet about it, and let him go? They always say that's the way to bring them back, don't they? I know how you feel, I do really; but Mummy used to say if you hang on to them too hard, they'll only stay away, once they've managed to get free."

As soon as the words were out I regretted them; I had been thinking only of Timothy, and of somehow persuading Carmel to do what would in the end hurt herself and the son the least; but now I remembered what my mother had been speaking about, and was afraid I had cut rather near the bone. But I need not have worried. People like Carmel are impervious to criticism simply because they can never admit a fault in themselves. She could see no reference to her own triple domestic tragedy, because nothing would ever persuade her to believe that any part of it was her fault; any more than those people who complain of being unloved and unwanted ever pause to ask if they are in fact lovable.

She said: "You haven't any children, of course. Doesn't Lewis want them?"

"Have a heart. We've not been married all that long."

"Two years? Plenty of time to start one. Of course," said Carmel, "he's not at home much, is he?"

"What have my affairs and Lewis's got to do with this?" I asked, so sharply that she abandoned whatever tack she had been starting on.

"Only that if you had children of your own you wouldn't be so gay and glib."

"If I had children I hope I'd have the sense not to put fences round them." That I still spoke sharply was not entirely due to exasperation with Carmel; the trend of this futile conversation was, minute by minute, reminding me of the fences that only a short while ago I had been trying to put round Lewis. I added: "Besides, Timothy isn't a child, he's what? Seventeen? I think it's you who don't understand, Carmel. Boys grow up."

"If they didn't grow *away* so. My baby son, it seems only yesterday—"

"When does his father want him to go?"

"Whenever he likes. And of course he's wild to go." She added, with a spite that sounded suddenly, shockingly genuine: "As a matter of fact I don't mind him *going*. I just don't want him to feel he owes it to Graham."

I counted ten and then said mildly: "Then send him off straight away, and let him think he owes it to you."

"I might, if I thought—" She checked herself, with a quick look I couldn't read. She was fiddling rather consciously again with the bosom of her dress, not her heart this time, but what lay more or less directly over it, the very beautiful sapphire and diamond brooch that had been one of Graham Lacy's guilt offerings to her. Then she spoke in quite a different tone: "As a matter of fact, Vanessa, I'm sure you're right. I *ought* to let him go. One ought to make oneself realise that one's babies grow up, and that one's own feelings hardly matter. After all, they have their lives to live."

I waited. It was coming now, if I was any judge of the signs.

"Vanessa?"

"Yes?"

She pricked her finger on the brooch, said a word which one never imagines that one's mother's generation ever knew, blotted the bead of blood on her table napkin, and met my eyes again, this time with a steely determination which didn't quite match the suppliant's voice she used. "I did wonder if you could help me?"

"I? But how?"

"I really do agree with all you've said, and as a matter of fact it would suit me quite well to have Timmy away for a little while just now, and I really *would like* to let him go, but you see, Timmy is such a *young* seventeen, and he's never been away from home before, except to a school camp, and that's different, isn't it? And I can't go with him myself, because it would be quite *impossible* . . . meeting Graham . . . I don't mean I wouldn't *willingly* sacrifice myself for him, but he was really quite rude when I suggested it, and if he did go off with Graham then *I'd* be on my own, and I hate foreign countries, they're so uncomfortable, besides not speaking English, and you can say what you like, I'm not going to let that child go alone among foreigners. So then I thought of you."

I stared at her. "Now I really don't understand."

"Well, it's quite simple. I knew you'd been going on holiday with Lewis this month, and then he had to go on business instead . . ." Being Carmel, she couldn't, even when she wanted a favour from me, quite repress that look of malicious curiosity . . . "But I did think you'd probably be joining him later, and if you were, then if you and Timmy could travel together it would solve everything, don't you see?"

"No, I don't. If Graham's in Vienna, I can't see how I—"

"The thing is, you'd be *there*, and you've no idea what that would mean to me. I mean, just letting him go off like that to meet Graham, with no idea of what their plans were or anything, and Timmy never writes, you know what boys are, and of course I'd sooner not be in touch with Graham myself, at *all*. But if I knew you and Lewis were somewhere around— I mean, Lewis must know his way about in foreign countries by now, and I expect he's fairly reliable on the whole, isn't he?"

She made it sound a rather doubtful quality. Just then Lewis was at rock bottom in my estimation, but I defended him automatically. "Naturally. But I can't go with Tim, I'm afraid . . . No, Carmel, please listen. It isn't that I wouldn't do it like a shot if I were going to Vienna, but we're going to Italy for our holiday, and besides—"

"But you could join him in Vienna first. It would be more fun, wouldn't it, and salvage a bit of the holiday you've missed?"

I stared at her. "Join him in Vienna? But—what do you mean? We can hardly ask Lewis—"

"If it's the fare, dear," said Carmel, "well, since you'd be sort of convoying Timmy, I'd expect to take care of that."

I said with some asperity: "I think I could just about manage it, thank you."

It was one of Carmel's most irritating characteristics to assume that everyone else was penniless, and that Lewis, who made what seemed to me a very good thing indeed out of his chemical firm, would hardly have been able to afford a car if it hadn't been run on an expense account. But then, my standards were not Carmel's. I added dryly: "I expect I'd be able to swop the tickets."

"Then why not? What's to stop you joining him out there, once his business is finished? It would save him having to come back here for you, and you'd get the extra time, and a bit of extra fun, too. I mean, I'd be happy to stand you both the difference in the fares. But you can see that it did seem the most marvellous piece of luck that Lewis was in Austria, and you might be thinking of joining him? As soon as I knew, I rang you up."

"Carmel. Look, stop these wonderful plans and just listen, will you? I'm not likely to be going to Vienna, now or later, for the simple reason that Lewis is not in Austria. He's in Sweden."

"In Sweden? When did he leave Austria?"

"He didn't. He's been in Sweden all along. In Stockholm, if you want to know. He went on Sunday, and I heard from him on Monday."

I didn't add that the only message in four days had been a very brief cable. Lewis was as capable as I was of holding tightly to a quarrel.

"But you must be wrong. I'll swear it was Lewis. And Molly Gregg was with me, and Angela Thripp, and they both said, 'Oh, that's Lewis March!' And it was."

I said: "I don't know what you're talking about."

"Well, yesterday." She made it sound as if I was merely

being stupid, as I had been over Timothy. "We were shopping, and there was an hour to Angy's train and we wanted somewhere to sit, so we went to the news cinema, and there was something—a disaster or something, I simply can't remember what—but it was Austria somewhere definitely, and Lewis was in it, as plain as plain, and Molly said to me, 'Oh, that's Lewis March!' and Angela said, 'Yes, look, I'm sure it is!' And then the camera went closer and it was, I'm quite certain it was. So of course I thought straight away of you, and I thought you might be going there too, any day, so when Tim got too maddening and sulky about it, I rang you up."

I must have been looking more stupid even than she had been implying. "You're telling me you saw Lewis, my husband Lewis, in a news-reel of something happening in Austria? You can't have done, you must be mistaken."

"I'm never mistaken," said Carmel simply.

"Well, but he can't be—" I stopped. My blank protestations had got even through Carmel's absorption in her own affairs: in her eyes I could see the little flicker of malicious curiosity flaring up again. In imagination I could hear Angela and Molly and Carmel and the rest of them twittering over it . . . "And he's gone off and she didn't know, my dears. Do you suppose they had a row? Another woman, perhaps? Because she obviously hadn't the *faintest* idea where he was . . ."

I glanced at my watch. "Well, I'll have to be going, honestly. I wish I could help you, I do really, but if Lewis has been in Austria somewhere it would just be a flying trip down from Stockholm. You wouldn't believe the way they push him about sometimes. I never know quite where he'll turn up next . . . " I pushed back my chair. "Thanks awfully for the tea, it was lovely seeing you. I must say I'm intrigued about this news-reel . . . Are you absolutely certain that it was Austria? Whereabouts, do you remember? And can't you remember what was happening? You said—a disaster . . ."

"I tell you, I can't remember much about it." She was rather pettishly fishing in her bag for her purse. "I wasn't really noticing, I was talking to Molly, and it was only when Lewis

17

came on . . . Well, that's that, I suppose. If you're not going, you're not going, and Timmy can't go either. But if you change your mind, or if you hear from him, you'll let me know, won't you?"

"Of course. If you're right, there may be something waiting for me at home." I hesitated, then said, I hoped casually: "Which cinema was it, did you say?"

"Leicester Square. And it was him, it really was. We all recognised him straight away. You know the way he has."

"I know all the ways he has," I said, more dryly than I had meant to. "At least, I thought I did. And you really can't remember what was happening?"

She was busy applying lipstick. "Not really. Something about a circus, and a dead man. A fire, that was it, a fire." She put her head to one side, examining the curve of her rouged lips in the tiny mirror. "But it wasn't Lewis who was dead."

I didn't answer. If I had, I'd have said something I'd have been sorry for.

$$\cdot \qquad \cdot \qquad \cdot$$

The news theatre was dark and flickering, and smelt of cigarettes and wet coats. I made my way blindly to a seat. At this time of day the place was half empty, and I was glad of this, as it meant that I could slip into a back row where I could sit alone.

A coloured cartoon was in progress, with animals quacking and swaggering across the screen. Then came some sort of travelogue; Denmark, I think it was, 'Hans Anderson's country', but I sat through it without seeing it. It seemed a long time before the news came round, and longer still before we had done with the big stuff, the latest from Africa, the Middle East, the Grand Prix, the Test . . .

All at once there it was. "Circus Fire in Austrian Village . . . Sunday night . . . Province of Styria . . . An elephant loose in the village street . . ." And the pictures. Not of the fire itself, but of the black and smoking aftermath in the grey of early morning, with police, and grey-faced men in thick overcoats huddled round whatever had been pulled from the wreck. There was the circus encampment in its field, the caravans, mostly streamlined and modern, the big top in the background, and behind it a glimpse of a pine-covered hill, and the glint of a white-washed church tower with an onion spire. In the foreground was a screen—a sort of temporary hoarding—with advertising matter pasted on it; a photograph I couldn't see, some man's name and something about '*Eine absolute Star-Attraktion*', and then a list of prices. Then something must have shoved against the screen, for it fell flat on the trampled grass.

Yes, it was Lewis. He had been standing in the shelter of the screen, and for a moment, obviously, had no idea that the cameras were now on him. He was standing quite still, on the edge of the crowd that was watching the police, staring, like all of them, at the burnt-out wreck, and at something which lay still hidden from the cameras. Then he moved his head in the way he had—oh yes, I knew that way—and amazingly, I saw the expression on his face. He was angry. Quite plainly and simply angry. I was all too recently familiar with that anger . . . but there, where every other man wore the same expression either of solemn respect or of shocked horror, the anger was somehow incongruous and disturbing. And this quite apart from the fact that this was certainly Austria and not Sweden, and that on Monday morning I had had a cable from him from Stockholm . . .

There was a girl beside him. As she moved, I saw her beyond him. A blonde, young and rather more than pretty in that small-featured, wide-eyed way that can be so devastating, even in the early morning and dressed in a shiny black raincoat with a high collar. Her hair hung in long, fair curls over the glossy black collar, and she looked fragile and small and lovely. She was pressed close to Lewis's side, as if for protection, and his arm was round her.

She looked up and saw the cameras on them both, and I saw her reach up and touch him, saying something, a quick whispered word that matched the intimate gesture.

Ninety-nine people out of a hundred, in that situation, would glance instinctively at the camera, before either facing it self-consciously, or turning out of its range. My husband didn't even look round. He turned quickly away and vanished into the crowd, the girl with him.

In the same moment the circus field vanished from the screen, and we were inside a sagging canvas tent, where an elephant rocked solemnly at her moorings, apparently muttering to herself.

". . . the two dead men. The police continue their investigations." the commentator was saying, in that indifferent voice, as the picture changed again to a bathing beach on the South Coast of England . . .

·   ·   ·

The *Mirror* had it—a dozen lines at the bottom corner of page six, under the headline: CIRCUS BLAZE RIDDLE.

Police have been called in to investigate a fire which caused a night of terror in a small Austrian village near Graz. Elephants ran amok when a caravan belonging to a travelling circus took fire, knocking down and injuring a six-year-old girl, and causing havoc in the village. Two men who had been sleeping in the van were burned to death.

The *Guardian* gave it eight lines just above the Bridge game on page thirteen.

Two men were churned to death on Sunday night when a wagon belonging to a travelling circus caught fire. The circus was performing in the village of Xlhalf?Wfen, in the Styrian province of Austria, near Graz.

Next morning, Friday, I did hear from Lewis. It was a note in his own handwriting, dated on Monday, and postmarked Stockholm, and it read: "*Have almost finished the job here, and hope to be home in a few days' time. I'll cable when you can expect me. Love, Lewis.*"

·   ·   ·

That same morning I rang up Carmel Lacy.

"If you still want a courier for your baby boy," I told her, "you've got one. You were quite right about Lewis . . . I've had a letter, and he's in Austria, and he wants me to join him there. I'll go any time, and the sooner the better . . ."

Chapter Two

Not yet old enough for a man, nor young enough for a boy; as a squash is before 'tis a peascod, or a codling when 'tis almost an apple: 'tis with him e'en standing water, between boy and man. He is very well-favoured, and he speaks very shrewishly: one would think his mother's milk were scarce out of him.

Shakespeare: *Twelfth Night*

Timothy Lacy had changed, in that startling way children have that one ought to expect but never does.

He had grown into a tall boy, resembling as far as I could see neither parent, but with a strong look of his grandfather, and a quick-moving, almost nervous manner which would weather with time into the same wiry, energetic toughness. He had grey-green eyes, a fair skin tending to freckles, and a lot of brown hair cut fashionably long in a style which his mother had deplored loudly, but which I secretly rather liked. The expression he had worn ever since his mother had officially handed him over in the main lounge at London Airport—much as she had handed over her spoilt spaniel in my father's surgery—had been, if one put it kindly, reserved. If one put it truthfully, he had looked like a small boy in a fit of the sulks.

He was fumbling now with his seat belt, and it was obvious from his unaccustomed movements that he had never flown before; but I dared not offer to help. After Carmel's tearful—and very public—handing over of her baby, it would have seemed like tucking his feeder round his neck.

I said instead: "It was clever of you to get these seats in front of the wing. If only there's no cloud we'll have a marvellous view."

He gave me a glance where I could see nothing but dislike. The thick, silky hair made a wonderful ambush to glower through, and increased the resemblance to a spoilt but wary dog.

He did mutter something, but at that moment the Austrian Airlines Caravelle began to edge her silky, screaming way forward over the concrete, and he turned eagerly to the window.

We took off exactly on time. The Caravelle paused, gathered herself, then surged forward and rushed up into the air in that exciting lift that never fails to give me the genuine old-fashioned thrill up the marrow of the spine. London fell away, the coast came up, receded, the hazy silver-blue of the channel spread out like wrinkled silk, then the parcelled fields of Belgium reeled out below us, fainter and fainter with distance as the Caravelle climbed to her cruising height and levelled off for the two hours' stride to Vienna. Clouds flecked the view below, thickened, lapped over it like fish-scales, drew a blanket across it . . . We hung seemingly motionless in the sunlight in front of our whispering engines, with the marvellous pageant of clouds spread, at no more than the speed of drifting surf, below.

"Angels' eye view," I said. "We get a lot of privileges now that only the gods got before. Including destroying whole cities at a blow, if it comes to that."

He said nothing. I sighed to myself, gave up my attempts to take my own mind off the situation ahead of me, and opened a magazine. Lunch came, and went, temptingly foreign, with *Apfelsaft* or red wine or champagne, the boy beside me so pointedly refraining from comment on what was obviously a burstingly exciting experience for him that I felt a flicker of irritation pierce my own preoccupations. The Caravelle tilted slightly to starboard; Nürnberg must be somewhere now below that cloud, and we were turning south-east for Passau and the Austrian border. The trays were cleared, people stood, stretched, moved about, and the trolley of scent and cigarettes was wheeled up the aisle in nice time to block the passengers' access to the lavatories.

The pretty stewardess in her navy uniform bent over me. "Would you care for cigarettes, madam? Perfume? Liquor?"

"No, thank you."

Her eyes went doubtfully to Timothy, who had turned back from his window. "Cigarettes, sir?"

"Of course." He said it promptly, and rather too loudly, and I caught the edge of a glance at me. "What kind have you?"

She told him, and he made his choice and fumbled for the money. As she handed him the statutory packet of two hundred, I saw his eyes widen, but he successfully hid dismay, if that was what he was feeling, and paid. The trolley moved on. With some panache, but without another glance at me, Timothy tucked the cigarettes down into his airline holdall, and got out a paperback mystery. Silence hovered again, conscious, ready to strike.

I said: "You know, I couldn't really care less if you want to smoke all day and all night till you die of six sorts of cancer all at once. Go right ahead. And as a matter of fact, the sooner the better. You have the worst manners of any young man I ever met."

The paperback dropped to his knees, and he looked at me full for the first time, eyes and mouth startled open. I said: "I know quite well that you're perfectly capable of travelling alone, and that you'd prefer it. Well, so would I. I've got troubles enough of my own, without bothering about yours, but if I hadn't said I'd go with you, you'd never have got away. I know you're sitting there fulminating because you've had a kind of nursemaid tagged on to you, but for goodness' sake aren't you adult enough to know that there are two sides to everything? You know you'd get on fine on your own, but your mother doesn't, and there's no sense in making gestures to reassure oneself, if they're only distressing other people. Surely all that really matters now is that you have got your own way, so why not make the best of it? We're stuck with each other till I get you—or you get me—safely into Vienna, and you meet your father. Then we're both free to go about our own affairs."

Timothy swallowed. The action seemed to use the muscles of his whole body. When he spoke, his voice cracked infuriatingly back for a moment into falsetto.

"I—I'm sorry," he said.

"I didn't want to make you talk if you'd rather read or watch the view," I said, "but as a matter of fact I always get nervous on take-off, and if one chatters a bit about things it takes one's mind off it."

"I'm sorry," said Timothy again. He was scarlet now, but his voice had got back to the norm required of a young man who could comfort a nervous woman on take-off. "I hadn't realised you were feeling like that. I was so—that is, it's all been so . . . I couldn't think how I was going to . . ." He stopped floundering, bit his lip, then said with devastating simplicity: "The cigarettes were for Daddy."

As an *amende honorable* it was superb. It also had the effect of taking the wind right out of my sails. And he knew it. I could see the glint in the grey-green eyes.

I said: "Timothy Lacy, you have all the makings of a dangerous young man. I'm not in the least surprised your mother's afraid to let you out alone. Now tell me what to call you. I know your mother calls you Timmy, but it sounds a bit babyish to me. Do you prefer Timothy, or Tim?"

"I'll settle for Tim."

"Well, mine's Vanessa."

"That's an awfully pretty name. Are you called after Vanessa Redgrave?"

I laughed. "Have a heart, I'm twenty-four. I don't know where they got the name from, probably just something my mother found in a book. As a matter of fact, it's a butterfly, or rather a family of butterflies, rather pretty ones, peacocks and painted ladies, and so on. Fair and fickle, that's me, born to flit from flower to flower."

"Well," said Timothy, "that's a bond between us, anyway. They used to call me Mothy for short at my prep. school. I say, you can see a bit now through the clouds. There's a river . . . Do you suppose it's the Danube?"

"Could be. We more or less follow it the last part of the way."

"If you're going to be frightened when we land," he said kindly, "I'll hold your hand if you like."

·   ·   ·

24

"Isn't she beautiful?" asked Timothy.

The clouds we drifted across now, a mile above our own shadow, were Austrian. They looked just the same. Timothy, slightly crumpled looking, and melting minute by minute into relaxation, had got to the stage of showing me photographs. This one was of a girl on a grey pony. It was an oldish print, fading a bit, and in the girl, plump and fair and sitting solidly in the saddle, I was a bit startled to recognise Carmel.

"Er, yes." Nothing that her son had told me up to now—and he had poured out a good deal about the Lacy *ménage* which I was sure Carmel would prefer me not to have heard—nothing had led me to expect the enthusiasm with which Timothy now held out his mother's photograph. I asked rather lamely: "How old was she then?"

"Pretty old when that was taken. About fifteen. You can tell by the tail."

"You can tell by the what?"

"The tail. Actually that pony's of the Welsh 'Starlight' strain, and they're pretty long-lived; they don't start to look old till they're dying on their feet." Then he recollected himself. "Gosh, listen to me telling you! As if you didn't know all that, being practically a vet."

"Not so much of the 'practically', please! I qualified just before I was married."

"Did you? I hadn't realised."

"If it comes to that," I said, "I was 'practically' a vet. as you call it, before I even started at the Dick Vet.—that's the Veterinary College in Edinburgh where I went. You can't be brought up all your life in a veterinary surgeon's house and not learn a heck of a lot about the job."

"I suppose not . . . it'll be like me, getting sort of brought up with the horses at my grandfather's place. Did you ever practise?"

"Officially, only for about six months, but in actual fact you do a lot of practical work as a student, especially in your final year. You travel out to farms, and handle the animals, and you learn to make your own diagnoses, use X-rays, assist operations

—the lot. After I got my diploma I started work as Daddy's assistant, but then I met Lewis and got married."

"What exactly does he do, your husband?"

"He's employed by Pan-European Chemicals. You'll have heard of it; it's not as vast as I.C.I., but it's getting on that way. Lewis is in the Sales Department. He's planning to change over now to another branch, because his job takes him abroad too much—he used not to mind, but we hardly seem to have seen each other since we were married. To begin with I used to go home while he was abroad, and work with my father, but then I started helping out now and then at the P.D.S.A.—that's the People's Dispensary for Sick Animals—near where we live in London, and that keeps my hand in."

"Gosh, yes: I'm sorry about the 'practically', it was a howling insult." He sat quiet for a moment, riffling through the remaining photographs in his hands. I saw that they were mostly of horses. He seemed completely relaxed now and at ease, his random remarks and silences coming as easily as among his contemporaries. Which, in fact, I now felt myself to be: oddly enough, this was the effect which my school-mistressy outburst had produced in both of us, as if we had quarrelled and now had made it up on equal terms, with a licence to say what we felt.

He said suddenly: "I hate London. It was all right when grandfather was alive, I was allowed to go there a lot in the hols. Mummy didn't seem to want me around so much then, when the girls were still home. If only she'd kept the place on . . . got somebody in to manage it . . . not just sold it . . ." He snapped the photographs together into a pack, pushed them into their envelope and tucked them decisively down into the holdall. "And now that I've left school, it just looked as if it was going to be London all summer, and I felt I couldn't stick it. So I had to do something drastic, hadn't I?"

"Like harrying your poor mother into parting with you? I shouldn't worry; she'll survive it."

He gave me a quick, bright glance, and seemed about to say something, but thought better of it. When he did speak, I felt sure this was not what he had been going to say. "Have you ever been to Vienna before?"

"No."

"I wondered if you were interested in the Spanish Riding School. You know, the team of white Lipizzan stallions that give those performances of *haute école* to music. I've wanted to see them all my life."

I said: "I know of them, of course, but I can't say I know much about them. I'd certainly love to see them. Are they in Vienna now?"

"They live in Vienna. The performances are put on in a marvellous building like a big eighteenth-century ballroom, in the Hofburg Palace. They perform every Sunday morning; only, I'm afraid, not in August. They'll begin again in September . . ." He grinned. "If I know anything about it, I'll still be here. But one can go into the stables any time and see them there, and I believe you can get to the training sessions and see the work actually going on. My father's been in Vienna now for six months, and I'm hoping he'll know a few of the right people by now, and get me in behind the scenes." He glanced away out of his window. "I believe we're beginning to lose height."

I looked thoughtfully at his averted profile. Here was yet another change. Now that he was launched on something that appealed to him, that genuinely mattered, his voice and manner had lost the remaining touches of awkward youth. This was a young man talking about his subject with the air of knowing far more about it than he was bothering to impart. But not quite, yet, with the air of knowing exactly where he was going: there was a lurking trace of defiance still about that.

I asked, to keep him talking: "Why is it called the 'Spanish' Riding School?"

"What? Oh, because the Lipizzan stud was founded originally with Spanish horses. I think it's about the oldest breed of horse we've got—they go right back to the Romans, Roman cavalry horses in Spain being crossed with Arabians and so on, and they were the best war-horses you could get, so they were sold right, left, and centre all over Europe in the Middle Ages, and when the Austrian Stud was founded at Lipizza they bought Spanish stock for it."

"Hence the name Lipizzan . . . Yes, I see. Didn't Austria give up Lipizza to Italy after the first war, or something?"

He nodded. "One gathers it was a marvel the horses didn't disappear altogether, when the Austrian Empire broke up. I suppose when the Republic was started nobody was much interested in a relic of, well, high life, but then they started giving public performances—they'd become state property, of course—and now the Austrians are frantically proud of them. The stud had a pretty ropy time at the end of the last war, too, when Vienna was bombarded; you'll remember how Colonel Podhajsky, the Director, got the stallions safely out of Vienna, then the mares were rescued from Czechoslovakia by the American Army, and the stud was set up in some barracks or other at Wels in the north, before they got re-settled at Piber."

"Yes, I knew that. Piber, was it? Where's that? Somewhere in the south, isn't it?"

"It's down in Styria, not far from Graz. What's the matter?"

"Nothing. Go on. Tell me about the stallions."

He looked at me for a moment as if to see whether I was genuinely interested or not, then he went on, his manner a rather touching blend of didacticism and boyish enthusiasm.

"Well, they're bred at Piber, then when they're four, the best of them go to Vienna to be trained. The others are sold. The ones at Vienna take years to train. I suppose one of the things that makes the performance so exciting isn't just that it's beautiful, but that—" He glanced at me again, hesitated, then said almost shyly: "Well, don't you think there's something a bit thrilling about the—the *oldness* of it all, movements and figures passed down right from the year One, right from Xenophon, you know, the *Art of Horsemanship*—isn't it rather marvellous to think of the idea of *haute école* going right back to the fifth century B.C.? But with the Lipizzans it isn't even ordinary *haute école*; after all, you can see normal dressage anywhere at shows . . . what's

28

so beautiful is the way they've blended the dressage movements in to make the 'figure dances' like the School Quadrille, and then of course the 'airs above the ground'."

"The what? Oh, you mean those marvellous leaps the horses do."

"Yes, they call them the *Schulen uber der Erde*," said Timothy. "They're as old as the hills, too. They were the old battle movements all the war-horses had to learn if they were to be any good—I mean, if you were using both hands for shield and sword or whatnot, you had to have a horse that would jump to order in any direction at a moment's notice. Half a minute— if you'd like to look at these . . ."

He bent to fish in his holdall. We were coming down through cloud, steadily losing height, and already people here and there were making small movements of preparation for landing. But even the novelties of flying seemed lost to Timothy now.

He straightened up, slightly flushed, eagerly producing a book heavily illustrated by photographs.

"See, there they are, these are the different figures." He pushed the hair back out of his eyes and spread the book open on my knee. "All the stallions can learn to do the ordinary dressage movements—like the *piaffe*, that's a sort of high trot on the spot; and that lovely slow trot they call the Spanish trot—but I believe only the best of them go on to the actual leaps. There, see? They're terribly hard to do, and some of the horses never do manage them. They take years to train, and develop terrific muscles for it . . . Look at that one there . . . he's doing the *levade*, it looks just like rearing, except for the way he bends his hocks, but I believe it's a terrific effort to hold."

"It looks it. That's like the pose you see in the old statues, and old battle pictures and so on."

"That's exactly what it is! If somebody took a swipe at you in battle your horse was supposed to go between you and him, poor thing."

"Well, I hope it had armour, that's all," I said. "These are lovely, Tim. Oh, he's a beauty, isn't he? Look at that head, and those wise eyes. He knows a thing or two, that fellow."

"I'll say," said Timothy. "That's Pluto Theodorosta; he was the absolute tops, I believe; he died just recently. He was Colonel Podhajsky's favourite. I don't know which is the top stallion now, I think it's Maestoso Mercurio. There, that's him, and that one's Maestoso Alea—you can see their heads are similar, coming from the same strain . . . That's Conversano Bonavista—he was a favourite of the last Director's. Look, isn't this a marvellous photograph? That's Neapolitano Petra doing the *courbette*; I believe it's the most difficult leap of the lot. There was some story, I think it was about him; they were going to present him to some Eastern potentate or something, for a compliment, but his rider killed him, and then shot himself so they shouldn't be parted."

"Good heavens. Is it true?"

"I don't know. They don't put that sort of thing in any of the books about the stallions, but I heard quite a lot about them from an Austrian trainer who was in England for years, and used to visit my grandfather. I've probably got the story wrong, but actually, I wouldn't be surprised. You know how you can get to feel about horses . . . and when you've worked as these men do, every day with a horse for—oh, lord, for twenty years, perhaps . . ."

"I believe you. There's a dark one, Tim. I thought they were all white?"

"He's a bay, actually, Neapolitano Ancona. They used to be all colours, but they've gradually bred the colours out, all except the bay, and now there's always one bay in the show by tradition."

"Where do they get their names? That's two Neapolitanos and two Maestosos."

"They all come from six original stallions. They take their first name from the stallion, and the second from their dam."

I said with genuine respect: "You seem to know an awful lot about them."

He hesitated, flushed, and then said flatly: "I'm going to get a job there if they'll have me. That's why I came."

· · ·

"Are there really six sorts of cancer?" asked Tim.

"Are there what?" After his last bombshell, I had not felt called upon to make, or even capable of offering, any comment, and a pause had ensued, during which the flight hostess announced in German and English that we were approaching Vienna, and would we kindly fasten our seat belts and extinguish our cigarettes . . .

We dropped out of cloud, and, it seemed close below us now, flat, cropped stubble fields of Austria unrolled and tilted. Somewhere ahead in a hazy summer's evening was Vienna, with her woods and her grey, girdling river.

And now Timothy appeared to be distracting me with cheerful small talk from the approaching terrors of landing.

"I meant the six sorts of cancer you can get from smoking."

"Oh, I remember," I said. "Well, I expect there are, but don't take it to heart, if you're worrying about your father. I dare say he can take care of himself."

"I wasn't worrying about him. At least, not in the sense you mean."

There was something in his voice which told me that this was not, after all, merely a bit of distracting small talk. On the contrary, the carefully casual remark dangled in front of me like bait.

I rose to it. "Then what are you worrying about?"

"Is your husband meeting you at the airport?"

"No. He—I'm to get in touch with him after I get there. I've booked a room at a hotel. So if I may, I'll beg a lift into town with your father and you. Unless, of course, you want to shake off your nursemaid before you meet him?"

But he didn't smile. "Actually, he's not meeting me."

"But your mother said—"

"I know she did. But he's not. I—I told her he was, it made it easier. It was a lie."

"I see. Well, then—" Something in his expression stopped me. "Does it matter all that much?" I asked.

"That's not all." He cleared his throat. "It's—I thought it would be all right, but now it's come to the point, I'm beginning to wonder. I dare say," he added with a sudden, fierce bitterness that disturbed me, "I dare say she's right, and I'm a stupid kid who shouldn't be out loose, but I—" He swallowed. "Did you say you'd got a hotel?"

"Yes. It's right in the centre. On the Stephansplatz, opposite St Stephen's Cathedral. Why? Would you like to go there first with me?"

"If you don't mind."

"Fine," I said briskly, "we'll do that. Look, have you room in your holdall for these magazines?"

"Yes, here, let me. Mrs March—"

"Vanessa, please. You know, you don't have to tell me anything you don't want to."

"I think I'd better."

"Here, Tim, relax, it can't be as bad as that. What have you done? Forgotten to tell him which day you're coming?"

"It's worse than that. He's not even expecting me. He didn't ask me to come at all. I made it all up, to get away. In fact," said Timothy desperately, "he hasn't written to me since he left. Not once. Oh"—at something which must have shown in my face— "I didn't mind, really. I mean, we were never all that close, and if he didn't want to, well, it was up to him, wasn't it? You're not to think I told all those lies to Mummy about him writing because I—because I felt he should have done, or something. I only did it so that I could get away."

He finished the terrible little confession on a note of apology. I couldn't look at him. It was all I could do not to state loudly and clearly just what I thought of his parents. "In other words," I said, "you're running away?"

"Yes. In a way. Yes."

"And now that you're stuck with a nursemaid who looks like handing you over personally, you've had to tell her?"

"It wasn't that." He looked grateful for the calm neutrality of my tone. "I could have got away from you easily. It just didn't seem fair, when you'd be the one to be left with all the row."

"I see. Thank you. Well, we'll have to think this out, won't we? How are you off for money?"

"I've got about twenty pounds."

"If your father didn't send you the money for the fare, where did you get it?"

"Well, I suppose I stole it." said Timothy.

"My poor Tim, you are breaking out, aren't you? Who from?"

"Oh, nobody. It was my Post Office account. I was supposed to leave it alone till my eighteenth birthday. That," said Timothy clearly, "is pretty soon, anyway."

"Am I to take it you didn't intend to get in touch with your father at all? Did you only use the fact that he lives in Vienna as an excuse to get away?"

"Not really. I've got to live somewhere till I get the job, and twenty pounds won't last for ever. I expect there'll be a bit of a turn-up, but you get over it."

He spoke without noticeable apprehension, and I was reassured. Perhaps he was tougher than I had thought. It seemed as if he might need to be.

I said: "Well, we'll go together to my hotel first, shall we, and have a wash and so forth, and ring your father up. I expect he'll come for you . . . That is, if he's home. I suppose you don't know if he's in Vienna now? It's August, after all; he may be away on holiday."

"That's what the twenty pounds is for," said Timothy. "The —well, the interregnum."

I got it then, with a bang. I turned to stare at him, and he, back in ambush behind the heavy lock of hair, eyed me once again warily, but this time—I thought—also with amusement.

"Timothy Lacy! Are you trying to tell me you've lied to your poor mother and gone blinding off into the blue without having the foggiest idea where your father even *is*?"

"Well, he does live in Vienna, I know he does. The money comes from there—the money to pay for school and so on."

"But you don't actually know his address?"

"No."

There was a rather loaded silence. He must have misunderstood my half of it, for he said quickly: "Don't think I'll be a nuisance to you. If it's too late to get hold of Daddy's bank or something, I'll just take a room at the hotel till Monday. You don't need to bother about me at all. I'll be fine, and there's masses of things I want to do. When's your husband joining you?"

"I don't quite know."

"You'll be telephoning him tonight?"

Another pause. I took a breath to speak but I didn't need to. The grey-green eyes widened. The lock of hair went back.

"Vanessa March!" It was a wickedly perfect imitation of the tone I had used to him, and it crumbled the last barriers of status between us. "Are you trying to tell me that you've lied to my poor mother and gone off blinding into the blue without having the foggiest idea where your husband even *is*?"

I nodded. We met one another's eyes. Unnoticed, the Caravelle touched down as smoothly as a gull. Outside the windows the flat fields of Schwechat streamed past, lights pricking out in the early dusk. The babel of foreign voices rose around us as people hunted for coats and hand-baggage.

Timothy pulled himself together. "The orphans of the storm." he said. "Never mind, Vanessa, I'll look after you."

Chapter Three

In all the woes that curse our race
There is a lady in the case.
         W. S. Gilbert: *Fallen Fairies*

In the event, Timothy's father proved very easy to locate. He was in the telephone book. It was Tim himself who discovered this, while I, sitting on my bed in the large, pleasant, and rather noisy room of the hotel Am Stephansplatz, was telephoning our first tentative enquiries down to the reception desk about banking hours in Vienna.

"It must be him," said Timothy, pushing the directory page under my nose. "Look, there it is. Prinz Eugenstrasse 81. The telephone number's 63 42 61."

"And the banks are shut now, so he may be there, or some-one'll be there who knows where he is. He'll have a house-keeper, surely?" I cradled the receiver, and swung my legs down off the bed. "Well, if only Lewis is as easy to find, all our troubles will be over by dinner-time. At least," I amended it, "some of them. Go ahead then, it's all yours . . . and the girl at the switchboard speaks English."

"It's not that. My German's not bad, I did it for 'A' levels; and as a matter of fact I'm panting to try."

"Well, then?" Then, as he still hesitated: "Be your age, Tim."

He made a face at me, then grinned and lifted the receiver. I went into the bathroom and shut the door.

Under the circumstances it seemed a remarkably short con-versation. When I went in again he had put back the receiver and was leaning on the window-sill, watching the crowds thronging the pavement outside St Stephen's Cathedral.

He said, without looking round: "He wasn't annoyed."

I opened a suitcase and began to lift my things out. "Oh, he was there, was he? Good. Well, that's one trouble on the way out. I'm very glad. Is he coming for you, or will you get a taxi?"

"He was just going out, as a matter of fact," said Tim. "He won't be in till pretty late. He's going to a concert with his fiancée."

I shook out a dress rather carefully and hung it away. "I suppose you didn't know about her?"

"No. I told you he never wrote. Her name's Christl. I think it's short for Christina."

"Oh? Austrian?"

"Yes. Viennese. It's a rather pretty name, isn't it?"

I lifted another frock from my case. "I don't suppose he'd tell you much about it on the phone."

"Not much. I told him you were here. He said he couldn't get out of the concert, but would we meet them afterwards for

35

supper at . . . I wrote it down . . . at Sacher's Hotel. It's by the Opera House. Eleven o'clock in the Blue Bar."

He had turned back now from the window and was watching me. His face gave no clue to what he was thinking. I raised an eyebrow. "Flying high on your first night out of the nest. 'Eleven o'clock in the Blue Bar.' It sounds like something out of Ian Fleming. What price the apron strings now?"

"Well," he said, "it's what I wanted, isn't it?"

"My dear," I said, "do you mind?"

"To be quite honest, I don't know. Should I?"

"It would be very understandable if you did. It's rather a thing to have thrust at one just like that, a parent marrying again."

"Yes, my mother's going to marry again, too."

It was one of those things to which there seems no reply at all. I couldn't think what to say. I just stood there with my hands full of stockings, and probably looking as stupid as I felt. "I had no idea," I said at last.

"Oh, it's not official, and as a matter of fact she said certainly not when I asked her flat out, but I'm pretty sure. In fact I'd take a small bet."

"Do you like him?"

"He's all right. It's John Linley, the publisher; do you know him?"

"No, but I remember your mother did mention the name." I hoped I hadn't sounded as relieved as I felt: compared with some of Carmel Lacy's 'men-around-town', a publisher sounded the height of respectability. Not that it mattered to me what happened to Carmel Lacy, but I was beginning to find that I rather cared what happened to Timothy.

He didn't pursue the subject. He said: "What does this hotel charge for bed and breakfast?"

I told him. "I suppose your father won't have had time to make arrangements for you? I was wondering whether we'd have to take your case along to Sacher's, or call for it here later."

"Well," said Timothy, "that's rather the point. He didn't say anything about my joining him. In fact, I got the impression that it was the last thing he wanted. Oh, I don't mean my coming to Vienna, he took that in his stride, after he'd got over the surprise; and as a matter of fact he was rather decent about it. He—well, he obviously isn't going to send me back or anything, and I've got a feeling he might even be pretty helpful about the job. There wasn't time to talk about it, because he was in a hurry getting ready to go out, and he just said something about work permits, and thinking it over later on, but why not simply have a holiday to start with, and was I all right for cash."

"I like the sound of that last bit," I said. "Well, anyway, I expect you'll get things fixed up when you see him tonight. He'll probably want you to move in there tomorrow."

"That's just what I wouldn't bet on," said Timothy. "I told you he was pretty nice about my suddenly turning up like this, but I think it rather threw him. He wanted to see me, all right, but I'm certain he didn't want me staying with him, and that's one reason why he was so dashed forthcoming about money." This wasn't cynicism, but merely a matter-of-fact observation of the kind that would paralyse most parents if they could know what their children know about them. "Actually," he added, "I got the impression that he has someone living with him already."

I looked at him for a moment, was satisfied with what I saw, and said: "Then let us hope, Tim dear, that it's Christl, or things will begin to get altogether too complicated."

"Poor father," said Timothy unexpectedly, and laughed. "I've put him in a spot, haven't I? I expect he's sweating on the top line now. Well, I'd better see if I can book that room. I hope they've got one; they've probably only got suites, or something with private bathrooms and all that jazz."

"Well, it's a bit late for you to find anywhere else, and I gather your father's prepared to finance you. I'd go ahead. Dash it, he owes you the night's lodging at least!"

"Dead right he does. And then there's always blackmail. I've a golden future, haven't I?" And Timothy crossed to the telephone.

Well, I thought, as I stowed away the last pair of shoes, this was indeed what he had wanted. But there must be easier ways of growing up than tearing oneself loose from the apron strings, and then being thrown into the cold and foreign winds by a careless male hand, with a few coins flung after you. It was surprising, really, how normal and nice Timothy appeared to be . . .

"That's all right," said Timothy, putting down the receiver. "Number 216, one floor up. That's me settled. Now, what about you? Are you going to stay and do your telephoning now, or go out and get something to eat first? I don't know about you, but I can't wait till eleven. I'm starving."

I glanced up. "You're being very tactful. Does it hurt? You must be wondering like mad what I'm playing at."

He grinned. "Well, I don't just feel I'm in a position to criticise."

I shut the wardrobe door and sat down in one of the armchairs. "If you can hold off from food for five minutes, I'll tell you."

"Only if you want to."

"Fair's fair. Besides, I'd like to tell somebody. It's very simple and rather depressing and probably a bit sordid, and I dare say it happens every day. Only I thought it wouldn't ever happen to me. We were going away on holiday, Lewis and I, and it was the first really long break since we were married just over two years ago. I told you he works for P.E.C., and they slave-drive him, only they pay pretty well, and he's always enjoyed the travelling. He never knew whether he'd be sent to Hong Kong or to Oslo next, and it suited him. Then we got married. And he said he'd change his job, only it would take time to train his successor, so we decided we'd just take it as it came for a couple of years. It was Lewis who suggested giving it up, not me. I know I've not behaved particularly well, but it was his idea in the first place. You see, we both want a family, and, the way things are now, it wouldn't be fair on them . . . the children."

He didn't say anything. He was back at the window again,

and appeared to be tracing out with his eye, stone by stone, the massive façade of St Stephen's.

"Well"—I tried hard to stop sounding defensive—"he told told me finally he was leaving the department in mid-August this year, and we were going to have a holiday, a whole month, and go just where I wanted—he didn't care, he'd seen it all, he said he just wanted to be with me. It was, you know, another honeymoon. The first was only ten days. Then, just before we we were due to go, they asked him to take on one more assignment. A week, two weeks, they couldn't be sure how long it would take. Just when we were getting ready to go; we'd got the tickets, I was packing, and everything."

"What a rotten thing," said Timothy to St Stephen's.

"That's what I thought. And said. The thing was, they couldn't order him, they made it a request, but he said he couldn't turn it down, he'd have to go himself, there was no one else. So I said what about the man they'd been training, but Lewis said this was something that had come out of his last job, and he'd have to do it himself. And of course I was so disappointed that I went all feminine and unreasonable and threw a scene, one of those classic scenes, 'you think more of your rotten job than of me', and that sort of thing. And I've always *despised* women who did that. A man's job is his life, and you've got to take it as it comes and try to be as loyal to it as he is . . . But I wasn't."

"Well," said Timothy, "I don't blame you. Anybody would have been upset."

"The trouble was, of course, that Lewis was furious, too, with having to change his plans. He said couldn't I see that he didn't want to go at all, and that it wasn't anything to do with not wanting to be with me, but that there was no alternative. So I said well, why couldn't he just take me with him this time for a change, and when he said he couldn't, surely I knew that by this time, I really blew up. Then he got furious, and we had the most dreadful row. I said the most awful things, Tim, I still think about them."

He looked at me with a gravity that somehow seemed

enormously youthful. "And now you're just torturing yourself all the time because you've hurt his feelings?"

"Lewis," I said, rather too carefully, and forgetting momentarily who I was talking to, "is selfish, obstinate, and arrogant, and has no feelings of any kind whatsoever."

"Yes," said Timothy, "I mean no. But if you know he doesn't want you to join him, why did you come, especially if you're still so furious with him?"

I looked down at my hands, which were clasped together rather too tightly on my knee. "That's more sordid still, I'm afraid. I think he's with a woman, and that's something I can't quite laugh off the way we did with your father."

"Vanessa—"

"I'm sorry, Tim, I'm not behaving well. I'm certainly not a fit and proper person to chaperon you, let alone preach to you, with the damned nerve I had, but I'm so unhappy I've got to do something. That's why I came."

"Please don't be unhappy." He was as awkward with his comfort as any man is at any age, but touchingly kind with it. "I'm sure you must be wrong. Whatever anyone's been telling you, you'll find there's nothing in it."

"Yes. Yes, I'm sure you're right." I sat up straighter in the chair, as if by doing so I could shake off my thoughts. "And it wasn't anything anyone told me, it was just an impression I got, and I'm sure it was wrong; all that's the matter with me is that I do feel guilty about the things I said. It would have been all right if he hadn't had to go straight away. When you get married, Timothy"—I managed a smile at him—"never part on a quarrel. It's hell. When I think about it now ... He just went storming out of the flat, and then, when he got to the door, he stopped, as if he'd suddenly thought of something, and came back to me. I wasn't even looking at him. He kissed me goodbye, and went."

I looked up at him sombrely. It was a relief to put it at last into words. "It only came to me afterwards, but it was the way a man would act if he knew he was going to do something dangerous, and he didn't want to part like that. And now I know that's true. That's why I came."

He was staring at me. "What do you mean? 'Dangerous'? What sort of danger could he be in? How can you know?"

"I don't know. Let me tell you the rest; I'll be as quick as I can." And I told him all about the news-reel and the chain of events which had made me decide to come out to Austria and see for myself what was going on.

He listened in silence, perched now on the arm of the other chair.

When I had finished, he was quiet for a minute or two. Then he pushed the hair back from his forehead with a gesture that I was beginning to recognise as a signal of decision.

"Well, as far as locating the circus is concerned, that'll be dead easy. There are hardly any tenting circuses—that's travelling circuses—left these days, and everyone in Austria will probably know where this one was. We can ask the hall porter, and we can go on from there. Shall we go and do it now?"

I stood up. "No, we'll eat first. We'll go out and find a real Viennese restaurant, and do ourselves proud, shall we? Then when we feel a bit stronger, I'll tackle the Case of the Vanishing Husband, and you can take on the Father and the Fräulein."

"We'll both tackle them both." He uncoiled his length from the arm of the chair and stood up. He was a half a head taller than I was. He looked down at me, suddenly shy. "I was an awful ass this morning. I—I'm terribly glad we came together after all."

"That makes two of us," I said, reaching in the wardrobe for my coat. "For heaven's sake, let's go and eat."

. . . .

Not only did Tim's German prove more than equal to the occasion, but the hall porter was every bit as helpful as the telephone directory had been. He identified the circus immediately as the Circus Wagner, and the village where the accident had taken place as the village of Oberhausen, situated some way beyond Bruck, in the Gleinalpe, the hilly region that lies to the west of the main road from Vienna to Graz and the Yugoslav border.

"Really, there's nothing to this detective business," said

Timothy, relaying this information to me. My own German is of the sketchy variety which allows me to understand public notices, and to follow simple remarks reasonably accurately if they are made slowly enough, and preferably with gestures; but Tim's schoolboy German, though certainly slow and liberally laced with pantomime, seemed fairly fluent, and it got results.

"Ask him about the fire," I said. "It may have been a serious one if they know so much about it up here in Vienna."

But no, this was not the case. The hall porter's very gestures were reassuring. The only reason he knew so much himself was because he himself came from the village near Innsbruck where the Circus Wagner had its winter quarters, and not only did he know the owners and some of the performers, but he seemed to have a fair idea of their summer route through the country. The fire? Ah, that had been a terrible thing; yes, indeed, two men had been killed, a fearful affair it was, a living-wagon burned in the night, and the men with it. Who were they? Why, one of them was the horse-keeper. The hall porter, it appeared, had known him, too, a good man, good with the horses, but he drank, you understand . . . No doubt he had been drunk when the accident happened, knocked over a lamp, been careless with the bottled gas . . . these things were too easy to do in such cramped quarters, and something of the sort had happened once before . . . The only reason they kept him on, poor old Franzl, was because he was some sort of relation of Herr Wagner himself, and then he was such a very good man with the horses . . .

"And the other man?"

But here the hall porter's information ran out abruptly. I didn't need German to understand the lifted shoulders and spread hands. This, he did not know. It was no one belonging to the circus, or the village. Herr Wagner himself had not known him; he had not known, even, that there had been a second man in old Franzl's wagon that night. There were rumours—he himself had heard them—that it had not been an accident, that Franzl had been involved in some crime, and that he and the other man had been murdered as a result; but then there were

42

always such rumours when the police would not close a case straight away; whereas anyone who had known old Franzl would realise that such an idea was absurd, quite out of the question . . . As for the other man, he believed that he had been identified, but to tell you the truth, he had not read about this in the papers, or had forgotten it if he had . . .

He smiled deprecatingly, and shrugged his wide shoulders once again. "It is over, you understand, *gnädige Frau*, and the newspapers lose interest. Indeed, they would hardly have taken the trouble to report poor old Franzl's death, if it had not been for the elephant . . . A circus is always news, and particularly if there is an elephant . . . You saw some of the stories, perhaps? The truth of the matter was that there was only one elephant, a very old one, kept just for the parades, and she had in fact broken her rope, but had gone only a little way into the village, and had touched no one. The little girl, who was reported to be injured, had fallen down while running away in terror; the elephant had not touched her at all."

"Ask him," I said, "ask him if he's ever heard of a man called Lewis March."

"Never," said the hall porter, for once mercifully brief.

I wouldn't have ventured the question but that it was obvious that the man was so delighted to have an audience for his story that it never occured to him to wonder at our interest. A few more questions, and we had gathered all that we had wanted to know. Two days ago the circus had still been in Oberhausen, detained there by the police; its next stop was to have been Hohenwald, a village some fifty kilometres deeper into the Gleinalpe. There was a train at nine-forty next morning which would get me into Bruck before midday, and it was even possible that the local bus service might operate as far as Oberhausen, or, if necessary, Hohenwald, by the very same night. It was certainly possible to find somewhere to stay in any of these villages; there was an excellent small Gasthof in Oberhausen itself, called (inevitably, one felt) the Edelweiss, and I must, also inevitably, merely mention the hall porter's name to Frau Weber, and I would be more than welcome . . .

43

"Gosh," said Timothy, as we let ourselves out of the hotel again into the brilliant noisy square, and turned towards the Kärntnerstrasse, "I wish I was coming with you. I've always wanted to get inside the works of a circus, if that's what you call them. You'll promise to ring me up tomorrow night, won't you, and tell me how you got on, and what's happened?"

"I promise—that is, if I know where to get hold of you."

"There's that," he agreed. "Well, if father and Christl won't have me, I'll come with you. I really don't feel you ought to be allowed to go all that way on your own! Are you sure you wouldn't like me to come with you and buy the tickets and find out about the buses?"

"I'd love you to. I might even hold you to that. And now, if we're to get to Sacher's in time, we'd better get a move on. Can you really eat another meal? I thought you were a bit rash with that *Hühnerleberisotto* at the Deutsches Haus."

"Good lord, that was hours ago!" Timothy had quite recovered his buoyancy with the meal; he charged cheerfully along the crowded pavement, examining the contents of every shop window with such interest and enthusiasm that I began to wonder if we would ever reach our rendezvous. "What is this Sacher's anyway? It sounds a bit dull, a hotel. Will there be music?"

"I've no idea, but it certainly won't be dull. Everyone who comes to Vienna ought to go there at least once. I believe it's terribly glamorous, and it's certainly typical of Old Vienna, you know, baroque and gilt and red plush and the good old days. It was started by Madame Sacher, ages ago, some time in the nineteenth century, and I believe it's still fairly humming with the ghosts of archdukes and generals and all the Viennese high society at the time of the Hapsburgs. I think I even read something in a guide book about an archduke or something who went there for a bet in absolutely nothing whatever except his sword and maybe a few Orders."

"Bang on," said Timothy, "it sounds terrific. What would my mother say?"

·   ·   ·

44

Sacher's Hotel was all that I had imagined, with its brilliantly lit scarlet and gold drawing-rooms, the Turkey carpets, the oils in their heavy frames, the mahogany and flowers and spacious last-century atmosphere of comfortable leisure. The Blue Bar, where we were to meet Graham Lacy and his lady, was a smallish intimate cave lined with blue brocade, and lit with such discretion that one almost needed a flashlight to find one's drink. The champagne cocktails were about eight and sixpence a glass. Tim's father produced these for the company with very much the air of one who was producing a bribe and trying not to show it. Christl, on the other hand, did her best to pretend that this was a perfectly ordinary occasion, and that she and Graham had champagne cocktails every evening. As, perhaps, they did.

Somewhat to my own surprise, I liked Christl. I don't quite know what I had been expecting, a predatory Nordic blonde, perhaps, on the model of the one I had seen with Lewis. She was indeed a blonde, but not in the least predatory, at least to the outward eye. She was plump and pretty, and looked as if she would be more at home in the kitchen putting together an omelette for Graham, than sitting in the Blue Bar at Sacher's, taking him for a champagne cocktail. She wore a blue dress, which exactly matched the colour of her eyes, and there were no rings on her hands. Timothy's father was still recognisably the man I remembered, with the years and the weight added to the florid good looks, and the extra heartiness of manner added by the embarrassment of his son's descent on his Viennese idyll with a presumably virtuous female companion.

That it was an idyll was not long in doubt. He was in love with the girl—she was some twenty years younger than he was —and he made it plain. He also (though to do him justice he tried not to) made it plain that Timothy's appearance in Vienna at this moment was, to say the least of it, inopportune. By the time he had shepherded us through the dining-room for supper I saw with misgiving that resentment or insecurity had brought the sullen look back to Timothy's face.

I saw that Christl was watching him, too; and saw the exact

45

moment at which—while Graham was busy with the menu and the head waiter— she set herself deliberately to charm him. It was beautifully done, and was not too difficult, since she was not much older than he was, was very pretty, and had in full measure that warm, easy Viennese charm, which (as Vienna's friends and enemies both agree) 'sings the song you want to hear'. Before the wine was half down in our glasses, Timothy was looking entertained and flattered, and eating as if he had seen no food for a fortnight, while his father, also visibly relaxing, was able to devote himself to me.

He had already thanked me very pleasantly for accompanying Timothy across the Continent, and skated skilfully enough over the reason why he couldn't offer his son his own hospitality that night. He asked now with civil indifference after Carmel's health, and with equal indifference about that of my family, but it was soon obvious that he was curious to know what I was doing in Vienna, and just how Carmel had managed to involve me in her affairs, so I gathered that Timothy had said nothing to him in their brief telephone conversation.

"Oh, I'm just on holiday," I said. "My husband was called away to Stockholm just as we were setting off for a holiday together, so I came on here myself, and he'll be joining me soon."

"In Vienna?"

"No, in Graz. We planned a motoring holiday in South Austria, and I'm going down there tomorrow myself. It was just luck that I happened to be heading this way at the same time as Timothy."

"Indeed," said Graham Lacy politely. "That should be delightful. Where were you planning to go?"

Since I had only that moment, so to speak, launched myself and Lewis on a motoring tour of Southern Austria, I naturally hadn't the faintest idea. But I had had two years' experience of the married woman's way out of any difficulty. I said immediately: "Oh, I left all that to my husband. He's worked out a route, and to be quite honest I can't really remember exactly where he plans to go. I just sort of relax and go along with him."

"Ah, yes," said Graham Lacy, and then, to his son: "And what are your plans, Tim?" Timothy, caught off guard by the direct question, swallowed, flushed, and said nothing. He had been listening to my string of lies with no betraying gleam of surprise, even perhaps, with amusement; but now, faced either with confessing that he had come to Vienna naturally expecting his father to take him in, or with himself inventing some spur-of-the-moment story, he was dumb. There was a painful pause.

I opened my mouth to say something, but Christl rushed into the pause, saying in her pretty, soft voice: "Well, of course, he has come to see Vienna! What else? Timmy"—she said it charmingly, *Timmee*—"I wish I could show Vienna to you myself! There is so much to see, I should love to take you everywhere—all the places the tourists visit, the Hofburg, Schönbrunn, the Prater, Kahlenberg, and then all the places that the Viennese themselves go to—but I cannot, I am going out of Vienna tomorrow. I am so very disappointed, but you see I have promised; it is so many months since I have seen my parents, and they have been pressing me, and I have promised to go."

"But—" began Graham Lacy.

She touched his hand, and he stopped obediently, but the look of surprise on his face was a dead give-away, and it was not difficult to interpret the look she gave him. It was quite obvious that she intended to clear herself out of Graham's apartment with the greatest possible speed so that he would be free—indeed, obliged—to do the right thing by his son.

"Well . . ." began Graham Lacy. He cleared his throat. "Tomorrow's Sunday, so I've a free day. What do you say, old man, shall I come along about eleven or so, and collect you and your stuff? Then after you've settled in we could go out and do some of the sights? I don't have a great deal of time during the week, but you'll soon find your own way about."

Timothy's glance went from one to the other. I realised that he had seen as much as I had. He was a little flushed, but he said composedly enough: "That's terribly nice of you, Daddy, but I

47

won't descend on you just yet. I'd actually planned to go south with Vanessa tomorrow."

If Graham or Christl felt relief, they neither of them showed it. Graham said: "Indeed? It's very nice of Mrs March to ask you, but if she and her husband are setting off for their tour, they'll hardly want——"

"We won't be starting for a day or two," I said quickly, "I'm still not quite sure how soon Lewis will be able to join me, so I'll have a bit of time to fill in before we set off. I'd love to have Tim with me."

"Don't worry, I shan't land myself on them," said Timothy cheerfully, and quite without irony. "In any case I've been planning to get down into Styria somehow and visit Piber, and see the Lipizzan stud there, so if Mrs March wants company, it'll be killing two birds with one stone. If you don't mind being called a bird in public, Vanessa?"

"Delighted," I said.

"Then," said young Mr Lacy calmly, "that's settled. I'll ring you up, Daddy, when I'm coming back to Vienna." And he turned his attention to the sweet trolley, from which he presently selected a quite enormous portion of *Sachertorte*, a rich and very sweet chocolate cake topped with whipped cream.

I had the strong impression that the company settled down to drink their coffee with a distinct air of relaxation and relief all round. When we finally left the dining-room, Timothy and his father vanished in perfect amity in the direction of the cloakroom, and, when they returned, I thought I could see from their differing expressions of satisfaction that Graham had 'come through' quite handsomely with funds, without his son's having to resort to the blackmail he had threatened.

"Well," said Graham, as we bade each other good night, "I hope you enjoy yourselves. Take care of Mrs March, won't you, Timmy? And let me know when you're coming back to Vienna. If only you'd thought to let me know this time . . ." He added, awkwardly, "I'm afraid this has been a rather odd welcome to my long-lost son."

The cliché, would-be jocular, fell rather sadly among the shadows of Vienna's midnight pavement.

Timothy said cheerfully: "I'll remember next time. And thanks for tonight, it's been smashing."

The Peugeot drove off. Timothy and I turned to walk back to our hotel.

"Do you mind?" he asked.

"You know I don't. I told you I'd be glad to have you. That, at least, wasn't a lie . . . And talking of lies, we brushed through that pretty well, wouldn't you say? She's a nice girl, Tim."

"I know that. I did mind at first. I couldn't help it. But I don't now, not a bit." We were passing the lighted windows of Prachner's bookshop: I saw that he had a look that I had not seen in him before, buoyant and clear and free. "After all," he said, "he's got a perfect right to his own life, hasn't he? You can't hang on to people for ever. You've got to let them go."

"Of course," I said.

Chapter Four

Ay, now I am in Arden; the more fool I. When I was at home I was in a better place; but travellers must be content.

Shakespeare: *As You Like It*

We drove into the village of Oberhausen at about five o'clock next day.

Now that Timothy was coming with me, I had abandoned my original plan of going by train to Bruck or Graz, and hiring a car from there. Moreover, it was Sunday, and I was not sure if such arrangements could be made on a Sunday afternoon. But in Vienna, it seemed, anything could be arranged at more or less any time, especially with the efficient and willing help of the desk staff of the Hotel am Stephansplatz.

So it came about that Timothy and I left Vienna in a hired Volkswagen shortly before noon next day, making our way out through the mercifully thin Sunday traffic with me at the wheel and Timothy, map on knee, guiding me with remarkable efficiency out along the Triester Strasse, past the car cemetery, and on to the Wiener Neustadt road.

It was a beautiful day. As we ran south-west from Vienna along the *Autobahn* the countryside, at first dull and scabbed with urban industry, began to lift itself by degrees from the flat monotony of the plain. Beyond Wiener Neustadt we found ourselves in a rolling landscape of forested slopes, green pastures, and romantic crags girdled by silver streams and crowned with castles.

It was a scene from the idylls rather than from romance, pastoral rather than Gothic. The valley bottoms were rich with crops, and the hayfields stretched golden right up to the spurs of the hills. Even when the road—magnificently engineered— began its twisting climb to the Semmering Pass, there was still nothing in the grand manner about the scenery; the great slopes of pine forest were only a shelter and a frame for the peaceful human picture below.

We ate at Semmering—a resort which, at four thousand feet, is sunny all winter and which now, in the height of summer, had air so dizzyingly clear as to make Timothy extra ravenous even by his standards, and to restore to me something of the appetite which had been taken away by the nervous tension that I hadn't yet admitted, but which increased steadily as we neared the end of the journey.

We were on our way again by three, descending through more and more beautiful country till, a few kilometres beyond Bruck, we left the main road and its accompanying river, and turned up the valley of a tributary.

I pulled off the road on to a verge felted with pine needles.

"You've got a licence, haven't you, Tim? Would you like to drive?"

"Love to," he said promptly. "Are you tired?"

"A bit. It's a bit over-concentrated, with the left-hand drive, and driving on the wrong side, and all the cars out for the Sunday afternoon stampede. I must say you were marvellous over the road signs. I hope I'll do as well for you, or have you got your eye in by now?"

"I think so," he said as we changed over. "It doesn't look as if there'll be much traffic up this little road, anyway."

He took a few moments to examine the controls and play with the gear-box, and then we moved off. Not much to my surprise—I had long since ceased to underrate Timothy—he turned out to be a good driver, so that I was able to relax and think about what lay ahead of me, while I pretended for pride's sake to be admiring the scenery.

This was not difficult. The road ran at first through pine trees with a widish tumbling stream to the right, then, rounding a green bluff, it began to climb, curling along under cliffs hollowed by quarries and heavily overhung by the forests above, while beside us the stream fell ever more steeply through a series of rapids, and on the far bank the rocks crowded in.

But soon we were out of the narrow defile into a wide placid basin girdled by hills. Here the road ran straighter, bounded to either side only by green meadows knee-deep in white and yellow flowers. Behind the meadows rose the hills; at first softly, furred with grass, their green curves framed by the pines which flowed downhill to fill every fold and crevice of the slopes, as if the high forest were crowding so thickly on the crests that it overflowed down every vein and runnel of the land below, like whipped cream running down the side of a pudding. At the upper limits of this dense crowded forest soared the cliffs again, shining escarpments of silver rock threaded in their turn by the white veins of falling water.

But these were still in no sense overpowering hills. They fell short of majesty, staying, as it were, on the periphery of vision, while the eye was held by the nearer landscape with its rolling, golden greens, and the cheerful domestic charm of the small houses that were clustered here and there round their churches and farms. The hay had been cut, and was drying, woven round its poles like dark gold flax round the spindles, while below it the shorn fields lay as smooth as plush. Here and there were shrines, like tiny churches cut off at the apse, with flowers in front of some painted statue, and martins wheeling in and out under the shingle roof. The village houses, too, were painted, the walls all washed with pink, or pale blue, or white, while every window had its window-box tumbling with petunias, geraniums, marguerites. Every house, it seemed, had its small orchard heavy with apples and peaches, and its apricot tree trained against the bright wall. Everything glittered, was rich, shone. The little village churches, humbly built of paint-washed plaster and roofed with wooden shingles, each thrust up a spire or an onion dome topped with a glittering gold weathercock. The cattle grazing peacefully in the fields were honey-coloured, and bore large, deep-ringing bells. The valley scene was so rich, so sunlit, and so peaceful, that the eye hardly strayed up to the rocks behind. They were only a background to this entrancing pastoral, painted in with the long shadows of late afternoon.

The first thing I saw, as we ran into the village of Oberhausen, was the poster, CIRCUS WAGNER, wrapped round a tree-trunk. The second was the circus itself in a field to the right of the road, a motley collection of tents, wagons and caravans, grouped in an orderly confusion round the big top.

Timothy slowed to a crawl as we both craned to see.

"Well," he said, "they're still here. That's something, anyway. What are we going to do first?"

"Go straight through and try to find the Gasthof. Didn't the hall porter say it was at the far end of the village? Let's find it, and get ourselves settled before we do anything else."

"O.K."

The village street closed in. It was narrow, with no pavements, apart from a foot or two of beaten dust which formed a verge to either side and which was separated from the road by trees. Here and there a gabled window, or a flight of steps, thrust out to the edge of the road, forcing the people to abandon the footpaths and walk among the traffic. This they did with the utmost casualness: in fact the road, being smoother walking, was fuller than the footways, as the slow aimless Sunday crowd strolled about it at will, crossing in front of the cars without a glance. Since (as in most Austrian villages) the use of the horn was forbidden, our progress was very slow and circumspect. Timothy's pungent but perfectly cheerful running commentary was mercifully audible only to me.

At length we emerged from the narrows into an open square where an old well stood, and seats were set under the trees that surrounded the cobbled space. Ahead of us a church lifted a pretty onion spire with a gilt arrow for weathercock. The road divided to either side of the church.

I said: "I think we'd better stop and ask the way. If we go up the wrong street among these crowds, heaven knows where we'll get to before we can turn."

He drew carefully in to the side, stopped in the shade of a plane tree, and leaned out of his window. He hadn't far to go for help: A cheerful trio of women was passing the time of day in the middle of the road with half a dozen children skirmishing round their skirts. They all answered him at once, with explicit gestures, while the children, apparently stricken dumb and paralytic at the sound of Timothy's accent, crowded round, staring at us with round blue eyes.

At length he drew his head in. "Don't tell me," I said, "let me guess. It's the road to the right."

He grinned. "And we can't miss it. They say it's very nice along there, and quiet, because the other road's the main one. I say, I like this place, don't you? Look at that thing in the middle, the well or whatever it is, with that wrought-iron canopy. It's rather fine. Gosh, do you see that *Konditorei,* the baker's shop with the café tables inside? I could do with some of those cakes, couldn't you? We could come out and buy something as soon as we get settled . . ."

He chattered on, pleasantly excited, hanging out of his window in the hot sun. But I had ceased to listen, or even to see. The pretty village, with it's lively, milling crowds, had faded away, to become a shadowy background only for one person. I had seen Lewis's blonde.

She was pausing beside the well to speak to someone, an old woman in black, who carried an armful of flowers. She was half facing the other way, and was some forty yards off, but I thought I could not be mistaken. Then she turned, and I was sure. This was the girl I had seen on the news-reel. Moreover, in the flesh, and in the bright light of day, she was prettier even than I remembered. She was of small to medium height, with a slender curved young figure, and fair hair tied neatly back in a pony tail. Gone was the 'kinky' look that the waterproof and dishevelled hair had given her; she was charmingly dressed now in the traditional white blouse, flowered dirndl, and apron. She looked about eighteen.

As I watched her, she bade a laughing goodbye to the old woman, and came straight towards the car.

"Tim," I said softly, "pull your head in and shut the window. Quick."

He obeyed immediately.

"That girl coming towards the car, the pretty one, the blonde in the blue dirndl—that's the girl I saw in the news-reel. No, don't stare at her, just notice her, so that you'll know her again."

She came straight towards us, through the banded shadows of the tree-trunks, and passed the car without a glance. I didn't turn, but I saw Tim watching her in the driving mirror.

"She's going straight on down the street. Shall I wait?"

"Yes. Try to see where she goes."

After a pause he said: "I can't see her any more, there are too many people milling about, but she was heading straight down the street, the way we came in."

"Towards the circus field?"

"Yes. Would you like me to do a quick 'recce' and see just where she goes?"

"Would you?"

"Sure thing." He was already half out of the car. "I've always fancied myself in the James Bond line, who hasn't? You stay there and pay the parking fine."

The door slammed behind him. I tilted the driving mirror so that I could watch his tall young figure striding back down the middle of the street with all the magnificent local disregard for traffic. Then he, in his turn, was lost to view.

I leaned back in my seat, but not to relax. It was no surprise to feel myself trembling a little as my eyes reluctantly, yet feverishly, searched the crowds.

It was true, then, that my eyes had not deceived me: so much of it was true. Now that I had this confirmation, I found it a profoundly disconcerting experience. The sight of Lewis and the girl in the dark cinema, that flickering brief scene still echoing with ugly tragedy and made more mysterious by its foreign setting, had been like a dream, something distant, unreal, gone as soon as seen, and believed no more than a dream in daylight. And as always, the light of day outside the cinema had set the dream even further apart from the world of reality. My own hasty action in coming out to Austria had seemed even while I did it as unreal as the dream itself; and up to now the enchanting strange prettiness of the country had helped the illusion that I was still far astray from reality.

But now . . . Oberhausen, the circus, the girl herself . . . And next, Lewis . . .?

"What, no parking ticket?" It was Tim, back at the window.

"No parking ticket. You made me jump. I never heard you."

"I told you I'd found my vocation." He folded his length beside me into the driving seat. "I shadowed your subject with the greatest possible skill, and she did go to the circus. I think she must belong there, because she went straight in through the gate and then round towards the caravans. The village people—quite a lot were there with children—were being allowed in, but they all went to the other side; there's a menagerie or something there, open to the public. There was a man taking the money at the gate, but I didn't ask questions. Was that right?"

"Yes, quite."

"And I've got news for you. They're leaving tomorrow. There was a sticker across the poster, last performance tonight at eight o'clock."

"Oh? We're just lucky, then. Thanks a lot, Tim."

"Think nothing of it. It was fun. I tell you, I've come to the conclusion I'll be wasted on the Spanish Riding School. James Bond isn't in it—though as a matter of fact, Archie Goodwin's my favourite detective; you know, Nero Wolfe's assistant, handsome and efficient and a devil with women."

"Well, now's your chance," I said. "If we don't fall over Lewis pretty soon, I'll send you after the girl."

"What they call 'scraping an acquaintance'? Can do," said Tim cheerfully. "Golly, if this road gets much narrower, we'll scrape more than that . . . Wait a moment, though, I believe this is it."

The Gasthof Edelweiss was charming, and, in spite of its name, without a hint of chichi. It was a long, low, single-storeyed house, with a shingle roof where doves sunned themselves, and window-boxes full of flowers. It lay at the very edge of the village, and in fact the road petered out in front of it to continue on past the house as a country track leading to some farm. Between house and road lay a space of raked gravel where tables stood under chestnut trees. There were a few people sitting there over coffee or drinks. Between their feet the doves strutted and cooed. Swallows, thinking already perhaps of the hotter south, wheeled and twittered overhead. One could smell the pines.

Timothy and I were offered adjacent rooms, giving on the wide veranda at the back of the house. Here the windows faced the fields, and the small spotless rooms were very quiet. Mine had a pinewood floor scrubbed white, with two small bright psuedo-Persian rugs, solid pine furniture, and one reasonably comfortable chair. There was a really beautiful old chest of dark wood with painted panels, a rather inconvenient wardrobe, and a lot of heavy wrought-ironwork in the lamp brackets, and on the door, which was studded and barred like something from a Gothic cathedral. On the walls were two pictures, bright oily colours painted on wood; one showed an unidentifiable saint in a blue robe killing a dragon; the other a very similar saint in a red robe, watering some flowers. It seemed that in Austria there was a pleasantly wide choice of saintly qualities.

I unpacked quickly. I had thought I would be glad to be alone, just to think about what was to come, but in fact I found that I was refusing to think about it. I had, as it were, switched my mind out of gear and was concentrating only on folding away my clothes, on selecting something fresh to wear, and on the drink which I would shortly have with Timothy under the chestnut trees.

But when I was ready to go, I still lingered. I pushed the long windows wide, and went out on to the veranda.

This was set only two or three feet above ground level, so that immediately beyond the rail, and directly, it seemed, beneath one's feet, the fields began. These had been recently mown, and the almost forgotten smell of new-mown hay filled the late afternoon. Beyond the stretches of shorn velvet the river ran, sunk deep in trees, and behind this feathered girdle of ash and willow rose the pines, slope after slope to the silver mountain-tops. One side of the valley was deep in shadow. It was nearly half past six.

A sound made me look round. Timothy had come out of his window on to his section of veranda. He had put on a clean shirt and looked alert and excited.

"There you are, I thought I heard you. I wondered if you'd decided what to do next?"

"Actually, I hadn't. I'm sorry. I'm afraid I'm a bit of a dead loss. I haven't got over seeing that girl. It was a bit of a facer if you want the truth, like seeing a ghost."

"You mean you didn't really believe in her till now? I know exactly what you mean," added Timothy surprisingly. "I felt a bit the same about Christl. But you know, I don't know why you're worrying, not about *her* . . . I mean, if there was any connection . . . seeing them together on the news-reel like that . . . it wouldn't be —" He hesitated, trying to choose his words, then abruptly abandoned finesse. "Dash it, she may be pretty and all that, but *you* don't need to worry about her! You're beautiful! Did no one ever tell you?"

It was a fact that, now and again, people had; but I had never been so touched—or so completely deprived of speech.

I said eventually: "Thank you. But I—it's not just that side of it that's worrying me, you know. It's just that I've no business to be here at all, and now I'm not so much wondering how to find him as what in the world to say to him when I do . . ." I turned my back to the fields, and straightened up with what might pass for decision. "Oh, well, it's done now, and the circus is the obvious lead. Did you say it started at eight? Then we've plenty of time. We can have a meal and talk to Frau Weber, and then walk down through the village. If this village is anything like our village at home, the bush telegraph's faster than the speed of light. In fact, if he's here still, he probably knew all about us within thirty seconds of my signing the hotel register."

"If this is the last performance, they'll start the pull-down the minute it's over, and they'll be clear of the place by morning." He eyed me. "I thought—shall I just go along there now, and see about getting tickets?"

"But if they've been stuck here a week there'll be no rush, and —" I laughed. "Oh, I see. Well, why not? If you do track down 'the subject', you won't do anything rash, will you?"

"The soul of discretion," he promised. "I won't say a word. I'll be back in good time for dinner."

"I bet you will," I said, but he had already gone.

Chapter Five

I see, lady, the gentleman is not in your books.
                    Shakespeare: *Much Ado About Nothing*

The shadows of the chestnuts lay lightly across the café tables, and there was a slight warm breeze which fluttered the red checked cloths. Curled in the roots of one of the trees, an enormous St Bernard dog slept, twitching slightly from time to time in his dream. The place was quiet and very peaceful. I sat sipping my vermouth, telling myself that I must think, must think . . . and all the time my eyes were fixed on the street up which presently, I was sure, Lewis must come.

So strong was my imaginative sense of his presence that when, in fact, Timothy reappeared, coming at high speed up the street, I was almost startled to see him. Next moment I was genuinely startled to see who he had with him. Not Lewis, but—inevitably, it now seemed—Lewis's blonde.

Next moment they were standing beside the table, and Timothy was performing introductions.

"Vanessa, this is Annalisa Wagner. She belongs to the circus . . . You remember we saw a circus in the field the other side of the village? Miss Wagner, this is Mrs —" Too late, he saw the pitfall. He stopped dead.

I said, watching the girl: "My name is March. Vanessa March."

"How do you do, Mrs March?" There was no flicker of expression outside the normal non-committal politeness. She had, I noticed sourly, a charming voice, and her English was excellent.

"Won't you join us for a drink, Miss Wagner?"

"Why, thank you. If you would please call me Annalisa?"

Timothy said. "What will you have?"

"Coffee, please."

"Only coffee? Not a vermouth or something?"

She shook her head. "You'll find that we circus people drink very little. It's something that doesn't pay. Just coffee, please."

Timothy lifted a hand to the passing waitress, who responded immediately—an unusual circumstance in any country, but in Austria (I had already discovered) a miracle. It seemed he was even going to pass the waiter test with honours. He and the girl sat down, Timothy telegraphing "Over to you" with a subdued air of triumph that had nothing to do with the waitress, Annalisa with a smile and a graceful spread of the blue-flowered skirt.

Seen at close range, she was still very pretty, with an

ash-blonde Teutonic prettiness quite different from Christl's. One could not picture Fräulein Wagner as altogether at home in a kitchen. She would seem more in place among those slim, tough beauties who win olympic medals for skating, or who perform impossible feats of skill and balance in the slalom. I wondered if the impression of fragility and helpless appeal that I had got from the news-reel had been assumed for Lewis's benefit, or if it had merely shown up in contrast to his size and air of tough competence. Or perhaps—I realised it now, more charitably—she had just been caught in a moment of shock and distress. It appeared that it was her circus, after all.

I said as much. "Your name's Wagner? The circus must belong to you, to your family?"

"To my father. Timothy says that you are coming to see it tonight?"

"Yes. We're looking forward to it. We've only just arrived, but I understand that you are leaving tomorrow, so we don't want to miss you."

She nodded. "We move on tonight, after the show. We have already been here too long." I waited, but she did not pursue this. She asked: "You are keen on circuses?"

I hesitated, then said truthfully: "Not altogether. I've never liked performing animals much, but I love the other acts— high wire, trapeze, the clowns, all the acrobats."

"Not the horses?"

"Oh, I didn't count the horses as 'performing animals!' I meant bears and monkeys and tigers. I love the horses. Do you have many?"

"Not many, we are a small circus. But a circus is nothing without its horses. With us they are the most important of all. My father works the liberty horses: we think ourselves they are as good as the circus Schumann, but of course, we have not so many."

"I'll look forward to seeing them, I always love them, and they're my friend's ruling passion."

She laughed. "I know. I found him down in the horse lines. I don't know how he got in."

Timothy said: "I took a ticket for the menagerie, but you couldn't expect me to look at parrots and monkeys when I could see the horses just round the corner."

"No, it is not a good menagerie, I know. It is just a side-show for the children."

I said: "What good English you speak."

"My mother was English. I still get plenty of practice, because a circus is a very mixed place, really international. We have just now all sorts: the clowns are French, and the high-wire act is Hungarian, and the trampoline artistes are Japanese, and there is a comic act with a donkey, which is English, and an American juggler—besides the Germans and Austrians."

"United Nations," said Tim.

"Indeed." She dimpled at him. "And on the whole really united. We have to be."

"Have you an act yourself?" I asked.

"Yes. I help my father with the liberty horses . . . and there is a sort of rodeo act near the beginning. But my own act is a riding one. I have a Lipizzan stallion —"

"You have a what?" Timothy's interruption was robbed of rudeness by his obviously excited interest.

"A Lipizzan stallion. This is a breed of horse —"

"Yes, I know about them. I'm hoping to get to Piber to see the stud, and later on to see a performance in Vienna. But do you mean you have a *trained* stallion? I didn't think they ever sold them."

"He is trained, yes, but not at the School. My grandfather bought him as a four-year-old, and my uncle trained him . . . and me also."

"In high school work?"

She nodded.

"And you have a riding act of your own? You're a—a what is it?—an *ecuyere*?"

She had soared, I could see, in Timothy's estimation, from being 'the subject' or 'Lewis's blonde', to star billing in her own right. I realised that my own estimate of her had been right: a young woman who was capable of the concentrated skill and strength needed to put a high school stallion through his paces was about as fragile as pressed steel. "Gosh!" said Timothy, glowing with admiration.

She smiled. "Oh, not what you will see in Vienna, I assure you! None of the 'airs above the ground' except the *levade*, and sometimes the *croupade* . . ." She turned to me. "This is a leap right off the ground where the horse keeps his legs curled up—is that the word?"

"Tucked under him," supplied Tim.

"His legs tucked under him, and lands again on the same spot. We tried to teach him the *capriole*, where he leaps in a *croupade* and then kicks the back legs straight out, but this is very difficult, and he cannot do it, so now I leave it alone. It is my fault, not his."

In view of the admiration in Timothy's eyes I half expected him to contradict this, but he didn't. He was, like her, dedicated enough to know that it is never the horse's fault.

She added: "But in the other exercises he is wonderful. He is one of the Maestoso line, Maestoso Leda, and he is so musical . . . but there is no need for me to tell you. You will see him for yourselves tonight, and if he is good tonight I will try the *croupade*, especially for you."

We murmured our thanks. Tim's eyes were shining. I was going to have my work cut out to keep Annalisa as Suspect Number One in my Case of the Vanishing Husband.

He was saying: "I can hardly wait. Was he with the other horses? I didn't see him."

"You were at the wrong end of the stable." She dimpled at him again, charmingly. "You should have trespassed first at the other end. Yes, he is there. Would you like to come round tonight after the show and see the horses? There will be time before we pull down."

"You bet I would!" Then recollecting himself, with a glance at me, "Vanessa—?"

"I'd like to very much," I said. "How many have you?"

"Altogether twenty-seven, and then the ponies. The liberty horses are very good ones, you'll like them, Timothy, they are palominos, and we have twelve, very well matched. There will be only ten of them fit to work tonight, but it is still very beautiful to watch."

"'Fit to work'?" I asked, wondering if she intended what the phrase implied, or if her English had its blind moments. "Is there something wrong with the others?"

"Not really, but they're so valuable that one must be extra careful. There was an accident last week, and some of the horses were hurt. One of the wagons caught fire in the night, quite near the stable lines, and some of the horses injured themselves, with fear, you understand." She added, quietly: "But it was more serious than a few horses hurt. There were two men in the wagon, and they were killed, burnt to death."

"How very dreadful. How did that happen?"

"We are still not very sure." I thought she was going to stop there, but then she lifted her shoulders in a shrug and went on: "But if you are staying in the village, you will hear all about it, everybody in Oberhausen talks about nothing else for a week. This is why the circus has had to stay here so long, because the police came, and made inquiries." She made a little face. "That is what they call it, 'making inquiries'—hour after hour they asked questions and raked about and only today they say, 'Tomorrow you may go. It is over.'"

"I'm sorry. It must have been very distressing."

"It was a bad time for my father." The blue eyes lifted to mine. "The wagon belonged to Franz Wagner, his cousin . . . my Uncle Franzl. I always called him that, though really he was my second cousin . . . I suppose he always seemed old to me. He joined us when I was a little girl."

I forgot all my preconceived feelings about her in a genuine rush of sympathy. "My dear Fräulein . . . my dear Annalisa, I'm sorry. I hadn't realised it was a relative . . . that's awful. You must have had a terrible time."

She shrugged again, not uncaringly, but dismissively. "It is over."

"And the other man? There was another, you said?"

"He was nothing to do with the circus. He must have met my

63

Uncle Franzl somewhere, and gone back to his wagon for a drink—a talk, who knows? We did not know there was anyone else there with him. They pulled my Uncle Franzl out . . . He lived for a little, only a few minutes. But it was only when the wagon was nearly all burned that they found the . . . the other one."

"I see." I was silent for a moment. Perhaps I ought not to press her, but though she had spoken sombrely, the subject didn't appear to distress her unduly now. She must have repeated all this a hundred times during the past week. "But they did find out who the second man was?"

She nodded. "He was an Englishman. His name was Paul Denver, and he belonged to some British firm which had a a branch in Vienna . . . I didn't understand what sort of work, but I think it was something to do with farming. My father had not heard of him, and we don't know how Uncle Franzl met him—we had only arrived that day in Oberhausen, you understand. We don't usually give a performance on a Sunday, so they think that Uncle Franzl went out that evening drinking somewhere, and met this man, and got talking to him, and then they came back together and . . . perhaps they talked late, and drank a little more . . . You can picture to yourself how it might be . . ."

She paused, and I said: "Yes." I could picture it only too well. The wagon would burn like a torch. And beside it the stables, the plunging, panic-stricken horses, the screaming from the menagerie, the chaos of shouting.

"It was the lamp that fell," she said. "Afterwards they found the hook had broken that held it. It was the noise from the horses that gave the alarm. Then people began shouting that there was someone else in the wagon, but it was burning hard by that time; and then the other Englishman came running out of the dark and helped to pull him out. It turned out that he knew him; he had come to Oberhausen to meet him."

It was Timothy who said: " 'The other Englishman'?"

"Yes. He works for the same firm and he had just arrived in Oberhausen, driving from Vienna, and he saw the fire, and came to help."

It was still Timothy who asked: "And when did he leave?"

"Leave?" said Annalisa. "He is still here. He—" Then she stopped and smiled, and with the smile the strained look lifted and the sparkle came back. She was looking beyond me, to where someone had come in from the street. "Why, here he is," she said.

A man had just turned in from the street under the dappled shade of the chestnut trees. He paused there, looking towards our table. I believe I was already half out of my chair, regardless of what Annalisa might think. I heard Timothy say something, some question. And then the newcomer moved forward from the patch of shadow into the sunlight, and I met, full on, his indifferent, unrecognising eyes, and slight look of surprise.

I think I said: "No, no it's not," to Timothy, as I sank back into my chair.

Across me Annalisa was calling out: "Lee! Come and join us!"

Then the newcomer was standing over us, and introductions were being made.

"Lee," said Annalisa, "this is Vanessa March. Vanessa, Mr Elliott . . . And this is Tim."

I murmured something, heaven knows what, and the two men greeted one another. Mr Elliott pulled up a chair next to mine.

"I take it you must just have arrived here, or we'd have heard all about you long ago. In a place this size every movement is reported."

I managed to pull myself out of the turmoil into which the appearance of the 'other Englishman' had plunged me, and answered him civilly, if slightly at random. "Oh, I can believe that. Yes, we've only been here an hour or so. We came from Vienna today by car."

"And what brings you to Oberhausen?"

"Oh, just . . . touring around." I caught Timothy's eye on me, worried and speculative even while he replied to some remark of Annalisa's, and made another effort. "Actually, we—I was expecting to meet my husband down here . . . that is, in Graz . . . but after we got there we heard that he couldn't make it after

65

all. So we thought we might as well take a run out to see the countryside while we were here . . . It's very lovely, isn't it?"

"Very. You're staying in the village, then?"

"Only for the night. We're here, at the Edelweiss. We'll go back . . . that is, we'll go in the morning. Tim's got plans to visit Piber, you know, the Lipizzaner stud, so we'll probably go back that way. I can put in the time till I get a message from my husband."

Some fragment of what I was feeling must have shown through the carefully social mask I had put on. He said, in a tone which seemed meant to sound comforting: "I'm sure that will be soon."

I managed a creditably bright smile. "I hope so! But meanwhile Tim and I intend to enjoy ourselves, starting with the circus tonight."

"Tim is your brother?" This was from Annalisa. "He didn't tell me his other name. Not March?"

"No, anyway that'd have made me a brother-in-law," said Timothy. "My name's Lacy. No relation. Just companion, chauffeur and general dogsbody."

"Dog's body?" She made two words of it, puzzled. "Why do you call yourself that? To me, it sounds not at all polite."

"It isn't." I said. "He's trying to make out that he gets all the work to do organising our trip. I must say I wouldn't have got far without his German. All right, dogsbody, organise a drink for Mr Elliot, will you?"

"If you can do that in under twenty minutes," said Mr Elliott, "you're worth your weight in platinum. Good God!" This as the waitress, obedient still to Timothy's lightest gesture, paused by our table. The three of them plunged into a discussion, Mr Elliott in what sounded like, and probably was, flawless German.

As she sped away, I turned to him, composed now.

He had taken a pipe out of his pocket and was lighting it. It made him look very English. Apart from this, in his nondescript and rather shabby clothes, he might have been anything, anybody, from anywhere. He was tallish, and toughly built, and when he moved it was with a kind of springy precision that indicated strength and muscular control. But his voice and personality, while pleasant enough, struck me then as being singularly colourless. His hair was brown, his eyes of an indeterminate shade somewhere between blue and grey. His hands were good, but I could see a broken nail, and dirt ingrained in them as if he had been working hard at some dirty job. Since I had gathered from Annalisa that he was here as a representative of his firm, this hardly seemed in character, but perhaps he had been lending a kindly hand around the circus. His clothes bore this out; they looked like cheap holiday clothes which had recently had rough and even dirty wear.

I said: "And you? I understand from Fräulein Wagner that you're down here on business. I was very sorry to hear about the accident."

"She told you about that, did she? Yes, one of the men who died was a colleague of mine. He'd come down here on a project investigating farming methods and use of fertilisers, and I was actually on my way to meet him when it happened."

"I'm sorry." We exchanged a few commiserating phrases, then I asked: "What is your firm, Mr Elliott?"

"Our Vienna connection is Kalkenbrunner Fertilisers."

"Oh? Perhaps you know my husband's firm, Pan-European Chemicals?"

"Of course, though I can't for the moment recall any of the people. Stewart, did he work for them? Craig? I may have met your husband, but I don't remember, I'm afraid. Is he in Vienna often?"

"I haven't the faintest idea," I said, with perfect truth, though not perhaps with perfect civility. I was feeling the strain of this polite conversation about nothing. "Here's your drink. Have you been here ever since the accident happened?"

"Yes. The police inquiries went on rather a long time, and since my firm was willing to give me leave till things were cleared up, I stayed and gave a hand where it was needed." He smiled. "Not with the police, with the circus. There's your definition of a dogsbody, Annalisa . . . what I've been doing for the past week."

"You? You have been marvellous!" The look she gave him was almost as glowing as the one Timothy had given her. "Mrs March, you've no idea . . . I told you we were a small circus, and this means that everybody has to work hard. And after Uncle Franzl's death . . . I think that we had not realised how much he did. Perhaps this is always the way when someone dies? He was not a performer, you understand. He was a wonderful rider, but he would do no circus work—I mean, he would not work an act . . . But he was in charge of the horses, and I told you, he trained Maestoso Leda, and taught me my act . . ."

It seemed to be some kind of release to her to talk, and we all listened quietly. Beside me, Mr Elliott sat very still and relaxed, his eyes never leaving the girl.

"I remember it well," she said, "when he joined us. It was ten years ago, when I was eight, and my grandfather was still alive. We were near Wels, in Upper Austria, and my grandfather had just bought Maestoso Leda, and the Lipizzans themselves were staying in Wels at that time, and we went to see them. You can imagine"—this to Timothy—"how excited they made me! There was also a big horse fair in Wels, and this was the lucky thing, because my Uncle Franzl happened to be there with a dealer he went with after he left the Czech circus where he had worked. I think before that he was in the Army . . . He had not been close to the family, you understand. But he came to see my grandfather, and when we went north that night, into Bavaria, he went with us." She smiled. "Now, I can hardly remember the time when he was not part of our circus. I even forgot that his name was not Wagner . . . My grandfather wished him to change it, and he did. He took charge of all the stable work, and the—what do you call the saddles and the bridles and things? Not harness . . ."

"Tack?" suggested Timothy.

"Thank you, yes, that's it. He was also the vet.—the doctor for the horses. So you can imagine what it has been like, with so many of the animals damaged with the panic on the night of the fire, and my father with so much to attend to. He had no time for the horses, and Rudi, that's the chief groom, broke his arm getting the horses out . . . So I've had to do it, and Lee has helped me. Of course some of the artistes have helped also, but they have to practise for themselves every day . . . It has not been easy."

"I'll say," said Mr Elliott with feeling. "Who was it said that hell was a paradise of horses?"

"Nobody," I said dryly. "They said England was a paradise for horses and a hell for women."

"Is it?" asked Annalisa, interested.

"It has its moments. Go on, Mr Elliott. Are we to understand that you've been grooming twenty-seven horses for a week?" For the life of me I couldn't help glancing at his clothes.

He saw it and grinned. "I have indeed. I have ministered, you might say, to every detail of their toilet. The grooming's the easiest part, once you've discovered that the hair grows from bow to stern, and you have to brush that way; from the bite to the kick, you might say. The extraordinary thing is, they like it. At least, one gathers they do most of the time. I've only been bitten once."

"You poor thing," I said. "And I believe ponies are worse."

"A Hungarian gentleman did them. He has the advantage of only being three feet high himself. Oh, its been a most instructive week, I shall be sorry to leave."

Annalisa said: "I wish you would not leave. We shall not know what to do without you."

"I must say it'll be a bit deadly to go back to the old routine," said Mr Elliott. He glanced at his watch. "Annalisa, I hate to break the party up, but I really think that we should be going. All those beautiful horses to get ready for the show."

"Goodness, yes!" She got to her feet. The waitress appeared at Timothy's elbow as we all followed suit, and there was the inevitable polite wrangle between Timothy and Lee Elliott over the bill. Timothy—I would have backed him anywhere by now —won easily.

"Well, thanks very much." said Mr Elliott.

"It's been lovely to meet you," said Annalisa, "and shall we see you later? When the show is finished, just ask anybody, they will tell you where to come." She laughed unaffectedly. "I shall feel like a prima donna with visitors coming to ask for me after the show. I hope you enjoy it. *Kommst du*, Lee?"

They went. We sat down. I said: "I thought you'd have wanted to go and help."

"I thought I'd better stay with you," said Timothy. He looked at me. "Do you feel all right? You look awfully funny."

"Funny? How d'you mean?"

"Well, when he came, you went as white as a sheet. I suppose you were expecting your husband."

I nodded.

"So was I. When she said 'the other Englishman' was still here, I thought we were home and dry."

I shook my head. "No. When she heard my name was March, she never reacted. If a Mr March were here in the village—"

"Dash it, how stupid can one be? I'd forgotten that!" Then he frowned. "But that was at the very start . . . before the Elliott chap turned up. Why did you still think that it could be Mr March, when she said, 'Here he is'?"

"I didn't. I thought it *was*. There's a difference . . . Listen, Tim—" I found I was clutching a fold of the tablecloth so tightly that my nails had gone through the thin material. I let it go, and began to smooth out the crushed fabric. "I—I've made a dreadful mistake. When I saw Mr Elliott first, I thought for a moment that it *was* Lewis. When he came nearer, into the light, I saw I was wrong. Now do you see what I've done?"

He did indeed. He was ahead of me. "You mean he—this Elliott chap—was the chap you saw with Annalisa on the news-reel, not your husband at all? That he's enough like him for you to—that he's a sort of *double* of your husband? Gosh!" For the life of him he couldn't quite suppress a gleam of pleased excitement, but this faded abruptly as he took in the further implications of what I had said. "Gosh!" It was a different intonation this time. "You mean that you've come all this way to Austria, and all the time he *is* in Stockholm, just where he said he was?"

"Just exactly that," I said.

There was a silence, so full of comment that it sizzled.

"It's . . . a bit complicated, isn't it?" he said.

"That, my dear, is the understatement of the year."

"What are you going to do?"

I said: "What would you do, chum?"

"Well, eat, to start with," said Timothy, unhesitatingly, and looked round for the waitress.

Chapter Six

To see a fine lady upon a white horse.
Nursery Rhyme

Understandably, there was something a little depressed about the Circus Wagner that evening. Normally, as Timothy pointed out, a small travelling circus stays only for one night in a place like Oberhausen, but the Circus Wagner had been obliged to stand for a week. I gathered that there had been no performance on the week-nights following the disaster of the fire, but the normal two Saturday performances had been permitted, and now with the Sunday show the circus was attempting to recoup some of its losses; but since most of the local people and those from the nearby villages had already been to yesterday's performances, attendance was thin, and Timothy had had no difficulty in getting what he called 'starback' seats for us. These, the best seats, were rather comfortable portable chairs upholstered in red plush, right at the ring-side. As we sat down I saw that the place was half full of children, many of them in the ring-side seats. It turned out that Herr Wagner had reduced prices all round for today, and the children from this and the surrounding villages were perfectly happy to fill the places and see the same show over again for the price. It was a good move; it brought in a little money, and saved the performers from the depressing echoes of an empty house.

A dwarf in a scarlet baggy costume sold us our programme and ushered us into our chairs. The tent was filled with music from some vast amplifier: as always in Austria, the music was pleasant; even in a small village circus we were expected to listen to Offenbach and Suppé and Strauss. The tent was not a big one, but the floodlights on the poles at the four 'corners' of the ring threw so much brilliance down into the ring that above them the top of the tent seemed a vast floating darkness, and very high. Caught by a flicker of light the high wire glittered like a thread. On their platforms near the top of the poles the electricians crouched behind their lights, waiting. There was the circus smell, which is a mingling of sharp animal sweat and trampled grass, and with this the curiously pungent smell of Continental tobacco.

The big lights moved, the music changed, and a march blared out. The curtains at the back of the ring were pulled open, and the procession began.

For a small circus, the standard of performance was remarkably good. Herr Wagner himself was the ringmaster, a short, stocky man, who, even in the frock-coat and top hat of his calling, looked every inch a horseman. The 'rodeo', which followed the procession, was an exciting stampede of horses—real old-fashioned 'circus' horses, piebald and dun-coloured and spotted—supporting a wild-west act with some clever rope-work and voltige riding. Annalisa appeared only briefly, barely recognisable as a cowgirl eclipsed by a ten-gallon hat, and riding a hideous spotted horse with a pink muzzle and pink-rimmed eyes, which looked as clumsy as a hippo, and was as clever on its feet as the Maltese Cat. Then came a comic act with a donkey, and after it Herr Wagner again, with his liberty horses.

These were beautiful, every one a star, ten well-matched palominos with coats the colour of wild silk, and manes and tails of creamy floss. They wheeled in under the lights, plumes tossing, silk manes flying, breaking and reforming their circles, rearing one after the other in line, so that the plumes and the floss-silk manes tossed up like the crest of a breaking wave. Rods and shafts of limelight, falling from above, wove and criss-crossed in patterns of golden light, following the golden horses. Light ran and glittered on them. They were sun horses, bridled and plumed with gold, obedient, you would have sworn, to the pull of those rods of light, as the white horses of the wavecrests are to the pull of the moon.

Then the tossing plumes subsided, the flying hoofs met the ground again, the music stopped, and they were just ten self-satisfied horses, queuing at Herr Wagner's pockets for sugar.

Timothy said in my ear: "You can't tell me those pampered darlings ever bit anyone."

I laughed. "You mean Mr Elliott, our horse expert? He did a good job of grooming on them, anyway. They look wonderful."

"If he's as green about it as he makes out, he's a hero to take on this lot. Funny sort of chap, didn't you think?"

"In what way, funny?"

"Odd. If he's an executive type you wouldn't expect him to stay on here and get down to a job of hard work like that. Bit of a mystery about it, I thought."

"Perhaps he's keen on Annalisa."

"He's too old—" indignantly.

"No man's too old till they hammer down the coffin lid."

"They screw down coffin lids."

"Goodness, the things you know. Come to that, he's no older than Lewis. Do you see him anywhere?"

"Who?"

"Mr Elliott."

"No," said Timothy. "He'll be out the back madly brushing Maestoso Leda from bow to stern and combing out his rudder. Did you mind coming tonight?"

"Mind? Why should I?"

"Well, you must be beastly worried. I must say you're taking it marvellously."

"What else can I do? If you want the truth I feel a bit punch-drunk; it's a right pig's ear, as they'd say at home. In any case, there's nothing I can do till tomorrow, so we may as well enjoy ourselves while we can."

Timothy said: "It occurred to me, if you cabled Stockholm—"

But here, with a deafening crash of brass, and a wild cheer, the clowns came tumbling in, and Timothy, clutching his programme and rocking with laughter, took a dive straight back into childhood. And so, to be fair, did I. It was an act which needed no interpreting, predictable to the last laugh, being a version of the old water act, and the wettest one I had ever seen, with a grand finale involving a very old elephant who routed the whole gaggle of clowns with a water-spouting act of her own which—to judge by the gleam in her clever piggy eye— she much enjoyed.

After the clowns a couple of girls dancing on a tight-rope with pink parasols. Then a troupe of performing dogs. And then Timothy took his finger out of his programme, turned and grinned at me and whispered, "Wait for it."

The trumpets brayed, the ringmaster made his announcement, the red curtains parted, and a white horse broke from the shadows behind the ring and cantered into the limelight. On his back, looking prettier than ever, serene and competent, and tough as a whiplash in a dark blue version of a hussar's uniform, was Annalisa. This horse was not plumed and harnessed as the liberty horses had been; he was dressed for business, but the bridle was a magnificent affair of scarlet studded with gold, and his saddle-cloth glittered and flashed with colour as if every jewel that had ever been discovered was stitched into its silk.

"Oh, boy," said Tim reverently.

His eye was on the stallion, not on the girl, and, remembering the picture of Carmel on her pony, I smiled to myself. But here the rider did deserve some of the reverence. I knew that all the steps and figures the stallion was now performing so fluidly and easily, took years of intensive and patient training to teach. Even though she had not herself done all the training, it took great skill to put a horse through these dressage movements as she did, without any of her own guiding movements being

74

visible. She seemed simply to sit there, part of the horse, light and graceful and motionless, as the white stallion went through his lovely ballet.

Prompted by Timothy's whisper, I recognised the movements; the slow, skimming, Spanish Walk; the dancing fire of the standing trot, or *piaffe*; the shouldering-in which takes the horse diagonally forward in an incredibly smooth, swimming movement; and then, as she had promised us, the 'airs above the ground'. The stallion wheeled to the centre of the ring, snorted, laid back his ears, settled his hind hoofs in the sawdust, then lifted himself and his rider into a *levade*, the classic rearing pose of the equestrian statues. For two long bars of music he held it, then touched ground again for a moment, and—you could see the bunch and thrust of the muscles—launched himself clean into the air in a standing leap. For one superb moment he was poised there, high in the air, caught and lit dazzlingly white by the great lights, all four legs tucked neatly under him, all his jewels flashing and glancing with a million colours, but not it seemed more brilliant than the gleam of the muscles under the white skin or the lustre of the steady dark eye. One looked for his wings.

Then he was on the ground again, cantering round the ring, nodding and bowing his head to the applause which filled even that half empty tent. Then, still bowing and pawing the ground, he backed out of the ring and was lost in the darkness behind the curtain.

I let out a long breath. I felt as if I had been holding it for hours. Timothy and I smiled at one another.

"What's the anticlimax?" I asked him.

He looked at his programme. "Oh, here's your *absolute Star-Attraktion*. . . . Sandor Balog, he's called. It's 'Balog and Nagy', the high wire."

"For goodness' sake, it always terrifies me."

"Me, too," said Timothy happily, settling back as the high wire sprang into the light and the two men started their racing climb towards it. The music swung into a waltz, one of the men started out along the wire, and in the carefully wrought tensions

of the act all other preoccupations fell away, and tomorrow—
Lewis or no Lewis —could take care of itself.

.　.　.

When we came out of the circus tent with the crowd we found
it was quite dark.

"This way," said Timothy, leading me round to the left of
the big tent. Here, earlier in the day, there had been an orderly
crowd of wagons and tents, but many of these had now gone.
Already workmen were attacking the big top, the tent-men
unhooking the sides or walls of the tent, rolling the canvas to
leave for the trailer-men to pick up. Lights were still on in the
big top, presumably to help the work of the pull-down. I saw
the two high-wire artistes now clad in sweaters and jeans and
plimsolls, dismantling their gear from the top of the king-poles.
The hum of the big generator had stopped, and a small donkey
engine had taken over, fussily supplying the remaining lights
by which the circus people worked. Men in overalls hurried
past us carrying ladders, boxes, crates, baskets of clothes. A
tractor pulling some large trailer churned its way slowly and
carefully over the uneven ground towards the gate.

"The lions, I think," said Tim. "Can you smell them? The
stables are round this way. Mind your foot."

I dodged a bit of rope trailing from some bundle that a
couple of girls were carrying. I recognised one of the dainty
young dancers from the tight-rope act looking no less graceful
but very different in close fitting black pants and sweater.

Next moment a welcoming shaft of light shone out across
the trampled grass in front of us. It spilled out from the door
of a caravan where, silhouetted against the light and holding
back the rough curtain which had covered the doorway, stood
Annalisa, peering out into the night.

"Tim, Mrs March, is that you? I'm sorry I couldn't come to
show you the way, but I was busy changing."

She ran down the steps. Gone was the smart young hussar in
blue velvet, and here once more was the slender girl with the
blonde pony tail. But she hadn't gone back to the blue dirndl.

She was wearing—like the other artistes we had seen—pants and sweater. Hers were dark blue. She had cleaned the circus make-up off her face, and this now looked fresh and scrubbed clean, without even any lipstick. She looked business-like and ready for work, but as feminine as ever.

"I'll take you to see the horses straight away. They will not be moving till they are taken to the morning train, but they'll be being bedded down now. Did you enjoy the show?"

"Very much indeed," I said, "and you most of all . . . That's quite honest, Annalisa, you were marvellous. It was a wonderful act, one of the best things I've ever seen . . . And thank you very much for the *croupade*, you both did it beautifully, we were terribly impressed."

"It was terrific!" Timothy chimed in with enthusiasm, and we both praised her warmly, and as we walked along between the lighted windows of the rows of vans, I could see how she glowed with unaffected pleasure.

"It is too much—you are too good . . ." She sounded almost confused by our praise. "He did do it well tonight, did he not? It was a good evening . . . I am glad for you . . . One cannot always be sure. I think, if there had been more time to train him, he could have been a very good horse. But in a circus, you see, there is no time; we cannot afford to keep a horse for all the time it takes to train them in the advanced leaps, they have to work, and this spoils them, they are never polished. In the Spanish Riding School they can train for years before they let them perform. Even then, some of the stallions never get to do the leaps. This is kept for the best ones."

"Well," I said, "it still looked pretty good to me . . . and the palaminos were magnificent."

"Oh yes, they are lovely. Well, here they are. I brought some pieces of carrot if you would like to give them . . .?"

The horses were housed in a long tent, which, on the inside, looked every bit as solid and permanent as a stable. A few lights burned, showing up rows of horses' rumps half hidden by their rugs, tails swishing lazily. There was the sweet ammoniac smell of hay and horses, and the comfortable sound of munching.

Farther down the stable a couple of men were working, one forking straw, the other, duster in hand, shining up the metal studding on a piece of tack hanging from a pole. From a corner in the shadows came the whicker of greeting, and I saw the beautiful white head flung up as the stallion looked round at Annalisa.

Shorn of his jewelled trappings and standing at ease, Maestoso Leda was still beautiful, even though not so impressive as he had been on parade. Seeing one of the famous Lipizzans now for the first time at close quarters, I was surprised to realise how small he was; fourteen hands, I supposed, give or take an inch, stockily built with well-set-on shoulders and sturdy legs and feet, big barrelled, big chested, with the thick stallion neck and the power in the haunches that was needed for the spectacular leaps to which these animals could be trained. Something about the shape of his head recalled those old paintings of horses that one had always dismissed as inaccurate—those creatures with massive quarters, round and shining as apples, but with swan-curved necks and small heads with tiny ears; now I could see where they came from. His was—if one could use the word—an antique head, narrow, and sculptured like a Greek relief, while the rest of his body was massively muscled. The eye was remarkable, big and dark and liquid, gentle and yet male.

He whickered again at the sight of the carrots and bent his head to receive them. Annalisa and Timothy fed him, and the two of them were soon busy with him, almost crooning over him as they handled him. I watched for a little, then wandered off down the lines to look at some of the others. They were mostly stallions, the palominos looking at this close range a good deal more impressive than the Lipizzaner, but all relaxed and resting comfortably. I noticed one or two bandaged legs among the others, and a nasty graze skinning over on one palomino rump, but on the whole it seemed to me that the Circus Wagner had got off lightly. Nothing terrifies horses so much as fire, and if even one or two, in their panic-stricken plunging, had lashed out or broken loose, they could have caused immense damage to themselves and others.

At the far end of the stable one or two of the horses were lying down already, so I didn't go past them, since no horse will allow you to pass his stall without his getting up, and I didn't wish to disturb them. But the ponies I talked to, mischievous shaggy little beasts, twice as quick and twice as naughty as their big brothers, and at this moment all twice as wide awake. By the time I had worked my way back to the beginning where Annalisa and Timothy still stood talking softly in the royal box, the two stablemen had gone, and all seemed settled for what remained of the night. In the stall next to the end one—opposite the white stallion—stood another horse of much the same height and build as the Lipizzaner, but very different to look at. He was a piebald, with ugly markings, and he stood with his head drooping and mane and tail hanging limply, like uncombed flax. I thought at first it was the clever ugly beast that Annalisa had ridden in the rodeo, then saw that this was an older horse. His feed was scarcely touched, but his water bucket was empty. As I watched, he lowered his head and blew sadly around the bottom of the dry bucket.

I spoke softly, then laid a hand on him and went in.

Annalisa saw me and came across.

"Because we spend so much time with the King horse, you talk with the beggar? I am sorry, there is no carrot left."

"I doubt if he would want it," I said. "He hasn't touched his feed. I wasn't just being democratic; I thought he looked ill."

"He is still not eating? He has been like this all the week." She looked from the full manger to the empty bucket, and a pucker of worry showed between her brows. "He was my Uncle Franzl's horse, the poor old piebald . . . Ever since the fire he has been like this; nobody else looked after him, you see, always my uncle. He is old, too; my uncle used to say they were two old men together." She bit her lip, watching the horse. "I think he is—what is the word?—weeping for my uncle."

"Fretting. That may be true, but I think there's something wrong physically, too. The horse is in pain." I was examining him as I spoke, running a hand down the neck, turning back the rug to feel the withers. "See how he's sweating; he's wringing wet over the withers and down the neck, and look at his eye . . . his coat's as rough as a sack, Annalisa. Has anyone seen him?"

"The vet. came from Bruck after the fire, and he has been twice more since then. On Thursday, he was here."

"And he looked at this one?"

"He looked at them all. Not this one, perhaps, after the first time, because there was nothing wrong." She looked doubtfully at me, then back at the old piebald. "Yes, I can see he does not look very good, but if there had been anything . . . anything to see . . ." She hesitated.

Tim said: "Vanessa's a vet."

Her eyes widened. "You? Are you? Oh, then—"

"Has the horse been working?" I asked.

She shook her head. "He doesn't work, he is old, I think more than twenty. My Uncle Franzl had him in Czechoslovakia even before he joined us ten years ago. They tried at first to use him—they had a liberty act then with mixed horses—but he was slow to learn, so he has done very little. He was a pet of my Uncle Franzl's, or perhaps my father would not have kept him. I told you, we cannot afford to keep a horse that does not work, so in the old days, before there was money for all the tractors and motor caravans, he helped to pull a wagon, and Uncle Franzl used to ride him, and give rides to the children. But now . . ." she looked distressed . . . "if he is ill—we are moving the horses in a few hours, and in three days we leave Austria and cross the frontier. I am afraid of what my father will say."

"You've found something?" said Timothy to me.

I had indeed found something. Just above the knee on the off foreleg was a nasty swelling. I showed this to them, investigating further, while the old horse stood with drooping head, turning once to nuzzle me as my fingers felt and probed the leg.

I said to Tim: "Hold his head, will you? Gently, there, old man."

"What is it?" asked Annalisa, peering over my shoulder.

"It's a haematoma, a blood-swelling. He must have hurt himself during the fire, or perhaps had a kick from a loose horse, and he's torn one of the flexor tendons ... Look, these, here ... It wouldn't show for a day or two, and if he isn't working nobody would notice. And the rug's been hiding the swelling. But he must be dealt with now. It's a very nasty leg."

"Yes, I can see, it looks terrible. But how 'dealt with'? What will you do?"

I looked up. "I? I'm not your veterinary surgeon, Annalisa. You'll have to get the man from Bruck. I ought not to interfere.

"He ought not to have missed it." said Tim roundly. "Anybody could see the beast's ill."

"No," I said, "be fair. I'm sure in the normal course of things somebody would have seen it, but the circus's own horse-keeper is dead, and Herr Wagner's had far too much on his plate this past week. I told you this wouldn't develop straight away, and if no one called the veterinary surgeon's attention to it later, it could easily have been overlooked."

"What will have to be done?" asked Annalisa.

"It ought to be lanced—cut—and drained, and the leg stitched."

"Could you do it?"

I straightened up. "If you mean do I know how, yes, I do. But you have a veterinary surgeon, Annalisa, you should get him."

"On a Sunday night? At nearly midnight? And we leave for the train at six?"

Tim said: "Couldn't you, Vanessa?"

"Tim, I shouldn't. I don't know what the etiquette is here, and I've no business to walk in and do the man's work for him. Come to that, it is professional 'work'. It's probably even illegal, without permits or something. Besides, I've no instruments."

"There are Uncle Franzl's things." said Annalisa. "They were saved. I have them in my wagon. *Please*, Vanessa."

"It's nothing to do with the chap from Bruck, anyway," said Tim. "He'll have been paid, won't he? Now the circus moves on, and that's an end of him."

"Yes!" She took him up eagerly. Between them the old

horse stood motionless, his coat rough under my hand. It felt hot and scurfy. "You will be our new vet! I appoint you, I myself! And if it is not legal, then nobody need know!"

A new voice spoke from the tent door, startling us all.

"If what is not legal?"

Chapter Seven

Dost think I am a horse-doctor?
Marlowe: *Doctor Faustus*

Herr Wagner himself stood there, a thick-set, powerful-looking man, with a big head and a mane of brown hair going grey. He had a ruddy, weather-beaten complexion, and brown eyes under fierce brows. These now took in the scene with lively curiosity.

Behind him was a taller man, a slim, wiry figure in black whom I recognised as the *Star-Attraktion* of the high wire, the Hungarian Sandor Balog. He had dark hair slicked back above a broad forehead with thin black brows 'winged' above eyes so dark they were almost black. The nose was flattish and the cheekbones wide, and when he smiled, the lower lids of his eyes lifted, tilting the eyes and giving the face a Mongolian look. The nostrils were prominent and sharply carved, the lips full and well shaped. A disturbing face, perhaps a cruel one. He wasn't smiling now. He was looking, not (as one might have expected) at the two strangers near the horse's head, but with fixed intensity at Annalisa.

"Who are your friends, Liesl?" asked Herr Wagner.

"Father! *Lieber Gott*, but you startled me! I never heard you! Oh, this is Mrs March, she is English, staying in the village, and this is Tim, who travels with her . . ."

She included the Hungarian in her introductions. I noticed that she didn't look directly at him, whereas he never took his eyes off her, except to brush me, momentarily, with an indifferent glance. Herr Wagner greeted us courteously, then his eyes went to the horse.

"But what was this about a vet? Did I hear properly? And what is 'not legal'?"

Annalisa hesitated, started to speak, then glanced at me. "You permit?" Then, turning back to her father, she plunged into a flood of German which, from her gestures, was the story of her acquaintance with us, and the recent discovery of Piebald's injury.

To all this, after the first minute or so, the Hungarian paid little attention. I noticed that as the name of Lee Elliott occurred in the narrative, his gaze sharpened on the girl, so that I wondered if Sandor Balog, like me, had credited Mr Elliott with 'intentions' in that direction. If so, he didn't like it. But after a bit, it appeared, the narrative bored him. He wandered into the next stall—the end one of the row, where harness hung and trestles stood with saddles over them—and stood there, idly fingering the bright jewellery on Maestoso Leda's saddle, but still watching the girl.

She finished her story on a strong note of persuasion, where I caught the word 'Bruck', and a significant glance at her watch.

But—not much to my surprise—Herr Wagner didn't lend his weight to her appeal. He turned to me and in broadly accented but quite fluent English, thanked me for what he called my 'trouble' and 'great kindness', but finally, 'believed he must not trouble me'.

"My daughter is young, and a little"—he shrugged his wide shoulders and smiled charmingly—"a little impulsive . . . She should not be asking you this thing. You are a visitor, a lady, this is not a thing to invite a lady to do."

I laughed. "It's not that. I am a veterinary surgeon, and I'm used to worse jobs than this, it was only that—well, it simply isn't my affair. You have your own man. He'd certainly come tonight if you telephoned. If you haven't got the telephone here,

I'll do it for you, if you like, from the Gasthof Edelweiss . . . or rather, Tim will. He speaks German."

Herr Wagner didn't answer for a minute. He had come into the stall and was examining the horse with some care.

". . . Yes, I see. I see. I am ashamed that this was not seen. I will speak to Hans and Rudi; but you understand, *gnädige Frau*, there has been so much . . . and always my cousin Franzl he sees to this old horse himself. The boys perhaps were doing their own work—their own regular horses, *verstehen Sie?*—and this old one, he is missed. The poor old one, yes . . ."

He ran a caressing hand down the horse's neck, gave it a pat that had something valedictory about it, and straightened up.

"Well, it is late. You will have some coffee before you go, eh? No, no, I mean it. My Liesl always makes the coffee at this hour . . . This is why I come to find her, she is neglecting her old father."

"Thanks very much," I said, "but if I'm to ring this man up for you, I'd better get straight back. It's after midnight."

Herr Wagner said: "I shall not trouble you, *gnädige Frau*."

It was Timothy who understood before I did, who had seen the significance of that farewell caress, and had added to it Annalisa's reiteration that 'no circus can afford to keep a horse which does not work'. One could not blame Herr Wagner for his decision to jettison old Piebald now; he hadn't earned his keep for quite some time, and, according to Annalisa, hadn't even qualified for a pension. A working circus cannot keep pets.

I saw Timothy stiffen, still holding the headstall, his eyes fixed on Herr Wagner. His free hand crept to the horse's nose, cupping round the soft muzzle in a gesture at once protective, and pathetically futile. The horse lipped his fingers. Tim looked at me.

I said: "Herr Wagner, I'll operate now, if you'll let me. It'll be over in half an hour, and once I've got the leg fixed up you can move him to the train. He'll be as right as rain and fit for work in three or four weeks."

Herr Wagner stopped in the tent doorway. I thought he was going to brush the matter aside, but Tim said, "Please," in a voice as young and unprotected as his face, and I saw the older man hesitate.

"Yes, father, please," said the girl.

The Hungarian said nothing. You would have thought we were all of us separated from him by a glass screen. He had Annalisa's saddle and cloth over his arm now, and was waiting to follow Herr Wagner out of the stable.

Herr Wagner spread his hands wide in a gesture of deprecation. "But we cannot ask you —" he began.

"I wish you would," I said, and smiled. I put everything I had into that smile. "That's all we need to make it legal."

Annalisa said suddenly: "No! It is I who ask! After all this talk, it is I! I had forgotten! This was Uncle Franzl's horse, so now it is mine . . ." She swung round on her father, hands spread in what was almost a parody of his own gesture. "Is this not so, father? Did not Uncle Franzl leave me all his things . . . all that were saved, the pictures, and his flute, and the parrot . . . and old Piebald, too? So if he is mine, and I ask Vanessa to look after him . . . and if he can go to the train . . . ?"

She finished back on the note of pleading, but her father was already laughing, his square brown face lit up and rayed with wrinkles.

"*So* . . . you see how she rules me, this child of mine? Always a reason she finds to have her way—like her mother she is, very the same as her mother. Oh, yes, it is true that Franzl wished you to have everything . . . it is true perhaps that the horse is yours . . ." He gave his great ringmaster's laugh, so that the sleeping horses stirred in their stalls, and the chains jingled and rang. "All right, all right, if you wish, if you wish, children all of you. What do you need, *gnädige Frau?*"

"The instruments Annalisa said she had. Hot water. Nylon suturing material. I'll have to give an anti-tetanus injection; have you got the stuff? Good. And more light. I don't want to move him, I'd rather do it in his own stall, it'll upset him less, but I must have some sort of spotlight."

"I have a good flashlight," said Annalisa. "It's in my wagon. And Sandor has one, too. Will you get it, Sandor, please?"

"*Natürlich.*" It was as if a puppet had spoken—or rather, a creature from the ballet stage, so remote from us had that black-clad, graceful figure been in the shadows of the end stall. His voice was curiously light and hard. He spoke pleasantly enough, without emphasis, and had turned to go, when I stopped him.

"No, please . . . Thank you all the same, but it doesn't matter. A flashlight won't be enough. I wondered if someone could rig a light down here off a long flex? You know, a wire."

"That is easy to do," said Herr Wagner, adding in German, "Sandor, would you be good enough to do this for them? You know where to find the flex and all the things you need. Don't lumber yourself with that saddle, just leave it here. Annalisa won't mind if it stays here for the night for once."

"I was going to take it to my own wagon to mend it. I see some stitching is loose."

Tim translated in my ear: "It's all right. He's only taking the saddle to dump in his own wagon, and then he's going to get a flex and rig the light. I say, I'm sure he was going to have the old horse put down."

"I thought so, too."

"Is this a bad operation?"

"Not at all. Have you never seen this kind of thing before?"

"No, only the usual minor things, fomentations and so on. I'm afraid I shan't be much help, but I'll do my best if you want."

"Herr Wagner probably knows all about it, but thanks all the same. I'd a lot sooner have you than the boy friend, anyway."

"Him? You don't think he is, do you?"

I laughed. "No, only that he'd like to be. He doesn't look the type to run errands for girls otherwise. And what else did he come here for? Just to carry her saddle away for her? He didn't look too pleased to be co-opted as lighting expert."

"If it comes to that," said Tim, "he offered to stitch it up for her, or something, if I got it right. His German's a lot worse than his English."

"Well, there you are," I said, vaguely, then forgot about Sandor Balog. What mattered now was the horse.

· · ·

Once Herr Wagner had made up his mind to let me operate, he was helpfulness itself. The stablemen had all gone off duty; they had the early start to face, and were getting their sleep. But Herr Wagner and Annalisa stayed, and we had a surprise helper in the shape of the dwarf who was the clowns' butt in the *entrée*. His name was Elemer, and like Sandor Balog he was a Hungarian, being, I supposed, the 'Hungarian gentleman' who 'had the advantage of only being three feet high' and who had been helping Mr Elliott with the stable work in the recent emergency. He certainly seemed to know where everything was, unlike Balog, who did bring flex and tools as requested, but thereafter restricted his help to watching the dwarf and lifting him to reach the light socket—this last with some comment in Hungarian which made the little man flush angrily and compress his lips. And when the light was finally rigged, the *Star-Attraktion* retired gracefully into the shadows of the next stall to watch the performance, while the dwarf bustled to help Annalisa and Timothy.

They had conjured up a Primus stove from somewhere, and on it had managed to bring a large enamel bucket full of water to the boil while the light was being rigged and I, with Herr Wagner watching, checked over the contents of the dead Franzl's instrument case.

It held everything I could want, scalpel, knife, dressing and artery forceps, suturing material, cotton-wool galore. All these went into the bucket to boil, while Annalisa and Timothy went off to her wagon for another pan for me to wash in.

In a quarter of an hour or so all was ready. The light was rigged and steady, the boiling water drained off the sterile instruments, and I had washed up and started work.

I noticed that Herr Wagner was watching closely. Even if he

did not value the horse, he was too good a horseman to hand over the animal to someone and then leave him unsupervised. He said nothing, but washed up himself and then stood near me, obviously constituting himself my assistant.

I clipped the horse's leg and cleaned the area with surgical spirit, then reached for the hypodermic. As Herr Wagner put it into my hand, I caught sight of Tim's face, taut and anxious, watching across the horse's neck. There was nothing for him to do, so he stood by the animal's head and spoke to him gently from time to time, but in fact the boy seemed much more disturbed by the operation than the patient, and looked so anxious at the sight of the needle that I gave him a reassuring grin.

"I'm going to give him a local, Tim, don't worry. He won't feel a thing, and twenty minutes from now he'll be doing a *capriole*."

"What d'you give him?"

"Procaine. It goes by some German trade name here, but that's what it is. That's it between the vaseline and that brown tube labelled 'Koloston'. I'm going to infiltrate the procaine right round the area. Now watch. You run the needle in under the skin, near the swelling . . . There, he never blinked, and that's the only prick he'll feel. Then you put it in again, at the end of the anaesthetised bit . . . see? He doesn't feel that . . . and run it along the second side of your square. This way, you deaden the whole area. Then the third side . . . and the last. Now, give it time, and when I incise the haematoma he won't feel a thing."

The beam of light shifted, sending the shadows tilting. I glanced up quickly, before I remembered that it was the dwarf Elemer who was holding the wooden batten to which the lamp had been hooked.

"That is better now?" His deep guttural came from elbow height, and I glanced down, self-conscious now and hating myself for showing it. He was in deep shadow behind the bright bulb, and I couldn't see the misshapen body or the tiny arms that clutched the batten, but the light reflected on his upturned

88

face, which was the face made familiar by so many of the old tales that take deformity for granted, *Snow-white*, *Rumpelstiltskin*, and the rest. Only the eyes were unexpected; they were dark, the iris as dark as the pupil, big eyes fringed with thick short lashes; eyes where thoughts could not be read but only guessed at. Not for the first time I reflected that the normal, let alone the privileged, have a burden of guilt laid automatically on them from the cradle.

I said: "Thank you, it's fine." In spite of myself, I spoke just a shade too heartily. I saw him smile, but it was a kind smile. I turned quickly back to the job.

"Scalpel, please," I said, and reached out a wet hand. Herr Wagner put the scalpel into it. The beam of light was steady on the haematoma. I bent forward to cut.

The cut was about four inches long. The swelling cut as cleanly as an orange, and, as cleanly almost as orange juice, the serum flooded out of it and down the horse's leg, followed sluggishly by the blood, which, in a week, had formed a sizeable, stringy clot. You could almost feel the relief as the thing split and the pressure was lifted. Old Piebald's ears moved, and Tim whispered something into one of them.

"Forceps," I said.

I don't know whether Herr Wagner knew the English words, but he obviously knew the drill; as he handed me the dressing forceps I saw from the corner of my eye that he also had the artery forceps ready in case of any seepage from my cutting. And when I had pulled away the clotted blood with the forceps, the cotton-wool was ready to my hand without my having to speak.

In a short time the wound was clean. I dusted it generously with sterile penicillin powder, and reached silently for the suturing needle. It was there. Six blanket sutures, and the thing was done, and Herr Wagner had ready the pad of dry cotton-wool rolled in bandage, to put over the wound for protection.

I smiled up at Timothy, who still watched rather tautly across Piebald's unmoving (and you would have sworn indifferent) head.

I said: "That's that. He's survived, and he hasn't bitten me—yet. You see this pad Herr Wagner's made for me? We call that a dolly. I stitch it on now —"

"You *stitch* it on? You mean you stitch it to the *horse*?"

"Where else? Only to the skin—and he won't feel it any more than he's felt the rest. Watch."

I laid the dolly—the size and shape of a generously filled sausage—along the line of the stitched cut, then knotted the nylon suturing thread in the skin to one side of it, carried the thread close across the dolly, and knotted another stitch in. It took four stitches, then the dry pad lay snugly over the wound.

"Won't he worry at it and pull it off?" asked Tim.

"Not unless the wound's infected, and starts to itch or hurt him, but it looked beautifully clean to me. It's my guess he'll never even know the dolly's there. It can come off in three or four days' time. Now, there's just his anti-tetanus shot and penicillin, and that will be that. Pull his mane across, will you, Tim, I'll put this in the neck . . . There you are, old darling, that's you . . ." I smoothed my hand down the drooping neck. "I think you'll live."

"Yes," said Herr Wagner, behind me, "thanks to you, *gnädige Frau*, he will live."

There was something in his voice that made it more than just a phrase. Timothy's eyes met mine, and his face broke into a grin. Old Piebald rolled a big dark eye back at me, and said nothing.

·   ·   ·

"You'll have some coffee now?" said Annalisa.

It was not so much a question as an order, and I didn't protest as she led the way to her wagon. I was suddenly very tired, and longing for the day to be over, but in the pre-dawn chill the thought of coffee was irresistible.

Behind us, in the stable, Elemer and Herr Wagner were settling Piebald for what was left of the night. Sandor Balog came with us. I gathered that it had been kind, even condescending, of an artiste of his calibre to have helped so far.

It seemed that this kindness—or his interest in Annalisa—didn't impel him to anything more domestic. He settled with me on the bench at the table in her wagon, and allowed her to serve the coffee alone. Timothy did offer help, but was refused, and sat down beside Sandor, looking round him with frank pleasure.

The living-wagon was—just at present—very untidy, but still rather attractive. Though it was a newish caravan, the pattern of circus life with its century-old traditions had modified its streamlined modernity to give it the authentic old gypsy wagon flavour. The stove near the door was of white enamel, and burned bottled gas, but the lamp swinging over it looked like an old converted storm lantern, and the little table was covered with a brilliant red cloth with a fringe, for all the world like a gypsy's shawl. A faded striped curtain hung over the forward doorway through which could be glimpsed the corner of a tumbled bunk covered with clothes; the light caught the edge of the blue velvet riding costume, and glittered off the jewelled handle of a whip. On a hook near one window hung the hussar's cap with all its amethysts and diamonds and its osprey plume which wavered and tossed a little in the warm draught from the stove. Between window and stove was the dressing-shelf, with candles stuck to either side of a square mirror with a chipped corner. The candles had guttered down into big blobs of grey wax and the shelf itself was smeared heavily with red and carmine and the white of powder. There was a splash of pink liquid powder across the looking-glass. A wicker cage, swinging from a hook and shrouded with a green kerchief, completed the gypsy picture. Our voices roused the inmate to a sort of sleepy croak, and I remembered Annalisa's saying something about Uncle Franzl's parrot.

"But this is terrific, it really is!" Timothy was enthusiastic, and very wide awake still. "It's just how I've always imagined it. Aren't you lucky? Gosh, fancy living in a house when you could have a wagon, and move on every day or so!"

She laughed. "I wonder if you would say the same thing at five o'clock in the morning? Sugar, Vanessa?"

"No, thank you."

"This is yours, Sandor. Sugar, Tim?"

"Yes, please."

I curved my hands round the hot blue cup. The coffee was delicious, fragrant and strong, and through the coffee-scent came, seductively, another even more delicious—the smell of hot, freshly baked bread. Annalisa put a dish on the table; *croissants*, flaky and rich, flat buns shining with sugared tops and still steaming, fresh sweet bread with new butter melting on it.

"*Gotterdämmerung*," said Timothy reverently, if inappropriately. "Did you make them?"

She laughed. "No, no! They come from the village bakery. Lee brought them."

Sandor looked up. "He is here still?"

"He goes back tomorrow. Oh, you mean is he here, in the circus? No. He came down to the stables while Vanessa was busy with the horse, but only for a minute."

"Did he?" I said. "I didn't see him."

"He didn't stay. He only watched for a minute, then he went to get the bread, but he wouldn't stay for coffee, either."

"Was he at the show?" asked Sandor.

"I don't think so. I didn't see him. Did you?" This to Tim and me.

"No."

To my surprise, this didn't please Sandor either, but then it appeared that a Lee Elliott safely anchored in a ring-side seat was preferable to a Lee Elliott at large back stage . . . possibly in Annalisa's wagon.

He said, with a savage intensity that seemed out of place and somehow shocking: "I don't know what he is doing here still. He did what he came for on Monday, then why did he not go back?"

"Because I asked him to stay." Annalisa's voice was light and cold. "More coffee, Vanessa?"

"Thank you. It's lovely."

"*You* asked him to stay?"

"Yes. Why not? What objection have you got, Sandor Balog?"

It was obvious that, whatever his objection was, it was a violent one. I thought for a moment that he was going to explode into words. The black eyes glittered, the nostrils flared like a horse's, but then the full lips folded sullenly over his anger, and he looked down, stirring his coffee in silence. I found myself hoping for Annalisa's sake that her cool manner hid no warmer feeling for him; he might be playing lapdog now, but it seemed to me a thin disguise for a creature much nearer to the wolf.

"Tim," said Annalisa, "have some more. Another *croissant*?"

"I'd love it. Thank you. Personally," said Timothy, muscling in on his third bun with undiminished zeal, "I'd say Mr Elliott had real executive sense. This is a terrific idea, raiding a bakery in the middle of the night. I must do it some day. Will you thank him for us if you see him again?"

"We shall be gone before he gets up. You may see him yourself."

"Where's he staying?"

"He sleeps over the bakery; it's the one in the square, there's a Frau Schindler who lets a room there."

"Big deal," said Tim. "I told you he was smart. I wish we'd thought of that."

"Gimme a bit, you greedy bastard," said the parrot suddenly, directly over my head. I jumped, and spilled coffee, and Annalisa and the parrot laughed heartily. The green kerchief, twitched aside by a powerful beak, came down over my head like an extinguisher.

"*Levez, levez*," said the parrot. "Shake a leg, Peter, *changez*, hup! Get your mane hogged, you goddam limey, you! *Gib mir was! Gib mir was!*"

"For pete's sake!" said Tim. He tore off a bit of *croissant*. "All right, old chap, here. No, not like that, you fool, like that. There."

"Put your comb up," said the parrot, accepting the bread.

"I'm not a flipping cockatoo," said Tim.

"Don't teach him any more words, please," said Annalisa,

93

laughing, "and keep your nose away from the bars, Tim, he's a terrible bird." She was helping me to emerge from the folds of the green kerchief. "I am sorry, he is so terrible . . . I do not know who had him before Uncle Franzl, but he's very . . . what is it? . . . he's a real *Weltbürger*, and from all the worst places!"

"A cosmopolitan," said Tim. "Dead right, he is! That bird's been around."

The parrot made a comment, this time in German, that got Annalisa to her feet.

"Please, we must cover him up again before he really starts! I'm sorry, Vanessa, did the scarf go in your coffee? It's quite clean."

"Let me," said Sandor Balog. He, too, was laughing, and it transformed him. There was (I saw it sinkingly, because I was getting to like Annalisa) quite a powerful animal attraction there. He and Tim draped the cage once more, while Annalisa tried to get me fresh coffee, but this time I refused.

"We must go. Look at the time, and you people have an early start. No, really, it was nothing, you're very welcome . . ." This as she began once again to thank me for what I had done.

"If you come near us again," she said eagerly, "please come to see us. We shall be leaving Austria in two or three days' time, but we go today to Hohenwald, and after that to Zechstein. If you are near us, on your motor tour, you will call, will you not? If you wish to watch the show again, it will be a pleasure, any time; we will keep you the best seats. But in any case, my father and I would be glad to welcome you."

Sandor Balog rose also. "I shall see you to the gate." When we protested that there was no need, he produced a slim flashlight from his pocket. "Yes, please. The ground is all muddy where the tractors have been, and there is not much light. Please allow me."

"In that case," I said, "thank you. Good night, Annalisa, and *auf Wiedersehen*."

"*Auf Wiedersehen*."

"*Merde, alors*," said the parrot, muffled.

Chapter Eight

The statements was interesting, but tough.
Mark Twain: *Huckleberry Finn*

"Probably just seeing us off the premises," said Timothy later, as we walked through the sleeping village towards the Gasthof Edelweiss. The air was still and cold. A clock in the church tower struck two, with a thin, acid sweetness. A chain jingled, and a dog grumbled in its throat somewhere. "I say, you don't really think there could be anything between him and Annalisa, do you? I thought he was an absolute wart."

"Not on her side, I'm sure. Anyway, you can leave our Sandor safely to Herr Wagner and the parrot."

He chuckled. "I rather cared for the parrot. I'd like to hear him—That's odd."

"What's odd?"

"I thought I saw someone over there . . . the other side of the square, by those trees."

"Well, why not?"

"I'm sure it was Mr Elliott."

"Well, why not?" I said again. "He's probably been down for some more buns for himself, and now he's walking off the indigestion. Come along, Tim, I'm just about dropping."

But tired as I was, when at length I was ready for bed I found sleep far away, and myself restless. I padded across the boards in my bare feet to open the long windows, and went out on to the veranda to look at the night. Next door to mine, Timothy's window was open, too, but his light was out already. In the distance the clock struck the half hour. Nearer at hand a soft chiming echoed it as a cow stirred in her stall.

The night was sweet, cold and clear. The stars seemed close to the mountain-tops, as if they were sharp points of reflection off some high snow struck by the moon, and their light showed the soft slopes of meadow and fir wood in silver monochrome and shadow. You could have traced the countryside by its scents alone. Immediately below the veranda the clover and mown hay; beyond it pines, and the cold scent of running water; faint food-smells from the Gasthof kitchen; somewhere a homely whiff of pig, and the sweet smell of the cows with their bells sleepily ringing in the byre.

It was still and peaceful and very lovely. Anybody should be able to sleep.

I padded back across boards already faintly damp with dew, and got into bed. The only covering was a large eiderdown, or feather puff, light and warm, but apt to expose the feet when one pulled it up under one's chin. I curled up facing the window, tucked the puff round me as best I might, and wondered about Lewis . . .

I don't think I was asleep, but I may have been floating into the edge of it, because the tiny noise from outside brought me fully awake with a start. I didn't move, but strained my ears. Nothing. But I was certain something—or someone—had moved out there.

Then the hand parted the curtains. He didn't make a sound, just slid between them like a ghost. As I sat up in bed, pulling the puff round me, he was already turning to draw the long windows shut. They latched with a tiny click. He stood there just inside the windows, quite still, listening.

"All right, Mr Elliott," I said, "I'm awake. What brings you this way? Couldn't you find your way to Annalisa's wagon, or was Sandor Balog standing guard?"

He came forward towards the bed. Even on the bare floors he moved without a sound, incredibly quietly, like a cat. "I think I'm in the right place."

"What makes you think that, Mr Lee Elliott? What makes you think that after what's been going on you have the faintest right to come wandering in here like a tomcat on the prowl, and expect a welcome?"

"Oh, well, if we're talking about rights . . ." said Lewis, sitting down on the edge of the bed, and taking off his shoes.

. . .

"And now," I said, "supposing you start? What in the world are you doing here, and what's your connection with Annalisa?"

"How like a woman to start at the wrong end," said Lewis. "I'll ask the questions, please. First of all, what are *you* doing here, and who is that boy?"

"Keep your voice down, he's next door."

"I know. I looked in when I came along the veranda. He was sound asleep."

"Efficient, aren't you? You know who he is; I told you, it's Tim Lacy. Don't you remember Carmel? I'm sure you met her once. She gave us that horrible decanter for a wedding present."

"Ah, yes, that fair fat female, I remember. All soft and sweet, and full of icy draughts at the edges, like this damned feather thing on the bed. Must you have all of it, incidentally? I'm getting cold."

"Then you'd better get your clothes on again. It would be bad enough if Tim or Frau Weber heard you and came in, let alone finding you like that —"

"I suppose I had. A life of sin is beastly uncomfortable," said Lewis peacefully, sitting up and reaching for his trousers.

"Well, for pity's sake, can't you tell me why we're having to lead it? When I saw you standing there tonight, I nearly fainted. I'd have yelled out in another second."

"I know. That's why I gave you the high sign to say nothing. I must say you passed it off very well. Did the boy guess?"

"No, but he told me I looked funny."

"Well, so you did. You looked as if you'd seen a ghost."

"Of course I did! It was the most unnerving thing that ever happened to me. As a matter of fact, for one dreadful moment, when you looked straight through me like that, I wondered if I could have been mistaken. Lewis, those clothes, where did you get them? They were absolutely disgusting."

"Yes, weren't they?" He sounded remarkably complacent about it. "Do you mean to tell me that you honestly did wonder whether you'd made a mistake or not?"

"Yes, truthfully."

"Well—damn, I can't find my sock—I hope I've convinced you now."

"Oh, yes. Same old technique, same old Lewis. It's you all right, I'd know that old routine anywhere."

He grinned. "Well, so long as you're sure . . . where the hell is that sock? Do you think I could put the light on for a moment?"

"No, I do not. If I'm not allowed to claim you as my husband with benefit of clergy here and now, I'm not going to let my reputation go straight down the sink by being discovered in bed with you. I've got Tim to think of."

"Oh, yes, Tim. You still haven't told me why you're here with him. Ah, there's the sock. Go on, your move, I'm listening."

"It's not in the least important how I got here, or why I'm with Tim," I said sharply, "but I should have thought it was perfectly obvious what brought me here. Lewis —"

"I'll tell you my part of it later. No, my darling Van, this matters . . . I must know how you found out I was here in Oberhausen. I'll tell you why all in good time, but you've got to tell me your end of it here and now. Of course it's obvious what brought you here; you knew I was here; now I want you to tell me how you knew."

"I knew you were with the circus, and when we asked in Vienna where it was, they said the accident had happened in Oberhausen. We came down. We thought the circus might have already left, but that people would know where it had gone."

He was pulling on his sweater now, a thick dark affair. As he emerged from it he paused for a moment, and turned his head. He said, in a stilled, listening voice:

"The news-reel cameras?"

"Heavens, how on earth did you guess so quickly? Yes, Carmel Lacy saw the news-reel, and thought she recognised you, and she wanted someone to convoy Timothy to Vienna, so she rang me up. She assumed I'd be joining you out here sooner or later."

"I see. I saw the camera, but I didn't know whether I'd got on to it or not, and of course I was hoping I wasn't recognisable.

I suppose you went to see it yourself?" I nodded. "How recognisable was it?"

"Fairly clear, I'm afraid. Does it matter?"

He didn't answer that. "Fancy your seeing it. It's one of those things." He was silent again for a moment. "It never entered my head it could get as far as you. But as soon as I saw you here in Oberhausen I realised you must have found out somehow, and that was all I could think of. Have you any idea if it got on to television?"

"Not in England, I'm pretty sure. I usually watch the news, and I haven't seen it. And I'm sure if it had been on, and anyone had recognised you, it would have got back to me." I sat up, hugging my knees, and pulling the feather puff round me. "Lewis, what *is* all this? I got your cable from Stockholm on the Monday. Did you send it?"

"No."

"I thought you couldn't have. And then there was the letter; that came on Friday. I suppose that was given to someone to post for you?"

"Yes."

"But—why Stockholm? Why not just Vienna anyway?"

"I had to have somewhere clear away from where you and I were going. It wouldn't have been easy to stall you off coming if it had been more or less on the way. As it happens," said Lewis a little bitterly, "I'd have done better to spare the extra few lies, if I was going to be so bloody careless as to get myself into the news."

"And you had to stall me off?"

"Yes."

I said miserably: "You can see what I thought when I saw the news-reel. I couldn't believe there was anything wrong between us, not really . . . but I—I'd been so unhappy, and after what we'd said to each other that dreadful afternoon —"

"That's over. We'll not talk about that any more." That it was over, had never even been started, had been agreed between us some half-hour earlier.

"No, all right. I love you very much, Lewis."

He made the kind of noise a husband considers sufficient answer to that remark—a sort of comforting grunt—then reached across to the pocket of his jacket where it hung over the chair, for cigarette and lighter, and lay down again beside me on the single bed.

"There. Decent enough for you? No, keep that beastly puff thing; wrap it round you, sweetie, I'm warm enough now . . . I see. You saw this news-reel thing, worked it out that I was here in Austria when I'd told you I was going to Stockholm; thought, presumably, that I might have been sent from Stockholm to Austria on business; but when you got the note allegedly written from Stockholm on the day you knew I was near Graz, you decided you'd come to see what it was all about. That it?"

"More or less. I think in a silly sort of way it was Carmel Lacy asking me to travel with Tim that really made me decide to come. It seemed to—well, to fit in so. It was as if I was being pushed to Austria, as if I was sort of *meant* to come. Besides, I had to know what you were up to. It was obvious there was something."

"And what did you think I was up to?"

"I didn't know. When I saw the girl—Annalisa—she was on the film too, you know —"

"Was she? Yes, I see." He sounded rather pleased than otherwise. He blew a smoke-ring which feathered up, ghostly in the frail light that showed through the gap in the window curtains. "Don't you trust me, then?"

"No."

"Fair enough," he said mildly, and a second smoke-ring went through the first.

I shot up beside him. *"Lewis!"*

"Keep your voice down, for pity's sake!" He reached a lazy arm and pulled me down close to him. "You can, as a matter of fact. I thought I'd just given you the best of reasons why you should."

"Or why I shouldn't."

"Depending on the point of view? There's something in that." He sounded no more than placidly amused. "Lie still, girl, and don't be unrestful. We haven't much time, and I want to hear the rest."

I obeyed him. "All right. And don't forget there's quite a lot that I want to hear as well." I told him, as quickly as I could, all that had happened. "After you'd left us this evening with Annalisa, I didn't know whether to tell Timothy the truth or not, but I thought I'd better wait until I'd talked to you, so I pretended I'd made a mistake. You'd given me a hint you'd be seeing me soon, so I half expected you at the circus."

"I came down later. I watched you operating."

"I know you did. My spies are everywhere." I felt him laugh quietly to himself. "What's the joke?"

"Nothing. I take it you got the buns?"

"Yes, thank you very much. You've a life-long admirer in Timothy; he thinks you show real executive sense. Why didn't you stay? You must have known I was looking round corners for you."

"I thought I'd keep out of your way till we could talk alone. Anyway, I was afraid of putting you off. You do a nice job, Mrs March."

"Poor old Piebald, Herr Wagner was going to put him down, I think. He was Franzl's, and he's pretty well useless. However, he'll be all right now, and officially, I gather, he's Annalisa's, and I've a feeling she'll let him end his days in peace for her uncle's sake. Incidentally, I warn you, you're about to lose her to Timothy."

"Well, I hope he can shoot straight," said Lewis. "Half the rodeo act and all the clowns are in love with her, not to mention that Balog character, and the dwarf. And if you say 'Are you?' I shall do you a violence."

"Are you?"

He tightened his arm round me, and I snuggled my cheek close into the crook of his shoulder, against the rough sweater. There was a long, comfortable silence. I heard the tiny hiss of tobacco as he drew on the cigarette, and the fire ate along the tube.

"As a matter of fact," I said, muffled, "I don't care any more why you're here. You're here, that's all. Darling Lewis. The only thing is, mayn't I stay with you? Can we have our holiday now, soon, here? Whatever it is you were doing, have you finished it?"

"Almost. Once I've reported back to Vienna, that's probably it."

"You're going there tomorrow?"

"Today. Yes."

"I gather you'd rather go alone. Then if I wait for you here — no not here, somewhere where you can be Lewis March — could you come back when you've made your report, and we could have our holiday together as from then?"

"It's possible. What about the boy?"

"Annalisa can have him," I said sleepily. "Fair exchange. Lewis, you're not lying on this clean bed with those ghastly trousers on, are you?"

"Good heavens, no. Those were the ones I wore for mucking out the stables."

"They looked like it." I chuckled. "Did you really groom the horses?"

"I did. Did I tell you one of those damned yellow ones bit me? The things I do for England . . . I should get both danger money and dirt money this time."

There was a silence.

"Well, I suppose it's my turn now. Listen, Van, my dear, I ought not to tell you even now, but as things are, I think I've got to, and in any case I know by this time I can trust you with anything I've got, and"—I heard the smile—"I'm quitting, anyway. Besides, I've been thinking, and I've a feeling I'll want your help." He stretched the other arm and stabbed out his cigarette in the ash-tray on the bed-side table. Then he put the hand behind his head. "Now, we haven't much time, because we must both get some sleep. I'll make it fast, and give you only the bare facts. You'll be able to supply the details for yourself, once you know the score. All this tangle about Stockholm, the cable, the letter, the Lee Elliott nonsense, the lies—you'll see why, when I've told you the rest."

He paused, then went on softly, his eyes on the ceiling, where the dark beams were swimming faintly into the first light of dawn.

"What I told you earlier this evening about my job in Oberhausen was true, as far as it went. Paul Denver and I worked for the same employer, and I was on my way down here to meet him, when the fire happened, and he died. I got into Oberhausen in the small hours of Monday morning. I knew Denver was in touch with the circus, and as soon as I got to the village I saw the fire in the circus field, and went straight in. When I didn't see Paul, and people were shouting about there being a second man in the wagon, I guessed who it was."

"Annalisa said you just came running out of the dark and helped them."

"Yes. When we got him out he was dead. Franz Wagner was still alive."

He was silent for a moment. "So much was true. Now for the rest. Here it is. My job at P.E.C. is a perfectly genuine one, but I also do other jobs from time to time for another employer, sometimes under other names. This was one of them. Some of my trips abroad are for my—well, call it my secondary job. P.E.C. don't know, of course, and I won't tell how the trips are fixed; nor will I tell you the name of my own Department . . . but take it from me, in the Sales Department of P.E.C. there's so much coming and going that all things seem to be possible." I heard the even, soft voice alter as he smiled. "There you have it, in all its sizzling drama. Some of my jobs—the ones I've refused to take you on—have been what you'd call cloak-and-dagger assignments."

"Cloak-and-dagger? You mean Secret Service? *Lewis!*" I struggled to take it in. "You mean you're a—an agent? A . . . *spy?*"

He laughed. "Take your pick of titles. We're not choosey."

"Lewis, it's—I can't believe—*you?*"

"As ever was. I'm sorry if it's a wild disillusionment." He turned his head sharply. "Why, darling, you're shivering! Honey, it's not dangerous . . . We don't all go roaring off in special Aston Martins loaded down with guns and suicide pills —more likely a bowler hat and a brief-case and maybe a roll of notes for bribing some snotty little informer. Good God, you've seen how dangerous this job is—grooming horses."

"'The things you do for England.'"

"Exactly that. And all that's happened is I got bitten by a palomino stallion."

"And Paul Denver died."

"And Paul Denver died." The smile left his voice. "Yes, I know what you're thinking, but there's no evidence that it's anything but an accident. Heaven knows the police have kept the circus standing long enough, while they went over everything with a fine toothcomb. Franz Wagner had had a small fire break out in his wagon once before—and he was a drunk. Mind you, that made him the person for Paul to get next to, if there was information to be got: another thing, I couldn't see Paul getting equally so sozzled that a fire could break out round him. But the reason for that wasn't far to seek. He'd had a crack on the head. Which is why, with my nasty suspicious nature, I've spent so long trying to find some shred of evidence that would make it something other than an accident. But I can't. On the other hand, there was evidence that the hook holding the oil lamp had broken, and the lamp had fallen, and it seems it could have knocked Paul silly for long enough to burn him to death, while old Franz, who was merely very drunk, survived long enough—he was farther away from the source of fire—to be pulled out. He was able to speak—just. One imagines that if there'd been 'foul play' he'd have tried to say something about it, but he didn't."

"I hadn't realised he was coherent."

"He was conscious, but I wouldn't say coherent, poor old chap. The shock had knocked the drink out of him, but he was in pain, and besides, there was a terrible flap going on, with men trying to get the horses out of the stable lines just beside where he was lying, and he could talk about nothing else but the horses and all the gear in the stable . . . There was a bit of a wind, and at one time they were afraid the stables might catch fire. We tried to question him, but all he would do was rave on and on about the horses—the Lipizzaner, mostly—and some precious saddle or other from Naples that he seemed to set store by."

"That was all?"

"As far as we could make out. We tried to tell him the horses were safe—the white stallion was out first of all, as a matter of fact—but I don't know if it got through to him. He was still talking about him—the Lipizzaner—when he died." He paused for a moment. "It was Annalisa he was trying to talk to . . . She was there all the time. It's fairly distressing to watch anyone die of burns, Van. Afterwards, when the police descended on them, and her father had to leave her . . ."

I knew he was trying to explain, without seeming to explain, the apparent swiftness of intimacy between himself and the girl. I said: "It's all right, I understand. You're a comforting person to have around. Couldn't she make out what Franzl was saying, then?"

"Not really. She says that none of the harness is Italian, it's all Austrian made, and there's nothing of any value, as far as she knows. It all seemed to mean nothing. So there's your mystery. Whatever Franzl had on his mind, it wasn't murder. Paul's death looks like one of those damned accidents that can cut right across the best-laid plans. If I'd got here a couple of hours earlier, I might have located him in time to stop whatever happened, and to hear what he had to tell me."

"You say you were already on your way to meet him. You'd been sent to get some information from him?"

"Yes. What seems to have happened is this: Denver's been in Czechoslovakia, and he came out a few days ago. He put in his report at Vienna Station—that's what we call our clearing-house for Eastern Europe—and then he went on leave here in Austria. As far as anyone knew, I gather, he was just doing as he said, and taking a holiday. All right. Next thing, the Department got a message—coded cable—asking for me to go out immediately, me and no one else. He had made contact with the Circus Wagner, and I was to pick him up there as Lee Elliott

(I'd worked with him under that name before). Well, what Paul asked for he usually got, so I came. The rest you know."

"And you've no idea why he sent for you?"

"The only clue I have is the contact he'd made with the circus —that, and the fact that he insisted on its being I who joined him. You see, the circus is crossing into Yugoslavia in two days' time, and Paul and I had worked there together before. I speak pretty good Serbo-Croat. Now, Paul's cover and Lee Elliott's are quite good enough to get across the border without burying ourselves in a circus, so I can only imagine that Paul had got himself into the circus because whatever he had found, and was following up, is centred there."

"Something or someone who *hasn't* got good cover, trying to get over the border?"

"That's the obvious conclusion. A circus is one group of people that tends to have the freedom of frontiers, even of Iron Curtain ones; but among all that crowd of men and goods and animals . . . Well, without a lead, it's hopeless. I've hung around and made myself useful, and fraternised madly—and I've found nothing."

"And that's your report? Just negative?"

"A nice useful negative. A splendid last assignment."

"Will they leave it at that? I mean, is there any chance they'd want you to stick with it—to cross the border?"

He stirred. "I don't think they'll send me, no. But . . . well, I can't think why else Paul insisted on the 'Lee Elliott' stuff, if he hadn't expected to go back there." His hand moved to ruffle my hair. "Don't cross bridges, darling, it may not be necessary. But if it were, the only risk would be another bite from that perishing yellow stallion."

I said: "What you're trying to tell me is, you might go for your own personal satisfaction?"

He said slowly: "If you put it like that, yes. I don't see that the Department will want me to take it further, as things are; but . . ." He hesitated for the first time. "My own satisfaction, yes, call it that. It isn't a hunch: I don't ride hunches. But I knew Denver, and if he had something to tell me, it's probable that it mattered. You'll have to forgive him. He had no idea that I was going on leave, or that I was quitting. I'm sorry."

"Don't. We've had all that. I'm not saying any of those things again. If it matters, it matters. The only thing is, I'll come too, this time. No, don't laugh at me, I mean it. If you're going under your own steam, there's no reason why I shouldn't, and I may even be able to help. I've got as good a connection with the circus as you have—I'm vet-in-chief, and I've been invited in any time I like. Besides, I've got a patient I have to see to."

"*Entendu.* Have you also got a visa?"

"No."

"Well, then . . . No, I'm not laughing you off; I told you I want your help, and I do want you to do just what you've said —stick with the circus till it leaves. Listen to me. I've got to go back to Vienna in the morning, and in any case my reasons for sticking around the circus are wearing a bit thin, and will hardly survive the pull-down, let alone the move across the border. But by the sheerest luck you're here, and you've got this cast-iron—and totally innocent—connection with them. They've got two more nights in this country, at Hohenwald, then Zech-stein, then the border. Now, if you and Timothy should just happen to be travelling much the same route as that . . . and if you happened to take such a keen professional interest in your old piebald patient that you felt you must look in on them again . . . That's all, don't ask any specific questions, just look and listen. Get in back stage, talk to people, move around and keep your eyes open. I told you I don't ride hunches, but I can feel it in my bones, there's something up . . . The point is that what-ever's wrong, whoever's wrong, they'll relax once they're rid of Denver's friend and colleague—me. And if they do relax, you may see or hear something."

"And if we do?"

"Do nothing. Understand? *Do nothing.* Wait for me."

"You'll come back soon?"

"Yes. Possibly tonight. Certainly by Tuesday night."

"What sort of thing, Lewis?"

"God knows, I don't. Anything that's out of pattern. There

may be nothing; but Denver asked for me, and Denver was heading for the border, and Denver died . . . You've got it clear? I don't want you to do anything, and certainly to take no risks at all. All you have to do is forget I was here, forget this conversation, and stay with the circus until I get in touch with you again. All right?"

"All right. And you needn't keep reassuring me, I'm not a bit nervous, just happy." I moved my cheek against the sweater. "You did say 'by the sheerest luck', didn't you?"

"That you were here? I did."

"Hush a minute, I think I heard Tim move." From next door came the heavy creak of the bed, as Timothy presumably roused and turned over. We lay still, clasped closely. After a while there was silence again.

He said very softly: "I ought to go. Damn!"

"What about Timothy?"

"Leave it for the moment. What he doesn't know won't hurt him. The trouble is this bloody alias . . . If you know his people, he'll find out who I am in any case, sooner or later, so we'll have to tell him. We can cook up some story for him—a special investigation for P.E.C. involving an insurance claim; something like that. I'll have to think. He may even decide for himself that I've some connection with the police, and that won't matter; it'll help to keep his mouth shut. He's all right, isn't he?"

"I'd trust him further than I can see."

"Fair enough, as long as we don't trust him with anything we haven't a right to. When I get back I'll talk to him. I'll really have to go." He sat up. "Now, final arrangements. Tomorrow, or rather today, you'll be at Hohenwald. You'd better keep in touch. Try to ring some time during the evening. The number's Vienna 32 14 60. I won't write it down, I want you to remember it. Got it?"

"I think so. Vienna 32 14 60. And do I ask for Mr Elliott?"

"Yes, please. If I'm not there someone else will answer. I'll tell them to expect your call. The next night you'll be at Zechstein, that's the take-off point for the border. I'll join you there. There's a hotel a couple of miles north of the village, a new one;

it's the old castle, and they've converted it, and I believe it's rather a fascinating place. Try and get rooms there, anyway. It's a fair distance out of the village, so that if I do come and join you there, I won't be seen and identified by half the parish ... Have you enough money?"

"For the time being, anyway. Will this castle place be very expensive?"

"Probably. Never mind, I'll see if I can get you on the strength! Book double, will you, in case I can join you as Mr March. Now I really must go."

"I suppose you must. Oh, Lewis, it's beastly cold without you."

"Is it, sweetie? Tuck that thing round you tighter, then, and go to sleep."

"I never felt less like sleep. I'll see you out."

I swung my feet out of bed, reached for my dressing-gown, and folded it round me. He had shrugged himself into his jacket, and was sitting down pulling on his shoes. They were, I noticed, rubber-soled plimsolls.

I dropped a kiss lightly on his hair. "You're too darned good at this, Casanova. Do you suppose you can get back into your own place without being seen and heard?"

"I'll try. In any case Frau Schindler will only think I've been helping the circus pull-down."

I unlatched the windows, and pushed them very quietly open. The cold scents of the dawn came in, as the starlight shivered and slackened towards morning. The breeze was rustling the grasses.

Lewis went past me like a shadow, and paused at the veranda rail. When he turned back, I went out.

He said softly: "The breeze'll help. Nobody'll hear me go." He kissed me. "Your reputation's safe a little longer, Mrs Prim."

I took him by the lapels of his jacket, and held on to them rather tightly. "Take care of yourself. Please take care of yourself."

"Why, what's this?"

"I don't know. Just a feeling. Take care."

"Don't worry, I'll do that. Now get yourself to bed, and go to sleep."

And suddenly, I was alone. I thought I heard, over the rustling of the grass, a deeper rustling, and then it was gone.

I turned back from the veranda rail, to see Timothy, in his pyjamas, standing at the open window of his room, staring at me.

·   ·   ·

For a moment, everything stopped; the breeze, the sounds of the night, the blood and breath in my body: for one long pulse of silence I could neither speak nor move.

He made no movement either, but, though I knew that Lewis had made no sound, I knew also that Timothy had seen him.

I suppose we stared at one another for a full half minute. It seemed like a year. He had not to be told yet; I had had my instructions; and at the unthinking level of fear which had prompted my last exchange with Lewis, I knew that they might matter. There was only one thing to do; assume that Timothy had seen nothing, and hope that he wouldn't dare broach the subject without my giving him a lead.

I said: "Hullo, couldn't you sleep?"

He came slowly out through the long windows until he was only a couple of feet away. In the growing light I could see him clearly. There was nothing in his face that one could put a name to, no curiosity, or embarrassment, or even surprise. His features had been schooled to a most complete indifference. He was going to play it exactly as I could have wished.

I think it was his very lack of expression that decided me. Boys of seventeen ought not to be able to look like that. Whatever Carmel and Graham Lacy had done between them to Timothy, I wasn't going to be responsible for adding another layer to that forcible sophistication.

And nothing would serve but the truth. It was emphatically not the time to ask, with exasperated affectation, what he thought I could possibly have been getting up to with Lee Elliott after half an hour's acquaintance. He had seen the kiss, after all. Besides, as soon as the first impact had worn off, he would certainly put two and two together, and arrive at the truth. He might as well have it now, and from me. Lewis would have to forgive me; but if Timothy could be trusted later, he could be trusted now.

I took in my breath and leaned back against the rail.

"Well, it's a fair cop," I said, lightly. "Now I suppose I'll have to confess I lied to you about our Mr Elliott."

"Lied to me?"

"Afraid so. You remember I told you he was my husband's double?"

"Yes, of course." His face had changed, emerging somehow from that pre-selected expression of indifference. I suppose his lightning conclusion was the obvious one, but somehow the relief and pleasure on his face made it a compliment. "You mean it *was* your husband, himself? You mean that chap Elliott—your husband *was* actually here all the time? The newsreel was right?"

"Just that. As soon as I saw him I realised he didn't want to be made known— and then Annalisa said, 'This is Lee Elliott', so I just shut up and said nothing."

"In disguise? Really? Gosh!" The old familiar Timothy was back; even in the cool half light I could see the sparkle of excitement. "I said he was mysterious, didn't I? No wonder you were punch-drunk tonight and wouldn't make plans about cables to Stockholm!" He took a breath. "But why? Was there something wrong about the fire, then, after all?"

"Don't ask me why, he didn't explain, only that there's something involved that his firm doesn't want to be made public, so for the moment we'll have to keep his secret." I gave a little laugh. "This'll be a great blow to his pride; he was so sure nobody'd heard him."

"As a matter of fact I didn't hear him. I'd woken up, and couldn't go to sleep again straight away, and I felt a bit hot under that eiderdown affair, so I just came over to open the window wider." He added, naïvely: "As a matter of fact I got a bit of a fright. I wondered what in the world he was doing snooping around here. I was just going to tackle him, and see if you were all right, when you came out of the window."

"And you realised it had been a reasonably friendly visit." I laughed. "Well, thanks for looking after me. Now you know all, as they say ... At any rate you know as much as I do, but keep it dark, there's a dear. I'm not supposed to have told you who he was."

"O.K. Good night."

"Good night."

And I went back to my cold bed.

Chapter Nine

Sometime he trots, as if he told the steps
With gentle majesty and modest pride:
Anon he rears upright, curvets and leaps,
As who should say 'Lo, thus my strength is tried.'
Shakespeare: *Venus and Adonis*

Next morning it was with a sense almost of shock that, as the car approached the other end of the village, I saw in place of the bustle and the big top of the circus, merely an empty field. There was the trampled circle, with the remains of sawdust and tanbark strewn where the ring had stood. Wisps of blowing straw were all that were left of the warm stable where the horses had slept, and where I had operated last night.

Tim stopped the car at the gate of the field.

"It's funny, isn't it? Like a field full of ghosts."

"I was just thinking that. It looks quite incredibly deserted, as if Aladdin or someone had rubbed a lamp, and the whole thing had been spirited away ... Like the end of a story." I looked towards the corner of the field, where the blackened grass and a few charred sticks indicated the scene of the tragedy. "And a sad story, too. I wonder if they were glad to get away? What did you stop for?" For he was getting out of the car.

"I thought I'd get something to eat on the way. I won't be long—that is, unless you'd like to come back with me, and maybe have a cup of coffee at the *Konditorei*?"

"I'll come."

The smell of fresh baking from the little bakery-cum-café was enough to snare anybody, and it would have been too much to expect Tim to pass it without a visit. The little window on the shady side of the morning square was filled with fragrant stacks of breads and excitingly foreign confections. Timothy gave them his earnest consideration, while I waited, trying not to look as if all my attention was fixed on the side door, where a notice saying *Zimmer frei* might indicate that the vistor had already left.

"Vanessa, do look at the names of these things! Aren't they marvellous? *Sandgugelhupf* . . . isn't that smashing? How about a nice *Sandgugelhupf* each? Or a *Polsterzipf*? Oh, look, it can't really be called a *Spitzbub*, can it?"

"I don't see why not, anything seems possible in this language. What about *Schokoladegugelhupf*—and I do rather care for the *Schnittbrot*."

"I think that only means sliced bread," said Timothy. "It is a marvellous language, isn't it?"

"I'm going to start learning it, as from today," I said. "I wish there was a shop where I could get a book, but there won't be one here, and we're not going through Bruck, either, today. Have you got one?"

"Only a phrase book, but you can borrow it if you like. It's quite a good one, as they go . . . Don't you just adore phrase books? The things they imagine one might want to say . . . they're almost as good as one's Greek grammar at school. I remember one of the first sentences I had to put into Greek was, 'She carried the bones in the basket.' I'm still wondering whose bones, and why."

"Well, there you are, it's stuck in your memory all this time, which is what I suppose school books are meant to do. I'll bet you remember that bit of Greek better than any other you did."

"As a matter of fact it's about the only bit I do remember, and just think how useful. The best thing I've come across so far in my German phrase book is in the section for 'Air Travel'. 'Will you please open the windows' seems to me a funny thing to say to anyone on a plane, somehow."

"Not seriously? You must be kidding. Is it really in the book?"

"Yes, honestly."

"Well, if all the phrases are as useful as that —"

"Good morning," said Lewis, just behind us.

He wasn't wearing the plimsolls this morning, but he had still moved very quietly. If it was getting to be a habit, I thought, it was a habit he could just get out of again. I didn't want to die of heart failure.

I said, "Good morning," a little breathlessly, wondering as I spoke if I should tell him straight away that Timothy knew, but Timothy was already greeting him with aplomb almost as professional as his own, and then it was somehow too late.

Timothy said: "Oh, hullo, Mr Elliott, good morning. You haven't gone yet? I wondered if you'd have left when the circus did."

"Too early for me. The last wagons were due to go at about five, I think. I didn't hear them."

"You must be a very sound sleeper," said Timothy cheerfully. "I imagined there'd be a lot of coming and going in the village during the night, but perhaps it doesn't disturb you?"

"Thank you," said Lewis, "no. I had an excellent night; far better than I had expected."

"Tim," I said quickly, perhaps even sharply, "you'd better choose what you want in the way of buns, and go in and buy them. We really ought to be setting off."

"O.K.," said Tim amiably, and vanished through the shop doorway.

"Honours about even," I said, "but will you please not score your points across my marriage bed? That boy knows, Lewis."

"Does he?" I was relieved to see that he looked, after the first frowning moment, no more than amused. "The little so-and-so, does he indeed?"

"I had to tell him. He saw you leaving last night."

"I must be slipping."

"No, it was pure accident. But I had to tell him."

"I suppose so. Don't worry. How much does he know?"

"Only who you are. He thinks it's some mysterious business mission for P.E.C. May I tell him you asked me to keep in touch with the circus?"

"I don't see why not. Tell him the firm may want more details about Denver's death, and I may have to come back, so meantime I've asked you to stick around. That's nothing but the truth, after all. You can refer any other questions to me."

"I doubt if he'll ask them. Tim's all right." It was a measure of what had happened in the last two days, that I knew that the phrase—and all it implied—was true. "When do you go?"

"I'm on my way now. You all right?"

"Fine. We're just setting off for Hohenwald, but Tim was afraid of starving on the way. Have you got a car here?"

He nodded to one which stood under the trees near by, a shabby fawn-coloured Volvo which nevertheless looked powerful. He was decently dressed this morning, I noticed, though still not recognisably Lewis March, my husband. This was still the anonymous and professionally insignificant Lee Elliott. I could see now that his very ability to melt into apparent insignificance was one of the tools of his trade, but nothing, I thought, could take from Lewis the precision and grace of movement which spoke always of strength and self-command, and could sometimes—when he allowed it—give him elegance.

He lifted his head, narrowing his eyes against the morning sun. "What's the boy stocking up with food for? You haven't a great way to go . . ." And then, very softly: "Stop looking at me like that, for goodness' sake, my dear girl. You look as if you were bringing me gold and frankincense."

"And why not? I has my rights too, Mr M." I added aloud:

"Exactly how far is Hohenwald, anyway? How far does a circus normally go in a day?"

"About thirty or forty miles. It's roughly fifty kilometres to Hohenwald. You should have a lovely run; the gradients aren't bad, and there's some beautiful country. Have lunch at Lindenbaum, and take your time."

When Timothy emerged from the shop with his arms alarmingly full of packages, Mr Elliott was giving me directions for a pleasant day's drive, with a map drawn on the back of an old envelope. I noticed that the envelope was addressed to 'Lee Elliott, Esq., c/o Kalkenbrunner Fertiliser Company, Meerstrasse, Vienna'.

"Well," I said, "we'll go. Have a good journey."

"And you," said Lewis. "Enjoy yourselves . . . *Auf Wiedersehen*, then, and remember me to Annalisa."

As we drove off, Timothy shot a sideways glance at me. "Was that just a crack?"

I laughed. "No. In any case, you're a fine one to talk about making cracks. I may tell you, Lewis knows."

He looked startled, then grinned. "Oh, you just told him? You mean he knows I know?"

"Yes, and leave it at that, will you, before I get muddled. All is now in the clear . . . and thank goodness we can talk."

This was the first chance we had had of private conversation since our daybreak meeting on the veranda. Breakfast had been a more or less public function in the Gasthof, with Timothy's devoted waitress watching our every move, but now, as we left the village behind us, we had not only the road, but the whole countryside, seemingly, to ourselves.

The road was, as Lewis had promised, idyllic. The morning sun cast long, fresh blue shadows, and the hedges were thick, and full of honeysuckle and white convolvulus. A hay cart had been that way, and the wisps of hay were hanging golden from the hedge in the still morning.

I began to explain to Timothy what Lewis had asked me to do, indicating merely that Lewis and his firm were not satisfied with the verdict of 'accident' on Paul Denver, and were still curious to know what connection—if any—the latter had had with the circus people, and if he could have incurred any enmities which might have led directly to his death.

"All he wants me to do," I said at length, "is keep in touch with the circus, as veterinary surgeon if they need me, or just as a friend. He's very emphatic that no questions are to be asked, or detective work done . . . there's no room for your Archie Goodwin act, Timothy. In fact I don't know whether you want to stay in on this or not? It chimes in exactly with what I'd like to do myself—I mean, if I can't join Lewis straight away, then I'm quite happy to stooge around here till he comes back, and maybe be a bit of help to him at the same time. And I do want to keep an eye on the old horse. But if you'd rather cut loose here and now, and go to Piber —"

"No, not a bit. Gosh, no, I'd love to stay, if you'd have me . . ."

His protestations were almost violently convincing, and only faded into silence when we caught up with the hay cart. This was enormous, and top-heavily laden, creaking along on its wooden wheels behind two plodding sorrel horses. The road was narrow, overhung with high hedges, and with ditches to either side.

". . . If you're sure you could do with me?" finished Timothy, as we negotiated the hay cart with three centimetres to spare on either side, and buzzed happily on up the next incline.

"I'm beginning to think I can't do without you," I said.

"That settles it then. Hohenwald it is."

.   .   .

The village of Hohenwald was much smaller than Oberhausen. It lay a mile or so behind the main road, in a pretty hanging valley, and was little more than a cluster of houses grouped round its church whose tower rose, crowned with a bell of grey-green shingles, above splayed roofs and gables of red tile. An arched stone bridge spanned a narrow mountain river, and led what traffic it could into the cobbled square. To south and west the land fell away in smiling orchards and fields of corn, some of them cut, golden among the greens, while to north and east the mountains lifted their stepped ramparts of pine forests. The verges of the gravel road were white with dust.

The sense of loss we had felt in leaving Oberhausen was cancelled here, even before we reached the village, by the sight of the now familiar posters wrapped round trees and gate-posts, and then by the Circus Wagner itself, settled in a field beside the river. It seemed odd to see, in this completely different setting, the same tents and wagons and big top, the whole build-up of the circus so exactly the same. It was indeed as if some genie's hand had picked it up complete and set it down again here, some thirty miles away.

It was mid-afternoon when we arrived, and the first performance would not start till five, but already children were crowding in a noisy and excited mob round the gate of the field. I saw the dwarf, Elemer, sitting on the gate and talking to the children, and making them laugh. He looked up and saw us as the car went by, and smiled and lifted his small hand in a wave of welcome. So the news would go before us.

There was some coming and going of tourists in the village, but for all that we got beds easily enough at another small and scrupulously clean Gasthof beside the church. Shortly after four, we walked back to the circus field.

As we passed the big top, I paused and looked inside.

The grass was fresh, the ring strewn with fresh sawdust, and on the platforms that crowned the enormous king-poles, electricians were busy putting the last touches to the wiring. The top itself, with its floating spaces, looked different, lit now from above with the curiously unreal diffused light of sunshine through canvas. The whole space echoed to the sound of hammering and shouting as the tent-men put up the last of the wooden tiers of scaffolding and arranged the benches on them. Someone on a high ladder was hanging the rear curtains in place, the crimson drapes through which the horses would come. A couple of clowns, already in costume but without their make-up, stood talking very seriously in the centre aisle.

In spite of the differences, it was hauntingly the same as last night, and though at the moment this was only a tent enclosing an alien air, I got the strongest feeling that it was full and echoing with the hundreds of past performances, the music of past songs and dances and laughter.

As we emerged again into the sunlight and I saw the strange gate, the strange village, the strange bell-shaped roof of the church tower against its backdrop of pines, I found myself experiencing a sudden sharp sense of loss – which I hadn't felt that morning – to realise that Lewis was not here. He was possibly already in Vienna. Last night's episode might have been a dream, gone to join the flickering unreality of that almost forgotten news-reel.

Annalisa was expecting us, and, to my relief, seemed pleased that we had come, and very eager that I should take another look at the piebald horse.

"But of course you are welcome! I wish I could ask you both in now, but I am dressing, as you see." All we had in fact seen of her so far was a face peering past the curtain that hung over the doorway of her sleeping-wagon. In spite of her welcoming smile and obviously real pleasure, I thought she looked pale— the gaiety and sparkle had gone. I wondered if she had had any sleep at all last night. "But you will come afterwards again and have coffee? You'll go to the performance, yes?"

"Timothy's going to see the show again, and if I know him, he'll see your act twice," I said, "but I don't think I will, thank you. I'll just go round to the stables. How's the patient?"

"Better, much better. He's a different horse already. He hardly limps at all, just a little, as if he was stiff . . . not a real limp at all."

"We call it 'going short'," I said. "Is he eating?"

"Not much . . . but he really does look better. I am so grateful to you."

"Think nothing of it. I take it you'll keep him now?"

I smiled as I spoke, and she responded, but (I thought) with a rather wintry charm, and said merely: "Then I shall see you later? *Also gut!* If you want to come in here and use my wagon, please do so, it's never shut. Come in and make coffee if you want it, anything. Just what you wish." The smile again, better this time, and the head vanished.

"She looks tired," I said. "I hope she manages her act all right. Well, see you later, Tim."

The stables, too, were uncannily the same. There was the same smell, the same rows of horses' rumps and idly swishing tails, but the sun was white on the canvas, and the air of sleepy peace was gone. The liberty horses were being prepared for the show. The rugs had been stripped off them, and their skins gleamed in the light. Half a dozen were already wearing their harness. Men hurried to and fro carrying rugs, surcingles, plumed bridles. The Shetland ponies, some of them getting excited, were beginning to fuss, nibbling one another's necks and switching their long tails. The Lipizzan stallion in his stall near the door stood placidly, head down, ears relaxed, taking no notice of the fuss and bustle. It was difficult to realise that in less than an hour's time he would be in the ring, magnificent in the spotlights, clothed with gold and jewels and flying through the air. Here in his dim corner he looked ancient and heavy with wisdom, and as earthbound as a horse of white stone.

Opposite him the piebald stood with drooping head, but as I approached his eye rolled back, and he moved an ear in greeting. What I had taken to be a boy was hunched in the next stall, busy over a piece of harness, but when he spoke, I realised that it was the dwarf Elemer.

"So you are back to see the suffering one." I don't know where the dwarf had learnt his English; it was guttural and stilted, but the vowels were cultured. His voice was deep and pleasant.

"Yes. He looks a lot better."

"He has eaten a little. Not enough. But he will mend . . ."

I went into the stall to look at the horse. "So Annalisa was saying."

". . . For what it is worth," the dwarf said. He lifted the jewelled saddle off its trestle, and began to hump it rather painfully across to the white stallion's stall. It almost hid him from sight, and the girth was trailing, but I thought I knew better than to offer help.

I turned my attention to the horse. The dolly was still in place, the swelling had vanished, and he accepted my hands without wincing. I moved him back a pace in his stall, and saw that he was putting the leg to the ground with more confidence already. The coat still stared, but his eye was brighter, and his general countenance very much better than last night.

I straightened up. "'For what it is worth'?" I wasn't quite sure if I had heard the guttural murmur aright. "Do you mean they *won't* keep him?"

He shrugged. The effect, with the tiny short arms and the big shoulders, was awful. I had to exert sharp control to stop myself from looking away. "Who knows?" was all he would say, and set one of those shoulders to the white stallion's hock to make him move over.

Then all of a sudden, it seemed, the show was on us. The horses went streaming out for the first act. I saw the 'cowboys' swing up into their saddles, and the 'Entry of the Gladiators' came thudding from the big top. The groom Rudi hurried into the Lipizzan's stall and, taking the saddle from Elemer, heaved it one-armed on to the stallion's back. I had been wrong about the dwarf's susceptibilities; the groom cracked some joke in German which, from the accompanying gesture, had some reference to Elemer's height, but the latter only laughed and went scuttling under the stallion's belly to fasten the girth. I straightened up from my examination of the piebald's leg, and stood fondling his ears, while I watched the white stallion putting on, jewel by jewel, his royal dress. Then the dwarf came across to me.

"They are starting. Are you going in to see the show again?"

I shook my head. "I was wondering . . . I suppose this old chap won't have had any exercise at all since the fire? Has he even been out to grass? I thought not. You know, a bit of gentle walking would do him a world of good, and a bit of grazing would do even more. I wondered if there was anywhere

I could take him? Do you think the verge of the road? Would it be allowed?"

"Of course," said the dwarf, "you must do as you wish, you know what is best. But do not take him to the road, there is too much dust. Go the other way." The little arm gestured towards the far door of the stable. "Behind this field there is a wood, but it is not a big wood just a—what do you say?—a belt of trees, perhaps twenty metres wide. There is a gate, and a path up through the trees, and above them is a little alp; it is common land, and there is good grass there. Nobody will stop you."

"Can I leave him grazing there till the pull-down?"

"Of course. You will not want to hobble him, no? Then if you wait one moment, I will get you the tether and a peg."

It was easy enough to find the place. At the far side of the field the ground lifted sharply away from the flat land where the tents stood, and the late sun gilded the young fir cones with amber and threw into deep shadow the path that wound upwards through the trees. The wood of the gate was damp, and it creaked a little as I opened it and led the old horse through. We went slowly. He put his off fore to the ground perhaps a little tenderly, but he was by no means lame; at most his gait was stiff, and as we made our way gently up the mossy track between the pines he seemed to go better with every step. He lifted his head, and his ears pricked with the first sign of interest he had shown. Even I, with my poor human senses, could smell the rich scents of that summer's evening.

Above the belt of pines lay the alp the dwarf had told me of, a long terrace of flat green, dotted here and there with bushes, and walled on every side by the dark firs. Someone had scythed down the long meadow grass, and the hay lay drying here and there in little piles; where it had been shorn the new grass was fresh and tender green, and full of flowers. The air smelt of honey.

The horse shouldered his way past me into the sunlight, dropped his head and began to graze. I left him to it, and carrying the slack of the tether took the peg into the middle of the meadow and drove it in, then moved a little way off and sat down.

The ground was warm with the day's sun. Faintly from below the belt of pines came the circus music, muted and made more musical by the distance. I sat listening, enjoying the last of the sunshine, while I contentedly watched the now greedy grazing of the old stallion. The grass was thick with familiar meadow flowers—harebells, thyme, eyebright, and, where the scythe had not yet passed, the foaming white and yellow of parsley and buttercups. What was not so familiar was the fluttering, rustling life of the meadow: the whole surface of the field seemed moving with butterflies—meadow browns, blues, sulphurs, fritillaries, and a few of my own Vanessas, the red admirals and tortoiseshells. Their colours flickered among the flowers, each vanishing momentarily as it clung and folded, then opening to its own bright colour as it fluttered on. Even the green roots of the grass were alive, as countless grasshoppers hopped and fiddled there. The air droned with bees, all zooming past me, I noticed, on the same purposeful track, as if on some apian *Autobahn* of their own. They were all making for a little hut, the size of a small summer-house, chalet-style and beautifully built of pine, and as full of tiny windows as a dovecot. It was, in fact, a bee-house, a sort of collective hive for several swarms, each one with its own tiny bee-door, behind which it made its honey in candle-shaped combs. Amused and interested, I watched the laden bees aiming like bullets each for its own door, remembering how, even a few years ago, in my own childhood, the English meadows, too, had been alive with wings, and how quiet now was the poisoned countryside.

From beyond the pines, sounding surprisingly remote, the cracked bell of the little church chimed six. There had been an interval of silence from the circus. I supposed it was the clowns' act, or the performing dogs: now, faintly and sweetly, but quite distinctly in the still clear air, the music started again. I heard the fanfare and recognised it; it was the entrance of Annalisa and her white stallion. The trumpets cut through the air, silver, clear and commanding. Old Piebald stopped grazing and lifted his head with his ears cocked, as one imagines a war-horse might at the smell of battle and the trumpets. Then the music changed, sweet, lilting and golden, as the orchestra stole into the waltz from *Der Rosenkavalier*.

There was some enchantment in hearing it at that distance on that lovely evening in the Alpine meadow. I settled my back comfortably against one of the little soft haycocks, and prepared to enjoy the concert; but then something about the old horse caught my attention, and I sat up to watch.

He had not lowered his head again to graze, but was standing with neck arched and ears pricked, in a sort of mimicry of the white stallion's proud posture. Then, like the white stallion's, his head moved, not in an ordinary equine toss, but with a graceful, almost ceremonial movement of conscious beauty. A forefoot lifted, pointed, pawed twice at the soft ground; then slowly, all by himself, bowing his head to his shadow on the turf, he began to dance. He was old and stiff, and he was going short on the off fore, but he moved to the music like a professional.

I sat among the lengthening shadows of the lonely meadow, watching him, somehow infinitely touched. In this way, I supposed, all old circus horses felt when they heard the music of their youth: the bowing, ceremonious dance of the liberty horse was something which, once learned, could never be forgotten.

And then I realised that this was not the movement of a liberty horse. It was not dancing as the palominos had 'danced'; this was a version, stiff but true, of the severely disciplined figures of the high school: first the Spanish Walk, shouldering-in in a smooth skimming diagonal; then the difficult *pirouette*, bringing him round sharply to present him sideways to his audience; then as I watched he broke into a form of the *piaffe*. It was a travesty, a sick old horse's travesty, of the standing trot which the Lipizzaner had performed with such precision and fire, but you could see it was a memory in him, still burning and alive, of the real thing perfectly executed. In the distance the music changed: the Lipizzaner down in the ring would be rising into the *levade*, the first of the 'airs above the ground'. And in the high Alpine meadow, with only me for audience, old Piebald settled his hind hooves, arched his crest and tail, and, lame forefoot clear of the ground, lifted into and held the same royal and beautiful *levade*.

And this, it seemed, had been enough. He came down to all four feet, shook his head, dropped his muzzle to the grass, and all at once was just an old tired piebald horse pegged out to graze in a green meadow.

Chapter Ten

This is the attitude in which artists depict the horses on which gods and heroes ride.

Xenophon: *The Art of Horsemanship*

"Tim," I said, "you're not proposing to sit through the whole of the second house too, are you?"

"No, I wasn't, though I'd have liked to see Annalisa ride again. Why, did you want me?"

"Yes, and I want you to skip Annalisa too, if you will. I've got something to show you, and it's something you won't want to miss. No"—in response to a quick, inquiring look from him—"nothing to do with that. Something purely personal. Will you come with me?"

"Well, of course. Where?"

"Away up the hill behind the field. I'm not going to tell you anything about it, I want you to see for yourself."

It was dark now, but the moon was coming up clear of the mountains and the trees. The air was very still, and the bats were out. The horse had moved on a little, grazing quietly.

"Oh, you've got old Piebald here," said Timothy. "Goodness,

he looks a different creature. He's eating like a horse, as they say."

"Exactly like a horse. But—*How noble in reason! how infinite in faculty! in form, in moving, how express and admirable! . . . the beauty of the world! the paragon of animals!*"

"What on earth's that?"

"*Hamlet*, with a dash of Noël Coward. Look, come over here, the grass is damp now, but there's a log; we can sit on that."

"What were you going to show me?"

"You'll have to wait for it. It's something that happened, and I hope it'll happen again. Here, sit down. Listen how clearly you can hear the music."

"Mm. That's the liberty act, isn't it? There, that's the end. Now it'll be the clowns. What is it, Vanessa? You sounded sort of excited."

"I am a bit. Wait and see. It may not happen, I—I simply don't know, and I may have been wrong. I can't help feeling now that it was all my imagination, but if it wasn't, perhaps you'll see it, too."

It was a beautiful night, the air clear and still. The butterflies had all gone, and the bees were quiet in their bee-house. In the silence I thought I could hear the cry of bats high up above the trees. The swish of the horse's hoofs through the grass, and the tearing sound of his cropping, were very loud in the still air. The moon rose clear of a low cloud that hugged the hill.

I said softly: "Listen, those are the trumpets. Don't say a word, now. Keep still."

At first I thought it wasn't going to happen. The trumpets shivered the air, distant, silver, brave: the old horse grazed. An owl flew low across the field, silent, ghostly white in the moonlight. The horse lifted his head to watch it. The trumpets called on unheeded.

The waltz from *Der Rosenkavalier* wound its way up through the pines. Beside me on the log Timothy sat obediently still.

The waltz beat on softly; five bars, six bars—and then it happened. The old head lifted, the neck arched, the forefoot went out in that arrogant beautiful movement, and the piebald glided once more into his own private and ceremonious dance. This way and that he went, his hoofs striking the turf softly. The moonlight flooded the meadow, blanching all colours to its own ghostly silver. The pines were very black. As the stallion rose in the last magnificent rear of the *levade*, the moonlight poured over him bleaching his hide so that for perhaps five or six long seconds he reared against the black background, a white horse dappled with shadows, no longer an old broken-down gypsy's piebald, but a *haute école* stallion, of the oldest line in Europe.

Timothy neither moved nor made a sound until it was over; then we turned and looked at one another.

"Am I right?" I asked.

He merely nodded, saying nothing. I had a suspicion that he was as moved as I had been by the sight, and was—boy-like—concerned not to show it. When he spoke, it was in a normal, even casual voice, but I knew I had been right. "The poor old chap," he said.

"He's been good, in his day," I said.

"I'll say." His voice sharpened, as he began to think. "But, here, I don't understand! If the horse was trained, why should they talk of getting rid of him?"

"He's old. I had a good look at him: he's over twenty."

"But nobody's given his age as a reason for putting him down, it's always been that 'he's no use, he can do nothing, the circus can't afford to keep a horse who does nothing'. You remember Annalisa said they'd tried him in the liberty routine and he was no use."

"If he was a highly trained dressage performer when they got him, he'd take badly to a new routine."

"Yes, but if he's 'highly trained', you'd think they could use him somehow. Or at any rate sell him. He'd fetch good money, even at twenty."

"Perhaps," I said, "they don't know he's a trained performer."

He turned to stare at me. In the strong moonlight it was possible to see one another quite clearly.

"Don't know?"

I said: "Well, they can't know, can they? You've just quoted the things they've said . . . and tonight, again, I got the impression they thought he was hardly worth my trouble," I told him what the dwarf had said.

He sat for a while, frowning down at the grass. "Well, where does this get us? We'll tell them, of course. They'll hardly —"

"I'm not sure that we should."

His head jerked up at that. "What d'you mean?"

"I've been thinking," I said. "This was Franz Wagner's horse. You remember what Annalisa told us, that he joined the circus ten years ago when it was somewhere in the north, and he happened to be working there with a dealer in a horse fair, and he brought this horse with him from the other circus, the Czech one. Now, you can't tell me that if he'd owned a horse trained like this one, and with this sort of talent, he'd have said nothing about it, if there hadn't been something wrong. Why, if he brings a performing stallion with him (and goes on riding him in private, apparently), does he say nothing, not even cash in on what could be a big asset? Well, it's certainly quite irrelevant to what Lewis wants to know, but Franz Wagner is part of Lewis's puzzle picture after all. 'Anything that's out of pattern,' he said, and from all points of view we could bear to know a bit more about old Franzl. If it comes to that, Tim, he changed his name, remember?"

"So he did. And refused to work an act . . . appear in public."

I said slowly: "What if the horse was really valuable, and he'd actually *stolen* it from the circus he was in before? I've a feeling that old Mr Wagner—Annalisa's grandfather—must have known about it, making him change his name and all that, but I'm pretty sure the others weren't told . . . Not that it matters now, it all happened a long time ago, and the man's dead; but if he stole one thing, he may have stolen others, and considering he's somewhere in Lewis's 'mystery', it might be worth following it up. If he'd done anything bad enough to lie low for, all these years, you might think that Paul Denver's connection with him was —"

"Wels," said Timothy suddenly. "She said Wels, didn't she?"

"I beg your pardon?"

"Annalisa said that when he joined the Circus Wagner they were playing at a place called Wels, in the north, near the Bavarian border."

"That's right, she did. I say, Tim, you remember she said that the circus was actually pulling down when he joined them? At least, she implied it. If he was actually on the run at the time, what better cover could he have? All the muddle and traffic of the horse fair in the town, and then the circus crossing the border that very night . . . One more man and a horse could easily —"

"The Spanish Riding School was in Wels till 1955," said Timothy.

The interruption was as brief and to the point as his last one, but, as before, I didn't get the implications straight away.

"Yes? She'd been to see them, she said. What would —?"

I stopped short, and I felt my mouth open as I gaped at him. I don't remember either of us getting to our feet, but I found myself standing there, while we stared at one another.

I said, hoarsely, "It can't be, Tim. It simply can't be. There'd have been a fuss—police —"

"There was." He sounded as dazed as I was. "Wait . . . listen . . . it's all coming clear now. You remember that story I told you on the plane, the one about the groom cutting his horse's throat and then killing himself? Well, I got it wrong. That's an old story, I don't even know if it's true, but I told you, it was never published, and of course I never knew the names. But there was another story which *was* published; I'd read it in one of these books I've got, and I'd got it muddled in my mind with the earlier story." He took a long breath. "Do you remember my showing you the photograph of Neapolitano Petra, and telling you he was the one who'd been killed? I was wrong. He disappeared, ten years ago this summer, and one of the stablemen disappeared along with him."

There was a silence. We both turned like puppets pulled by wires, to look at the old piebald grazing at the other side of the field.

"The markings," said Timothy. "How would he do it?"

"I don't know, it would be easy enough—hair dye, something of that sort." I swung back on him suddenly. "That would account for it!"

"Account for what?"

"The feel of that horse's coat. I noticed today it was still feeling rough and sort of harsh even though the fever had gone, and his coat shouldn't have been staring any more. I'm sure it was one of the black patches I was touching, you know how brittle and hard hair feels when it's dyed often. It bothered me a bit, it didn't feel quite right. We won't see much at this time of night, but I'd like to take a look at those black patches by daylight! Tim —" I checked myself. "No, look, it's nonsense, all of it! I still don't believe it!"

"Neither do I," said Timothy, "but it fits, you know, it really does. Just think, if it was Franz Wagner, how easily he could do it; take the stallion out somehow—I've read that conditions at Wels were sometimes a bit chaotic for the Riding School, and the local horse fair would make it a bit more so—disguise him, and then simply melt into his uncle's circus, which was luckily just on the pull-down. Perhaps he did it just on impulse, because the cover was there handy . . . he may even have been drunk . . . and then, when he realised what he'd done, he didn't dare confess. And he daren't let the horse perform in public, either, or do so himself; but he couldn't resist riding him in private—it's obvious he's kept him in practice of a sort."

"But why? If he was going to make nothing out of it, why steal the creature?"

He said slowly: "I can't help thinking it was partly bloody-mindedness, a sort of revenge. That's what comes through the story as I read it: it said 'the stableman' had joined the Riding School from some Army company in Styria, and he'd worked his way up to junior *Bereiter*—that's a rider—but he was a bit wild always, and quarrelled with the senior riders, and then got the idea they had a grudge against him and he wasn't being given a chance. Then he did get his chance at a performance, and turned up drunk, and was put right back to stable-hand on the spot. I expect he'd have been sacked, but they were having a job to get people at all in those years, and he was good with the horses when he was sober."

Another of those silences. "'Turned up drunk,'" I said softly. "'An Army company in Styria.' I suppose the Czech circus was just a story they made up for cover . . . Merciful heavens, it does fit. Of course, none of the books would mention the man's name?"

"No, but it could be found out."

"Yes . . . yes. That's the side of it we'll have to think over."

"You seem sure they don't know."

I said: "I can't believe they do. They gave no sign of it over all this business of the haematoma, with the spotlight—literally—on the old stallion . . . Besides, we can't say a word to them one way or the other till we're sure, and I don't know quite how to set about it. The National Stud aren't likely to tell us the name of the groom and if we ask the police they may wonder why we want to know, and we might get Herr Wagner and the circus into trouble. If you look at it the other way, we ought to tell them first, I suppose."

"I think we can find out fairly easily on our own," said Timothy.

"No, we mustn't. We can't afford to go round asking all sorts of questions, for Lewis's sake. I told you the Archie Goodwin stuff was out."

"Not that. It's much simpler. We can find out here and now. The real Lipizzans—the Riding School Lipizzans, that is—are all branded. I've always felt myself that it was rather a pity to disfigure a white horse with a brand, but they each carry three. There's a big 'L' on the near-side cheek, that's for Lipizzan, obviously. If he's bred at the National Stud, there'll be a crown and a 'P' for Piber on the flank. And on the side they do some sort of hieroglyphic which gives the actual breeding, the sire's line, and the dam. I'm not at all sure that I could decipher that, but I think if we find he's got all three brands, we can be pretty sure we're right."

"Well," I said, "what are we waiting for?"

The moonlight threw our shadows long and black across the turf as we walked over to the grazing horse. He was out of the moonlight now, and in the shadow of the pines, his black patches showing very dark and hiding his real shape so that he looked, not like a horse, but like floating patches of some moving ectoplasm.

I said: "You may be right, dear heaven, you may be right. You notice what a lot of black there is on his near side? The cheek, the ribs, the flank—all the places where you said the brands would be?" The horse lifted his head as we reached him, and I took hold of the halter. "They're horrible great ugly marks, too . . . You'd think it would go to his heart to . . ."

My voice trailed off. The horse had pushed his muzzle against my chest and Tim had run his hand gently but quickly down past the forelock, past the eye and over the near cheek. I saw the boy's fingers, pale in the moonlight, moving over the black skin. They felt, hesitated, then slowly traced out the shape of a big 'L'.

He said nothing. Nor did I. In silence as he dropped his hand I put mine on the horse's cheek. The skin was damp where the dewy grass had brushed him. There, ever so slightly ruffling the hair, I could feel the outline of the old brand. It was there, the 'L' for Lipizzan. And so was the crowned 'P' for Piber. And so was some complicated pattern on the ribs, where, faintly, could be traced something that might be an 'N' and a 'P' . . .

Neapolitano Petra blew gustily at the front of my dress, pulled his head away, and took another mouthful of the dew-wet clover.

Still in silence, Timothy and I turned and left him there, and made our way slowly down the path between the pines.

Here the moonlight didn't penetrate and it was very dark. For a time we picked our way in silence. Then Timothy said rather inadequately: "Well, it is."

I said: "I was just remembering the parrot."

"The parrot? Oh, yes, I remember, those French commands he gave; they were the traditional high school ones. He'd have picked them up from Franzl."

"Were they? I didn't know that. I was thinking of the 'Peter'. It could be his name for the horse."

We had reached the wicket gate leading from the wood to the circus field. As Timothy swung it open for me, excitement broke from him in a little laugh.

"We're getting good and loaded with secrets, aren't we? Do you suppose this one'll be any good to your husband and P.E.C.?"

"Heaven knows, but I can hardly wait to unload it on him! It's no good ringing him up again tonight: I tried earlier, and they said he wouldn't be available. But he's coming south as soon as he can, they said, and when he does, all our troubles will be over."

"Famous last words," said Timothy, and in his hand the gate creaked shut with what sounded like a mocking echo.

Chapter Eleven

A castle, precipice-encurled . . .
Browning: *De Gustibus*

Our arrival on the following day at Zechstein had about it the same curious quality of familiarity that we had encountered at Hohenwald: the circus posters, the slow lumbering of the last wagons and caravans into place in the fields on the outskirts of the village, the big top already up against its background of green; and the now familiar faces and vehicles seen everywhere.

The village lay in a wide valley where a river meandered lazily southward. At this point the valley floor was less than a mile wide, the ground rising on each side at first gently, with rounded hills, then more steeply into slopes of mixed forest— oak and chestnut, beech and holly—towards the precipitous fir woods and, finally, towering silver crests of rock. Spurs thrust out here and there from the valley walls, forcing the river to wind in shining detours round their rocky bases. The village, with its pretty church, its bridge, its mill, its wine shop with the bush hanging outside, was cradled in one such curve of the valley, and it was not until the road rounded the bluff beyond the village that we could see the castle.

On the far side of the river another great buttress of the mountain had thrust out to deflect the course of the river sharply back on itself. At the end of this buttress was a crag, itself rugged and crenellated like a castle, its precipitous outer side dropping sheer to the river which here slid dark and deep round the base of the cliff. This high promontory was connected to the mountainside by a narrow hogsback ridge crowded to the top with pines, rank on rank of them, dark and beautiful, contrasting vividly with the sweet green of the meadows below and the blazing blue of the afternoon sky. And, perched on the outermost edge of the crag, like something straight out of the fairy books of one's childhood, was the Schloss Zechstein, a miniature castle, but a real romantic castle for all that, a place of pinnacles and turrets and curtain walls, of narrow windows and battlements and coloured shields painted on the stone. There was even a bridge; not a drawbridge, but a narrow stone bridge arching out of the forest to the castle gate, where some small torrent broke the rock-ridge and sent a thin rope of white water smoking down below the walls. The castle was approached by a narrow metalled road which, branching at right angles off the main road in the valley below, led between heraldic pillars and over another graceful bridge, thereafter zigzagging steeply up to disappear in the thick mountain woods. For all its rugged approach and its carefully preserved mediaeval fortifications the place was not in the least forbidding. It was charming—not a castle for the guide-books, but a castle to be lived in.

When at length our little car had roared its way up the winding road to the ridge we found that the bridge to the castle gate was nothing like so slender as it had appeared from below. It was a stout well-kept structure, wide enough to take one car at a time. We drove over it and in through an archway into a small cobbled courtyard.

There was very little sign in the hall of the castle that the place was now a hotel. It was a biggish square hall with a stone-flagged floor and panelled walls, and a wide staircase leading up to a gallery. All the woodwork was of pine. There was a green porcelain stove in one corner, unlit at this time of the year, and a heavy wooden table on which stood the register and various other bits of hotel paraphernalia. A man in shirt-sleeves and green baize apron carried our luggage in for us and showed us where to register, then picked our bags up and prepared to lead us to our rooms. I started towards the stairs, but he stopped me, saying with an over-casual air that did not conceal his pride:

"This way, *gnädige Frau*. There is a lift."

I must have shown my surprise. In a place like this, one hardly counted on modern plumbing, let alone such conveniences as lifts. He smiled. "One would not expect it, no. It has just been put in. This is the first summer that we have had it. It is a great convenience."

"I'm sure it is. How marvellous."

"This way. I am afraid there is a little way to go down the passage here, towards the kitchens, but you will understand the Count did not wish such modern things to spoil the centre part of the castle. It would have been a pity to cut the panelling in the hall."

As he spoke he was leading us down a long dim corridor, its flagged floor covered with rush matting. I said: "The Count?"

"The Count and Countess still live here," the man explained. "You understand this has been their family home for many generations. They have, themselves, their own rooms in that part of the castle, the other side." He nodded his head back the way we had come, indicating the rooms to the opposite side of the central hall. The kitchen corridors we were traversing were in the north wing; no doubt the Count and Countess had kept the southern wing for themselves, while the main block of the castle, the centre block which faced the entrance and the bridge, was used as a hotel.

I said: "Do they run the hotel themselves, then?"

"No, madam, there is a manager, but the Countess herself takes a great interest. Here is the lift."

He had stopped in front of what looked like a massive pine door with the huge iron studs and hinges which I was beginning to expect everywhere in Austria. Hidden in the stone to one side of it, in another tangle of wrought iron, was an electric push button. The lift arrived without a sound, and proved to be one of the most modern possible variety, the self-service kind of which I am always stupidly terrified, and which has a panel of controls and buttons and switches that look every bit as complicated as the business end of a computer. But it took us safely and smoothly and, it seemed, in about three seconds, to the third floor.

My room was impressive and rather beautiful, placed about centrally on the main corridor, in a jut of the eastern wall which allowed its windows a magnificent view of the valley. It also appeared to include one of the charming pepperpot turrets that give the castle its fairy-tale appearance, the main part of the room being square, but with a wide round embrasure in one corner which had been charmingly furnished with a little writing table and two chairs. There was also in the embrasure a narrow door which must give on to some kind of balcony, or more probably—and much more romantically—the battlements.

Just as I had finished my unpacking, a tap on the door heralded Timothy.

"This is a smashing place, isn't it? But I must say it scares me a bit. Do you suppose one dares to ask for some tea?"

"I expect so, though heaven knows how. Perhaps you blow a peal on a slughorn, or beat on your shield with your sword— or, I'll tell you what, if you look around you'll find a long embroidered tassel, and if you pull it you'll hear a bell clanging hollowly in some dark corridor a million miles away, and then some bent old servitor will come shuffling in —"

"There's a telephone by the bed," said Timothy.

"Good heavens, so there is. How disappointing. Never mind,

you go ahead and order tea. Do you want it up here? I want to look outside this little door if I can."

The turret door was unlocked, and it did indeed lead to the battlements. There was a narrow walk which joined my turret with another about fifty yards away on the south-east corner of the castle. The walk ran along the eastern wall of the castle, between the battlements on one side which crowned the sheer drop to the river, and the steep pitch of the roof, and ended at the south-east turret in a narrow spiral of stone steps which corkscrewed up round the outside wall and led presumably to the tiny battlemented roof at the top. My own turret was charmingly crowned with a spire like a witch's hat, and had as weathercock a flying dragon. The roof slopes and gables were tiled with red, the castle walls were of honey-coloured stone, and every spire was tipped with gold—here a globe, there a flying swan, above my head a dragon. I leaned over the battlements: the stone was hot with the afternoon sun. A cool little breeze stirred the air, and in it I could hear the deep sound of the river below the cliff.

Timothy said behind me: "Tea's coming. I say, what a terrific view! Can you see the village?"

"No, but those farms down there must be on the very edge of it. Look, can you see that little white chalet affair, up in the pines on the other side? I think the circus field must be somewhere below that. I remember noticing the chalet as we came past."

"How far away do you suppose it is?"

"As the crow flies, only about a mile, but by that road, heaven knows. Isn't it a heavenly place?"

"Couldn't be better. Your husband's a picker, isn't he?"

"Invariably."

"All right," said Tim, grinning, "I bought that one. Well, I agree. What time do you expect him?"

"I don't know, and they told me nothing when I phoned. I suppose it's even possible he won't be able to come tonight, but he did say he would for sure, and the circus goes tomorrow. I'm just hoping." I didn't add that I was praying, too. It was also still possible that he would have to follow the circus into Yugoslavia, and the prospect filled me with fears that were probably absurd, but none the less real. "I'll ring up later," I added. "If he's already on his way I suppose they'll tell me."

"At least I'm supposed to know him now. I'm sure it would have been a bit of a strain."

"On me, perhaps," I said dryly. "You two seem to take deception in your stride; it's horrifying."

"I got the impression he'd take most things in his stride, as a matter of fact."

"You could be right."

"So our next move—after tea that is—is the circus?" He glanced at his watch. "There's bags of time, it's only three now. We can talk to them before the first house."

We had discussed the affair of the old piebald at some length that morning on our leisurely drive from Hohenwald in the circus's wake, and had made what was really the only decision, that we would have to tell Herr Wagner and Annalisa what we had discovered, without waiting for Lewis's possible arrival.

("Because after all," Timothy had said, "Franz Wagner's dead, and he's the criminal, not them. And the circus crosses into Yugoslavia in the morning, and after that into Hungary, so if there's to be any question of returning the horse it'll have to be decided today.")

"Yes," I said now, "we can be down there well before four. Oh, listen, isn't that the tea coming now? Go and let him in, there's a dear."

It was the same servant with the green baize apron. He carried an enormous tray on which was a beautiful antique silver tea service, and on a Dresden plate some remarkably small and rather dry-looking biscuits

I had followed Timothy back into the room. "Oh, thank you very much. Would you mind putting it here, on the writing table? Thanks. Are you doing all the work here today?"

He grinned as he set the tray down. "It feels like it, madam, but you could say that this was almost a holiday for us. We've had a big party of Americans who left this morning, and now there is nobody but yourselves, so many of our people are taking time off. There's a circus in the village, and most of them want to go to see it."

"It's a very good circus, too," said Tim. "We saw it at Hohenwald."

"Oh, indeed? I shall go myself at five o'clock, and then come back to let others go. Most of the servants here are from the village, and they go back to sleep at their homes at night."

An exclamation from Timothy made me turn. He had been standing beside the window embrasure, and now stared out northward. "What in the wide world's that? Look over there, over the top of the trees, clouds of smoke. Do you suppose it's a forest fire?"

I looked over his shoulder. Farther north, up the valley, in the opposite direction from the village, there were indeed clouds of black smoke apparently pouring out from among the trees, high up on the hillside.

I said: "Surely there are no houses up there. What on earth can it be? Do you really think it could be a forest fire, er —?" This to the servant.

"My name is Josef, madam. No, that is not a fire, it's just what we call *Die Feuerwehr*, the 'fire-engine'."

"The 'fire-engine'?"

"It has a lot of names, *Der Flügelzug*, the 'flying train', or some people call it *Der Feurige Elias*, 'Fiery Elijah', after the other one in the Salzkammergut. It is a little mountain train."

"You mean a train, a real train?" asked Timothy. "Right up there? Why, that's hundreds of feet up, maybe thousands."

"Yes, it is high, but this is one of those mountain railways, I don't know the English word for them—nowadays they build cable cars, and chair lifts, to go up these slopes, that's the modern way, but this old railway was built, oh, many many years ago, nearly a hundred years ago. It runs up on a small wheel that holds it, a cog, is that the word?"

"Rack and pinion," said Timothy. "Works on a pinion wheel and a cogged rail. We call it a rack railway."

Josef nodded. "That is it. A rack railway, I'll remember that.

It's very popular, partly"—he laughed—"because it's so old-fashioned; the Americans like it. It starts, oh, away down the valley, perhaps five or six kilometres from the village here. There's a little lake farther along, and one or two small hotels, a place for tourists. It's called Zweibrunn Am See. In the summer it can be very crowded."

"Where does the railway go to? Right up the mountain?" I asked.

"Yes, right to the top." He pointed again. "You cannot see the summit from here, though you can from the back rooms. From your room, sir, you will see it. The railway goes right up between this hill and the next, to the highest peak, and up there there is a little Gasthaus—a place where you can have refreshments. You can imagine the panorama. You can see right across the mountains into Yugoslavia, and into Hungary. If you are going to be here for a few days, madam, you must make this trip. The best time is early in the morning; the first train goes up at seven."

I said: "I should love to go up, but I'm quite sure I shan't manage it at seven. Well, thank you very much, Josef."

"Is that all, madam?"

"Yes, thank you. Oh, no, just a moment, please. Has there been any word when my husband is expected, Mr Lewis March?"

"I had no message, madam, and there is nothing at the desk."

"I see. Thank you."

As the door shut behind him I turned to see Timothy eyeing the tea-tray with dismay. "Is that what they call tea?"

"For goodness' sake, it's barely three o'clock. Don't tell me you're hungry again after that colossal lunch?"

"That was hours ago. I say, do you suppose he's gone? Do you think I could nip along to my room and get some of the things I bought? Thank goodness I had the sense to lay in some stores. You wouldn't say no to some really nice *Gugelhupf*, would you?"

"As a matter of fact, no, I'd love it. Where is your room, anyway? Next door?"

"No, it's on the other side, about two down the corridor. The single rooms aren't nearly as grand as this, and mine looks out over the courtyard, but it's still lovely. You can see right away up to the mountain-tops. D'you think it's safe to go now?"

The door shut cautiously behind him. I sat down and began to pour tea.

•   •   •

There was nobody in the hall. Somewhat to Timothy's derision, I refused to go down in the lift with him, but the descent of the wide staircase was sufficiently rewarding in itself, giving as it did on every floor a magnificent and slightly different view of the valley. Timothy had already gone out to the car, and I didn't follow him immediately, but went down the dim corridor towards the kitchen.

I got as far as the lift door without catching any glimpse of the man in the baize apron, or anyone else. Ahead of me the corridor stretched blankly with the doors shut and silent. I went along as far as the next corner and there hesitated for a moment, but just as I turned to go back towards the hall I heard a door open, and next moment an old man came into view. He saw me hesitating there, and approached.

"Good afternoon. Is there anything I can do for you?" His English was only very slightly accented, and his voice was gentle. He had a thin face and white hair worn rather long, and he walked stoopingly. His clothes—of some foreign-looking country tweed—were of curiously old-fashioned cut.

I said: "Oh thank you, but I didn't want to bother anyone. I know you're short-handed today; I just wanted to give a message to Josef—the man who took our luggage up."

"Ah, yes, he has gone to the other part of the house. If you come this way I will send him to you." As we went back the way I had come, towards the hall, the old man added: "My wife sent for him, but I don't think she will keep him long."

I realised then who he must be. "Forgive me, but are you—perhaps you are—?" I hesitated, not sure how properly to address an Austrian Count. He bent his head in a courteous

141

gesture, which was at once a nod and slight bow. "I am Graf Zechstein, at your service."

We had reached the hall, and he was leading the way across this towards a heavy carved door on the opposite side with 'Private' engraved on it in Gothic type, but I stopped.

"Then perhaps—if you could spare me a moment, please, it was actually you I was wanting. I was only looking for Josef to ask him to take a message to you."

"Of course. Is there some way in which I can help you?"

I hesitated. "It's rather a long story, and of course I'll willingly tell it to you, but what I wanted to ask you was simply this: is there a stable here at the castle, or anywhere a horse could be housed for a night or two—or perhaps, better still, somewhere where it could be put to graze? You might say I've . . . well, sort of come by a horse, and I need somewhere to put it at least for tonight. If it's at all possible?" I finished a little doubtfully.

He showed not the slightest surprise. "But certainly there are stables, and if you wish to stable your horse, naturally there will be a place. You have only to tell Josef. And if you wish to graze him there is no difficulty about that; anywhere outside on the mountain you will find grazing; we are not so very high here, and there are many spaces in the forest where the grass is good. Josef will see to this for you. When your horse is brought, just ask Josef where everything is. I myself will give him the message now."

I had opened my mouth to explain a little further when I realised that he neither required nor expected any further explanation. It could be that one simply did not query the eccentricities of one's guests, or perhaps he himself still vividly remembered a past when everyone arrived with horses; or it might simply be that he as Count Zechstein had never had to deal with any such request before in person. This was for Josef—like, it appeared, everything else. The Count was already nodding and smiling to me and turning away, so I contented myself with thanking him, and then went out to where Timothy waited with the car.

"Sorry to keep you waiting, but I was finding out if we could house old Piebald, if the circus does decide to leave him with us. I saw the Count himself, and it's all right; there's a stable still in commission, and he says there's plenty of grazing outside. He never even raised an eyebrow—in fact, I've a strong feeling that he rather expects his guests to roll up in barouches, or coaches and six, or something of that sort. Anyway, poor Josef's got to see to it. I'm wondering if he'll get to the circus after all. Are you going to drive?"

"Driving up that little road is one thing," said Timothy, "and driving down is another. I rather think it's your turn. I don't want to be selfish. And I may say if you think a coach and six ever got up to this castle in its whole history you've a stronger imagination than I have."

"One thing has been occurring to me," I said. "If you're really serious about wanting a job at the Spanish Riding School, you could hardly make a better start than by bringing home one of their long-lost stallions."

He grinned. "The thought had entered my twisted little mind."

"Then you are serious? Good for you. Well, in you get, then, let's be on our way. I wonder if they've ever had a Lippizzan stallion stabled here before?"

"'Airs above the ground'," he quoted, as the little car nosed its way across the narrow bridge. "Well, I'll bet the great Neapolitano Petra's never been stabled higher in his life, that's one thing. Incidentally, how is he going to get up here?"

"You're young and strong," I said cheerfully, "you're going to lead him. I'm sorry I can't say ride him, but that's not possible yet."

"I had a feeling you had something like this laid up for me," said Timothy, "when you said you couldn't do without me. There's always a comeback to that one. What a good thing I had that *Gugelhupf* for tea, isn't it?"

Chapter Twelve

When the foeman bares his steel,
        Tarantara, tarantara!
We uncomfortable feel,
        Tarantara.
             W. S. Gilbert: *Pirates of Penzance*

"But what on earth are we going to do?" asked Annalisa.

It was barely half an hour before the first performance was due to start. We were all in her wagon, Timothy, myself and Herr Wagner, rotund and perspiring, already dressed for the ring and looking extremely worried. Annalisa, in her cowgirl's costume for the first act, was hurriedly making up her face in front of the mirror. Timothy and I had told our story, and to our surprise Herr Wagner had accepted it immediately.

"I believe you," he said, "I believe you. I do not even need to see the brands . . . No, no, I knew nothing, and I suspected nothing, but you might say I *felt* it . . . here." A hand gestured perfunctorily towards his brawny chest. "I do not pretend that I ever thought about Franzl's horse, why should I? I am not a curious man . . . and what a man has done, where he has been, that is his own affair. If my dear wife had been alive, ah, that would have been different. But I, I ask nothing."

He paused, head bent, apparently studying the table-top, then looked up and nodded at us, slowly, though neither Timothy nor I had spoken.

"My father? Oh, yes, he must have known. But what would you? He was a man who cared all for his family, and nothing for the law. What would you have him do? Franzl was his nephew, his sister's son, and one must look after one's own. The penalty for stealing such a horse would be very heavy; a trained stallion is beyond price, and besides, it is State property . . ." He lifted his wide shoulders. "Tell you the truth, I did not know until now that Franzl had been in the *Spanische Reitschule* . . . We had heard nothing for many years, you understand: I thought he had learned his dressage with the cavalry at Wiener Neustadt. He used to speak of his service there. I tell you, in a circus we have many people, of many kinds; they come, and they go. If they tell you of themselves, then you listen . . . But you do not ask. No, you do not ask. We are artists, we of the circus, and we have our own affairs which take all our time, our lives, our—what shall I say?—our whole strength. I think you have a saying, 'Live and let live.' In the circus, we let live." He mopped his brow with a vast red handkerchief. "Do you understand me?"

We assured him that we did, which appeared to relieve him enormously. He became practical then, and brisk, with one eye on his watch, and the other on Timothy and myself, and I I knew quite well that he was thinking of his circus's schedule (not the performances, but the frontier passage in the morning) and trying to weigh up what our attitude was going to be.

"There is only one thing to do," he said, "there is only one thing that is both right and convenient, and that is to return the horse where he belongs." He rolled a brown knowing eye at me. "I am a business man, *gnädige Frau*, but I am also honest, when occasion permits. When honesty and business go together, then I am grateful to the good God. To me, to the circus, the horse is useless. It therefore seems"—he checked himself—"it seems to me right, in whatever case, to confess the whole to the Directors, and return the horse. Especially as there cannot well be any trouble for the circus now. Do you not agree?"

"Certainly."

"Don't stick your neck out," said the parrot.

Herr Wagner gave a surreptitious glance at his watch.

"But you also see my difficulty? Tomorrow we cross the border, and we do not return to Austria until the winter, when we come back to our permanent home near Innsbruck. So, as you say, with the best will in the world, I do not know how this thing shall be done."

I had a look at my watch, too; it was twenty minutes to five.

Having found out all we needed to know about Herr Wagner's reactions, I decided to cut this short. I said: "If you would trust Timothy and myself with the horse, and leave him in our care, we would be delighted to do all that was required."

Herr Wagner's look of astonished delight did him great credit. So did his protestations, which even managed to sound genuine. But we persuaded him, and he allowed himself to be persuaded. If we really meant it . . . if we could really find the time . . . there was no one with whom he would rather leave the animal . . . he was sure that the *Herr Direktor* of the National Stud would be so overwhelmed that he would render us every possible assistance . . .

And finally, amid a torrent of mutual goodwill, it was all arranged. Even the parrot contributed, though not with noticeable helpfulness. The only person who had said nothing was Annalisa.

"There is only one thing," said Herr Wagner. "This is after all a valuable horse, and he was stolen, and his value has been much diminished. Though I myself and the circus cannot well be blamed, there will be questions, and there may be a certain unpleasantness . . . There may even be proceedings. If this should happen —"

"Don't worry about that now," I said. "Neither Timothy nor I will get into trouble, and I don't see that you can, either. In any case, if they want to see you, you'll be coming back before winter. Be sure we'll make it very clear that neither of you knew a thing about it till we told you."

"That's right," said Timothy.

Annalisa, her face bright with paint, but still with that strained look about the eyes, had been sitting down, listening in silence to the conversation. Now her eyes lifted, and she said, very quietly:

"I did know about it."

Her father swung round. "*You knew?* You knew about this?"

She nodded. "Two days ago I knew."

"Two days? Then you mean—it was not from Franzl —"

"No, no, indeed not. It was only when Vanessa operated, on

146

Sunday night. She wanted the instrument case for the operation, and afterwards, when I washed the instruments and put them away, I found . . . these."

From the bench beside her she lifted the instrument case, opened it, and pulled out the bottom drawer, where one usually keeps papers—prescription forms, folders about new drugs, and so on. She lifted some of these out, and there underneath was a bundle of newspaper clippings. Naturally I couldn't read them, but I could see the repetition of the name 'Neopolitano Petra' and the photographs, in different poses, of the great stallion; and Timothy told me afterwards that they all related to the stallion's disappearance. These, now, Annalisa spread before us on the table, with the gesture of one who does in literal fact throw her cards on the table, and herself on the mercy of her audience.

"And there is this," she said.

She dropped the last piece of paper on top of the rest. This was a photograph, yellow and frayed at the edges, of a white horse standing by a stable door, and beside him a man in the uniform of the Spanish Riding School.

As Herr Wagner reached for it, she laid her final trophy on the table, the brown tube labelled 'Koloston', which had fleetingly caught my eye while I was operating.

I picked it up. "What's this? I saw it there, and I just thought it must be the German trade name for some sort of ointment. Don't tell me . . . It's hair dye?"

She nodded dumbly, then turned to her father. "*Papa* —"

He took no notice. He was shaking his head over the cuttings, looking at once shocked and deeply touched.

"Franzl," he said. "So it is true . . . All this time. Poor Franzl."

I said gently to Annalisa: "Why are you worrying so? You could have done nothing. In any case, we'll say you didn't know till we told you. Even if you'd wanted to, you couldn't have done much before today."

"I know. But it is not this"—with a gesture to the clippings —"that troubles me." She turned her eyes back to her father, and I saw they had filled with tears. "You see, when poor Uncle Franzl was dying, he must have tried to tell me. Now, when I read these papers, I know what he said. He was trying to tell me about the horse. He said its name . . . over and over he said its name, and he spoke of 'the Lipizzaner', but of course I thought he meant Maestoso Leda. I thought he was worrying in case Leda was hurt in the fire. We could only hear a few snatches of what he said; he spoke of Vienna, and 'the Lipizzaner', and even of his harness . . . and now I know he was telling us to take Neapolitano Petra back to Vienna, even his saddle and bridle, which came with him. '*Neapolitano Petra's Sattel*', he said, and we thought he spoke of a 'Neapolitan saddle', and this puzzled us, because there is no such thing here. But this is what he must have meant. It is the one I use for Maestoso Leda." A tear ran glassily over the blackened lashes. "We did not understand, and he was trying to confess, to make . . . to make . . ." She faltered over the word.

"Reparation," I said.

Her father patted her hand. "Do not trouble yourself, my Liesl, we shall make it now." He added some soft phrases in German which made her nod, and dry her eyes, then, with another glance at his watch, he became again his brisk self. "I shall have to go. If you would prefer to stay, and talk again later . . . ?"

I shook my head. "There's no need, if you're satisfied. We'll take the horse straight away, if we may, and deal with the next stage of the problem as it comes. The only thing that bothers me is what we're going to do if they don't want him back at the Stud now?"

Timothy said promptly: "I'll have him."

"And if you don't get your job, what then? Ship him back to England? What would your mother say?"

He grinned, and made a little grimace which showed all too clearly how far in the last couple of days he had come from those apron strings.

Herr Wagner was on his feet. "They will take him. You need have no fear of that. Their stallions live for thirty years, and when they die they are remembered. His name will still be on his stall, and fresh straw waiting. And now I must go. It is time. But there is a little matter of recompense; there will be all the trouble to which you will be put, the trouble and expense that we cannot expect you to bear for yourselves. This is ours. There will be the matter of a horsebox on the train from here to Köflach, for Piber, and other things. You will let me know."

I started to say something, but he waved it aside with sudden, unanswerable simplicity.

"You must allow me to make this reparation at least. My cousin Franzl would rest more easily if he knew."

"Very well," I said, "I'll let you know the cost."

He fished in some inner pocket and produced a card. "Here is my address, the most permanent address I have; our winter quarters near Innsbruck. And perhaps you will leave yours with us? Now, there is also the matter of your own professional services towards the horse —"

But this I would not allow, and he made no attempt to override me, but merely thanked me again, and then, with more protestations of goodwill and gratitude, relieved and beaming, he took his leave.

We went with Annalisa down to the stable tent. Elemer was busy with the white stallion, while the ugly pied horse she used for the rodeo was saddled and waiting, with Rudi at its head.

Annalisa plunged into rapid explanations in German, while the other horses, ready for the ring, were already streaming past with tossing manes and tails, and the music sounded loudly from the big top. Old Piebald flung his head up and whickered at the sight of me, and we went into the stall, where presently Annalisa followed us.

"I have told them—not everything, but that you are to take the horse. Elemer will help you—Oh!" Her hand went to her mouth.

"What is it?"

"The saddle! I was forgetting the saddle . . . You must take that, too." She swung back to the men. "Elemer, Rudi —"

"Look," I said quickly, "if it's on your horse, why not leave it? I'm sure it doesn't matter. We can take another if you insist, but I doubt if they'll bother about a thing like that."

But she persisted, obviously intent on purging the Circus Wagner of theft as completely as possible. She directed another flood of German at Elemer, and Timothy crossed the stable to help him lift the jewelled saddle off the white stallion. "In any case," said Annalisa to me, "you may need a saddle, and I wish you to take his own. But you see how we have decorated it for the circus . . . all those jewels . . . If I had had time to take them off —"

I laughed. "I see what you mean. It's not exactly what they're used to at the Spanish Riding School! But don't worry about it, I'll take them off before we send it back. If you want the jewels back, you'll have to tell me how to send them. Would the Innsbruck address be all right, the one your father gave me?"

She shook her head. "No, they're nothing, they are glass, stage pieces only. Please keep them, and do as you wish with them. Some of them are quite pretty, and I should like you to have —" But there Rudi interrupted with something in German, and she said quickly: "There is the music. I must go. Goodbye, goodbye and thank you. God be with you both."

She leaned forward suddenly, light as a dandelion puff, and kissed Timothy on the mouth. Then, with a hand from Rudi, she was up in the saddle, and the pied horse, with a jingle of curb chains and a thudding of hairy hoofs, was gone through the curtains at the back of the big top.

Timothy, laden with the saddle, stood staring after her. Elemer said something to Rudi, who, smiling, went off down the stable. The dwarf came across.

"I have sent him to get a bridle. How will you take the horse?"

"We're staying up at the castle," I said. "Tim's going to lead him up there, and I've made arrangements for him to be stabled. I can take the saddle up myself in the car."

"I'm afraid you will have a lot of work to make it plain again."

"Think nothing of it, I'll do it tonight. Look, are you sure she won't want the trimmings back? Some of them are awfully pretty . . . Look at this one. You know, that would look lovely on a dress—stage jewellery, of course, but it's really very pretty, with the gold filigree and tremblers, and anyway, it wouldn't matter if it didn't look real: who'd wear a sapphire that size, apart from Grand Duchesses?" I fingered the jewel; it was a big brooch, loosely stitched to the pommel, and flashed in the light as I touched it.

"Why don't you wear it, then? It will suit you. It's loose anyway." And before I could protest, the dwarf had produced a knife from somewhere, and had cut the 'jewel' from the pommel, and handed it to me with a little bow that was unspeakably grotesque, and yet not comic at all.

"Wear it and remember us all, *gnädige Frau*. It is a pretty thing, but your eyes make it look dim. I wish it could be real. Here is your bridle. Let Rudi put the saddle in the car for you. *Auf Wiedersehen, mein Herr*," this to Timothy, and then, taking my hand and kissing it: "*Küss die Hand, gnädige Frau*."

The ungainly little figure shambled out with its comic red costume flapping round the tiny legs.

As far as I could see, from an examination of Piebald's leg, there was nothing to stop Timothy leading the horse the couple of miles uphill to the castle. As I told him cheerfully, the exercise would do them both nothing but good. "I'll go straight up there myself now, and I'll expect you when I see you. Are you going to stay to see the high school act again?"

"I don't think so. I—I feel this is a good moment to leave on, somehow," said Timothy, very creditably. For a first kiss it had been a pretty good one, and public, at that.

"For both of us," I said. "Then *auf Wiedersehen* yourself, Tim, and take care of our horse."

I had left the car, unlocked, just outside the field gate. By the time I reached it Rudi had already left the saddle on the back seat, and gone back to his job. I could hear the bursts of applause for the clowns' *entrée*. Soon the trumpets would sound, and the white stallion would be making for the ring—tonight with only half his jewels.

I got into the car, and was reaching for my handbag to get out my key, when I realised that I had left the bag in Annalisa's wagon. Annoyed with myself for the delay—for I was anxious to find out if Lewis had arrived yet—I got out of the car and ran back to the wagon.

The bag was just where I had left it, on the seat under the bird cage. The parrot, which was sulkily eating a tomato, cocked its head to one side, and made some remark in German which sounded extremely rude.

I said: "Get stuffed, mate," picked up the bag, and ran down the wagon steps.

I collided with Sandor Balog. Whether he had just been passing, or whether he had been intending to go up into the wagon, I didn't know, but we were both moving fast, and I almost fell. His hands shot out and steadied me. They were remarkably strong, and, startled as he was, he must have gripped me harder than he had meant to; I remember that I cried out, not only with the start he had given me, but with the pain of his grip.

He muttered something, and let me go.

In my turn I had started some sort of breathless apology when his voice broke curtly across mine. "Where have you been?"

I stared at him in some surprise. "What do you mean?"

He jerked his head towards the wagon door. "She's not in there. She's in the ring, or will be in a moment. What were you doing?" His eye had even flicked down to the handbag which I held.

I said, coldly: "What do you think I was doing? Stealing something?"

"You were talking to someone."

"Yes, I was. Him." It was my turn to jerk my head towards the wagon door.

He gave me a queer look from those narrow black eyes, then took a swift step past me, peering up into the lighted doorway. He was dressed ready for his act in the striking black costume that I had seen poised so spectacularly in the lights and shadows of the big top, and he had wrapped a long cloak round himself, in which he looked rather splendid and satanic—and as if he would be the first to think so.

He turned back, looking a little at a loss. I got the impression that he had started something he hadn't meant to—that some other urgent preoccupation had jerked him into speaking as he had done, and that now he was out of his reckoning.

"Do you mean that damned bird?"

"Who else?"

"Get stuffed, mate," said the parrot, and threw a piece of tomato accurately at the door-jamb. It ran soggily down the wood.

The Hungarian opened his mouth, thought better of what he was going to say, and shut it again. He moved out of the parrot's range, trying to keep it casual. For my part, I was trying not to laugh. If the circus hadn't been crossing the border next morning I would have sent the parrot a crate of tomatoes with my compliments.

"I'm sorry," said Sandor Balog at length. The apology sat even more badly on him than the aggressive inquiries had done. "I did not for a moment realise who it was. You . . . are differently dressed. We get many strangers who come round, and . . ." He shrugged his wide shoulders, not finishing the sentence. "Is the boy here?"

"Yes, he's down in the stable." I left it at that. I could see no reason why I should offer any further explanation to Sandor Balog. I wondered why, if he had not at first recognised me, he had seen fit to address me in English; but this was another question which I did not particularly wish to explore.

Behind him the music of *Der Rosenkavalier* swayed and swung in the shadows. Fleetingly, I wondered if old Piebald was doing his *pas seul* down in the crowded stable. I rather thought not. It was something kept for solitude.

I said, pleasantly enough: "There's Annalisa's music now. It'll be you next. I shan't be seeing you again, so I'll say good night, and good luck."

But he didn't move. "Where did you get that?" He was looking at the jewel on my frock.

"Now, look," I said, "I told you I hadn't been stealing. That was a present, a parting gift if you like to call it that, a souvenir.

But don't worry, it isn't real, it's off the Lipizzan's saddle. I've had quite a bit of loot tonight, one way and another. Good night."

I turned away abruptly and headed for the gate. I thought for a moment that he was going to say something more, but the applause from the big top warned him and held him back. He turned with a swirl of his black cloak and went rapidly the other way.

The parrot started, in an unpleasant, wavering falsetto, to sing 'O for the wings of a dove'.

Chapter Thirteen

He found a stable for his steed,
And welcome for himself, and dinner.
W. M. Praed: *The Vicar*

It was the Count himself who greeted me on my return to the castle.

It was dusk now, and here and there in the castle lights pricked out yellow in the gloom. A lamp over the arched gateway cast a small pool of light on to the bridge: there was another over the main door, and others, here and there in the narrow windows, threw a pattern of light and shadow over the cobbled court. High up in a turret a solitary lighted window made one think of fairy tales again; Curdie's grandmother might sit spinning there, or Rapunzel of the long hair, or Elsa watching for the seven swans.

As I parked the car prosaically at one side of the court, and mounted the steps, the Count came out of the great door.

"Ah, Mrs March," he greeted me, then stopped, looking past me at the car almost as if he had never seen such a thing before.

I remembered our theory that his guests normally came in a coach and six. "Did I not understand that you proposed to stable a horse for the night?"

"Oh, yes, please, I do, but he'll be brought up later. Timothy —that's the young man I was with—he'll be bringing him."

"Ah, your man will bring him. I see." Now his eye fell on the saddle lodged in the back seat of the car. If he noticed the vulgarity of its jewelled and tinselled trappings he made no sign. "I see you have brought your saddle up yourself. Josef will carry it in for you, but meantime I am sure you will want to see for yourself where we shall house your horse."

"I think —" I began, but he had already turned away to cross the courtyard towards the west side, the side nearest the mountain, where the entrance archway divided into two what must be the store-rooms and outbuildings of the castle. From the gate to the north-west corner I could see a line of smaller arches; one or two of these were shut by heavy studded doors, but the three nearest the corner were open. I saw something which could have been the bonnet of a car, gleaming in the darkness behind the centre one of these, and in the bay to the left of it the glint of some brightly spoked vehicle which I couldn't see properly, but which from its height I guessed might even be the coach and six.

The Count pushed open one of the doors in an arch which might have belonged to a young cathedral, and took down a lantern from its hook. This, he proceeded to light—not, to my disappointment, with a tinderbox, but with a perfectly ordinary match. Then, with a brief apology for leading the way, he went ahead of me, holding the lantern high.

Not even the brushed and combed tidiness of Tim's grand-father's racing stables had prepared me for such splendour as I now saw. This was a decayed and cobwebbed splendour, it was true, but in the wavering light cast by the lantern held high above the old man's head, the empty magnificence of the stables was impressive in a haunted Gothic way that the comforts of modern living had dispelled from the castle itself. This was the real thing, a sharply evocative glimpse of a whole vanished way of life. Almost the only thing that had survived from this corner of that way of life, I reflected, was the unbreakable rule which still held good; that you attended to your horse's comfort before you saw to your own.

Nothing, it seemed, had been too good for the Zechstein horses. The place was vaulted like a church, the interlaced arches of the ceiling springing from pillars of some dark mottled stone which could have been serpentine. The walls were panelled up to the proper height with what could only be black oak, and the partitions between the boxes—there were no stalls—were of the same wood faced and inlaid. On the wall over each box was carved a large shield surmounted by a crest, and on the shields, dim in the shadows, I could see Gothic lettering. I couldn't read it, but I guessed that these were still the names of the vanished horses, each above his box. It was no surprise to see that the mangers appeared to be made of marble.

The place was, of course, by no means empty. Since the inmates had disappeared the clutter of years had gradually built up in the boxes and the fairway. Through an open door at the far end of the stable I could see—as the Count led me that way —what I had guessed to be the coach and six, standing in the arcaded coach-house beyond. It was indeed a carriage of some kind; the edge of the lantern's glimmer caught the gold picked out on the wheels and doors. Parked beyond it, and looking less incongruous than one would have imagined, was the sleek gleam of the modern car.

The box at the end of the stable was empty, and looked swept and clean. The manger had been scoured out, and beside it was a bale of straw. As the old man held the lantern up I saw the name on the carved shield above the box: 'Grane'. The Count said nothing, and I didn't ask, but I had a strong feeling that the loose-box had not just been swept out and the manger scoured for old Piebald: I thought it was kept that way. The name looked freshly painted, and the metal corn bin against the wall by the coach-house door was comparatively new.

"You will see," said the Count, "that there is a peg for your bridle here at the side of the box. Josef will show your man the saddleroom, and the feed."

I had already decided that the horse would be better out grazing for the night, and I had noticed a pleasant little alp, just nicely sheltered by trees and less than a hundred yards from the bridge, but I certainly hadn't the heart to say so. I thanked the Count, admired the stable, and listened for a while to his gentle reminiscences of past days as he led me back towards the door. Here he stood back for me to pass him, and then reached up to put the lantern, still lit, back where it had hung before.

"Your man will doubtless put it out when he has finished here." Then, as the light swung high, something about me seemed to catch his attention. I saw that, like Sandor a short time ago, he was looking at the 'jewel' on my lapel.

He was a good deal more civil than Sandor had been.

"Forgive me, I was admiring your jewel. It is a very pretty thing."

I laughed. "It's not really a jewel at all, I'm afraid, it's just a trinket. It was given me by someone down at the circus in the village as a souvenir. Perhaps I should have told you before—the horse I'm looking after has been with the circus for a little, and he was hurt, so they're leaving him in my care for a day or two." I touched the brooch. "I suppose this is a little token of gratitude for what I did; it's only glass; I admired it and they took it off the horse's saddle for me. It is pretty, isn't it?"

"Very pretty." He peered more closely, with a little apology. "Perhaps, yes, perhaps one can see that it is, after all, not real. I suppose that if it were, you would not be wearing it, but it would be safely locked away. A jewel that one can wear without fear is after all the best kind of jewel. No, what drew my attention was that it looked familiar. Come with me, and I will show you."

He led me at a brisk pace back across the courtyard, up the steps and across the hall through the door marked 'Private'.

The private wing of the castle was in its own way rather like the stables—no dust or cobwebs or clutter, but with the same general air of having stepped back about half a century. The same dim lighting was also still in evidence, for, though the castle's electricity did extend as far as this, it seemed to have been put in by someone with a dislike of modern innovations. The bulbs were small, faint, few and far between. The old Count, walking briskly ahead, led me up a gracefully curved staircase to a wide landing lit by a forty-watt bulb, and stopped in front of a canvas on the wall, so big that—though we could have done with the stable lantern—I could see it fairly well. It seemed to be painted mostly in shades of brown varnish, but, properly cleaned and with better lighting would turn out to be a portrait, a good deal larger than life, of a lady in the frilled and ruffled satins of the era of the Empress Maria Theresa.

"You see," said the old man, pointing.

And indeed I did. Perhaps originally the brooch had been painted more brightly than the rest, or perhaps some freak of time had left the varnish a little more transparent on this piece of the canvas, but in the dim painting it stood out remarkably clearly; a big brooch pinning the lace at the lady's bosom. And as far as one could make out, almost exactly like the one I was wearing. There was the gold filigree work, the central blue stone, the mass of small brilliants, and the same five dangling 'tremblers'. The only real difference was that about the painted lady's jewellery there could be no possible doubt; no one with that pale hard eye and Hapsburg jaw would have worn anything off a circus saddle.

"Goodness, it is like, isn't it?" I exclaimed. "Who is she?"

"She was my great-grandmother. This same jewel appears in two of the other portraits, but alas, they are not here, or I could show them to you. They are both in the *Alte Pinakothek* in Munich."

"And the jewel itself?"

Any wild thoughts I may have had of stolen treasure turning up as circus jewellery and ending up on my shoulder came to a speedy end at his reply. "Also, alas, in Munich. Most of my family's jewels are there. You may see them some day, perhaps." He smiled. "But meantime I hope it will give you pleasure to wear the most famous of them. It was a gift from the Czar, and there are romantic stories about it which are almost certainly not true . . . But romance persists, and the jewel has been much copied."

"I'll make a special trip some day to Munich to look at it," I promised, as we turned away. "Well, that's really rather exciting! Thank you very much for showing me the portrait: I'll treasure my present all the more now because it'll remind me of Zechstein."

"That's very charming of you, my dear. Now, I won't keep you; you will perhaps want to see your man. But perhaps some time you will give me the pleasure of showing you the rest of the castle? We still have quite a few treasures here and you may find it interesting."

"I shall be delighted. Thank you."

With the same air of slightly abstracted gentleness he saw me down the stairs and back into the hall. There was a woman there now, behind the big refectory table which did duty as a hotel desk. She had been writing, and was leafing through a stack of papers which were clipped together with a big metal clip. She was middle-aged, with a squat, dumpy figure and greying hair drawn tightly back. She had pendulous cheeks, and a little beak-mouth pursed between them like an octopus between two stones. I took her to be the receptionist, or perhaps the housekeeper, and wondered why, when she looked up and saw me preceding the Count from the south wing, her face, far from expressing the conventional welcome due to a hotel guest, showed what looked like cold surprise.

The Count's gentle voice spoke from behind me.

"Ah, there you are, my dear."

"I've been to the kitchens. Were you looking for me?" This, then, must be the Countess. Perhaps the white blouse and flowered dirndl which she wore, suitable perhaps for someone of Annalisa's age, were her concession to her new status as owner of a hotel. She spoke, as her husband had spoken, in English. Her voice in contrast to his was rapid and a little sharp, seeming to hold a perpetual undertone of exasperation.

She turned the exasperation, perhaps tempered a little, on to me. "Nowadays, it seems, one has to see to everything oneself. How do you do? I hope you'll be comfortable here. I am afraid, just at present, the service is not what it should be. But in these country places things become more and more difficult every day, even with the modern improvements. It's very difficult indeed now to get local help, and we find that the servants we get from the town don't wish to stay in any spot quite so isolated as this . . ."

I listened politely as she went on to tell me of her domestic troubles, murmuring something sympathetic from time to time. I had heard this kind of thing before many times from hotel-keepers in my own country, but never delivered with quite this air of grievance. I began to wonder at what point I should be made to feel that I must offer to make my own bed. When she paused at last, I said soothingly: "But it's charming, it really is. My room is lovely. And the whole place is so beautiful and really seems admirably kept. I find it so exciting to be able to visit a real castle like this. It must have been wonderful in the old days."

The tight lines of her face seemed to slacken a little. "Ah, yes, the old days. I am afraid that now they seem a very long time ago."

The Count said: "I was showing Mrs March the portrait of Gräfin Maria."

"Ah, yes. I am afraid the best of the portraits are no longer here. We have to live as best we can, in ways which we would once have considered impossible." She lifted her shoulders, solid under the frilly blouse. "The best of everything is gone, Mrs March."

I murmured something, uncomfortable and even irritated as one always is in face of a determined grievance. This, it seemed, was one of those angry natures that feeds on grievance; nothing would madden her more than to know that what she complained of had been put right. There are such people, unfortunates who have to be angry before they can feel alive. I had sometimes wondered if it were some old relic of pagan superstition, the fear of risking the jealousy and anger of the gods, that made such people afraid of even small happinesses. Or perhaps it was only that tragedy is more self-important than laughter. It is more impressive to be a Lear than a Rosalind.

I said: "Have you had any word yet from my husband, Countess? He hoped he might get here tonight."

"From Mr March? Yes . . ." She began again to riffle through the papers in front of her. "One moment . . . He sent a telegram to us. Ah, here it is." She handed a telegraph form across to me. It was, of course, in German.

"I wonder if you'd please translate it for me?"

"It only says: 'Regret must cancel tonight's reservation'," said the Countess, "but there is another for you, if I can find it . . . ah, yes, here."

I took it. This one was in English, and it ran: "Very sorry unable join you yet will get in touch love Lewis."

I let it drop to the table. I saw the Countess's hard little grey eyes watching me curiously, and realised that my face must be showing a disappointment quite startlingly intense. I pulled myself together.

"What a pity. He just says he can't join me yet, but that he'll get in touch. I suppose he may telephone me tomorrow, or perhaps even tonight. Thank you very much . . . I think I'll go outside now, and see if my young friend is on his way up with the horse." I smiled at the Count. "Thank you again."

I turned quickly to go. I was in no mood to stay and explain all over again to the Countess about the horse. But if she had been going to query my last statement she got no chance, because her husband was already speaking to her. "Did you say you were expecting another guest tonight after all, my dear? Who is this?"

"Another Englishman. A Mr Elliott."

By the mercy of heaven I had my back to them, and was already hurrying across the hall, for nothing could have hidden from them the surprise that must have showed unguarded on my face. In counting the hours to seeing Lewis, I had quite forgotten his alias, and that he had implied he might still have to use it.

The name had brought me up short for a moment, but I managed to pretend I had stumbled over the edge of a rug, and then simply kept going to the door without looking round. But I didn't hurry now. As I reached it, I heard her add:

"He has just telephoned. He can have Room (some number I didn't catch); it is ready. We must tell Josef when he comes back." She had dropped into German now, but I thought I understood the next bit as well. "He will not be here for dinner. He couldn't say what time he would get here. He thought it might be late."

.   .   .

It didn't take as long as I had expected to cut the jewels off the saddle. I carried the lantern into the stable, where I sat down on the bale of straw to do the job, with a small pair of very sharp scissors that I usually carry in my handbag. I'd have taken it upstairs to my room, where the light was better, but it was heavy, and Josef was at the circus, and I hadn't seen anyone else to ask; and besides, it smelled rather too strongly of horse.

So I sat in the lantern light picking at the jewels, while the tiny noises of the stable rustled round me.

The stones were loosely sewn, and came off easily enough. The tinselled braiding at the edge had been half stitched, half glued, and left a mark when at last I managed to pull it away; but nothing, I thought, to matter. The saddle, of soft pale leather with a rolled pommel, had obviously been a good one originally, but it was now very shabby, and both lining and leather showed signs of much mending.

All the same, when I had finished, and dropped the glittering handful of glass into my pocket, I looked round for a peg to hang the old saddle on, safely out of reach of marauders. The rustling in the recesses of that elaborately baroque stable hadn't been imagination; nor had it just been mice. Shabby or no, I wasn't going to leave the *Spanische Reitschule*'s saddle to the mercy of the Zechstein rats.

The only peg that was big enough was broken. It was no use perching the thing astride a partition, and I didn't believe in the old Count's saddle-room—at least, not in working order. In any case I didn't want to wait for Josef, or go looking for it myself in the dark. But the metal corn bin was rat-proof and roomy, and Piebald would not need corn tonight. I lifted the lid and put the saddle carefully down on the corn, then hung the lantern where I had found it, and went out to meet Timothy.

.   .   .

I went out through the archway on to the bridge, and stopped there, leaning over the parapet.

Above me, shadowy, soared the walls and spires and turrets of the castle, pricked here and there with windows full of yellow light. Beyond the bridge, shadow after shadow soared the pine-woods, sharp with their evening scent, and away down below in the dim valley clusters of lights marked the outlying farms. Apart from these the only sources of light in the veiled land-scape were the river which still showed as a faintly luminous ribbon sliding along the valley floor, and just below me the pale juts of rock on which the bridge was built. From some-where beneath came the trickling, splashing sound of the falling stream, but the big river at the foot of the cliff was silent.

The night was so still that if Piebald were already on his way I thought I should have heard the clip-clop of his hoofs, but there was silence, not broken this time by distant music from the circus. Even the faintest echo of this was cut off, I supposed, by the bluff that hid the village from view.

The distant sound of a motor engine broke the silence first, and I saw the lights coming along the valley road from the direction of the village. Then it had passed the road junction at the river bridge, and the lights curled along up the valley, and were lost to sight. Not Mr Lee Elliott. Not yet.

In any case—I had been trying to think it out—he would come from the north. Approaching from Vienna he would not have to pass through the village, but would turn off at the bridge for the castle. If he arrived while the performance was still going on he was unlikely to meet any of the circus people, and if he came after eleven the wagons would be moving south.

It was extremely unlikely that anyone who had known Mr Lee Elliott would see the man in the closed car driving rapidly up to the Schloss Zechstein; and indeed, in hoping to arrive as 'Lewis March' he must have reckoned on this.

His use of the disguise, then, could only mean that he planned to make another contact with the circus. And in twelve hours from now, the circus would be out of the country.

At that moment, faint and far away, I heard the sound of hoofs, the slow clip-clop, clip-clop, of a walking horse. They must have started up the steep road. The hoof-beats were steady and quite regular; it seemed that old Piebald was no longer 'going short'. I straightened up and strolled off the bridge and on down the road between the pines to wait for them.

Someone had put a stout wooden seat at the edge of the road, in a gap between the trees, facing outwards over the valley. I felt it cautiously; the wood was still dry, the damps of night had not yet reached it. I sat down to wait. The clip-clopping hoofs grew momentarily fainter as Timothy and the horse rounded some curve of the road, and trees crowded between to deaden the sound. Then, a few minutes later, they emerged nearer and louder.

It was all the scene needed, I thought, looking up where, on my left, the turrets rose dark and faintly lit against the stars . . . the silence, the stars pricking out, the charmed hush of the trees, and now the slow sound of the approaching horse. One almost expected De la Mare's Traveller or some wandering knight in armour to emerge from the pine-woods into the star-light.

The last stretch of the road must have had its verges heavily felted with pine needles, for when Timothy and the horse at last appeared rounding the bend in the road below me, they seemed to be moving as silently as any story-book apparition. It occurred to me then that this—this mundane appearance of mortal boy and horse, treading cautiously up the soft verge to save the lame leg—was every bit as dramatic as any romantic legend . . . the old stallion, deposed, menial, debased by his ugly coat, a sort of Frog Prince who might soon be back in his own royal place. He came now, plodding beside the boy through the moon-thrown shadows, the steely light that slithered across his pied coat making of him just another barred silver shadow. But the black would soon be gone; I had noticed tonight that it was growing out already. As I called out and moved I saw his head jerk up and his ears prick forward sharply, so that for a moment he looked a young horse again. He actually quickened his pace, and then I heard him give that lovely soft whickering through his nostrils. I remembered what Herr Wagner had said: "His name will still be on his stall, and fresh straw waiting." I hoped he was right, and, more even than that, I hoped that Timothy and I were right. There would be certain difficulties if the Frog Prince turned out just to be a frog after all.

Then his muzzle had dropped softly into my hand and I was caressing his ears and telling Timothy across him what the arrangements were—including those for Mr Lee Elliott—for the coming night.

I didn't add what was very much in the forefront of my own mind regarding Mr Lee Elliott—which was that, if Timothy and Lewis and I were the only occupants of the central part of the castle, at least tonight Mr Elliott would be able to prowl into my bedroom without any fear of discovery.

Chapter Fourteen

I girdid up my Lions & fled the Seen.
Artemus Ward: *A Visit to Brigham Young*

I must have been asleep when at last he came.

After the usual pattern of Continental hotels, my room had double doors where the bedroom, originally very large, had been reduced in size so that a bathroom could be added between it and the main corridor. I never heard the opening and closing of the outer door, but when the inner door of the room opened I was, it seemed, instantly awake.

The room was dark; the heavy curtains drawn close across the window and the turret embrasure completely shut out the moonlight. I heard the door close softly behind him, then he hesitated, presumably getting his bearings. He didn't feel for a light switch, and he must have been able to see something, for I heard the ancient floorboards creak as he approached the bed.

I said sleepily: "Darling, over here," and turned, groping for the bed-side light.

The sound stopped abruptly.

"Lewis?" I said. My hand had just found the switch.

A thin pencil of light from a small pocket torch shot out to dazzle me. It caught me full in the eyes. A swift whisper came: "Keep still. Take your hand off that switch." But even as he spoke, instinctively, I had pressed the switch and the light came on.

It wasn't Lewis. Standing about eight feet away from the foot of my bed was Sandor Balog, with the torch gripped in his hand.

"What are you doing here? Who are you looking for?"

Shock and fright made me speak loudly and shrilly. He had stopped exactly where he was, no doubt sensing that if he had moved a single step, fright would have got the better of me and I would have screamed. Now he thrust the torch back into his pocket. "Keep quiet, will you? Keep your voice down, and if —"

I said furiously: "Get out of here! Get out at once! Do you hear me? Get out of my room immediately!" And I rolled quickly over to reach for the bed-side telephone.

And now he did move. In two swift strides he was beside the bed, and his left hand shot out to grip my wrist just before I could touch the receiver. It was the second time that evening that I'd felt the strength of those hands, and this time the grip was both violent and cruel.

"Stop that, I tell you!" He wrenched my arm brutally aside, and flung me back bodily against the pillows.

I screamed then, with all my strength. I think I screamed Lewis's name, as I tried to throw myself out the farther side of the bed away from Sandor, but he pounced again, grabbing my flying arm once more with that brutal hand, and wrenched me back on to the pillows, and as I opened my mouth to scream again he hit me hard with his other hand across the mouth.

The blow slammed me hard back against the head of the bed. As my head and body were driven back, he hit me again. I don't think I fought any more; I hardly remember. In any case it would have been futile. The next few moments were a daze of shock, fear and pain, in which, abandoning the attempt to call out or run for help I cowered back against the pillows trying, uselessly enough, to protect my face with my free hand. I'm not even sure if he hit me again. I think he did, but eventually when he saw that I was cowed and quiet he dropped the vicious grip on my arm and moved away from me, back to the foot of the bed.

I put both hands to my bruised face, and tried to stop my body trembling.

"Look at me."

I didn't move.

His voice altered. "Look at me."

Slowly, as if by doing so I would tear away the skin from my cheeks, I pulled away my hands. I looked at him. He was standing now at the foot of the bed, just at the edge of the pool of light cast by the bed-side lamp, but I knew that I was still well within reach of that lightning athlete's pounce of his; and even without that I couldn't have hoped to run out of range of the gun which he now held in his right hand.

The gun shifted fractionally. "You see this?"

I didn't speak. I was biting my lips together to stop them shaking, but he could see that I could see it.

He said: "You've just seen how much use it is to scream in a place like this. There are two doors to this room, and the walls are half a metre thick, I should think, and in any case there's only that boy here, isn't there, the other side of the corridor, and quite a long way away? He'll be sleeping like a baby . . . but if you did manage to wake him, madame, that would be too bad for him. Do you understand?"

I understood very well. This time I nodded.

"All right . . . and if you try to touch that telephone again it will also be too bad for you."

"What do you want?" I had meant it to sound furious, but my voice came out in a sort of thin whisper, and I cleared my throat and tried again. It still didn't sound like my own voice at all, and I saw him smile. At the smile, some tiny seed of anger stirred somewhere inside me, sending a flickering thread of warmth through the cold and the fear.

"You were expecting someone, weren't you?" The smile grew. "Or do you welcome all comers to your room, madame?" He lounged against the foot of the bed, holding the pistol carelessly, his look at once contemptuous and appraising. Deep inside me the little flame caught and began to burn. I said, and was pleased to hear how steady and cold my voice sounded: "You can see how much I welcomed you."

"Ah, yes, the virtuous lady. You thought the husband had managed to get here after all, yes?"

So the first remark had been no more than a thug's routine insult. He contrived in some way to make the second sound equally offensive, and I managed to wonder fleetingly why any normal woman hates to be called 'virtuous'. But this was no more than a passing irony; with his mention of my husband, the immediate fears for myself had fled, and I had begun to think.

The thug knew that Lewis had been due. He had discovered that Lewis was delayed. Therefore, apparently, he had broken into my room to tackle me alone . . . Without knowing anything further, I accepted Sandor Balog at this point as the enemy in Lewis's shadowy assignment, as the centre of the circus 'mystery'. No doubt I should know soon enough if he had come to find out from me anything about Lewis . . .

My heart was beating in my throat somewhere. I swallowed, and said, fairly creditably:

"You didn't come here to be offensive. What did you come for? What is it to you when my husband is expected?"

"Nothing, my dear lady, except that perhaps I could not have come . . . like this . . . if he had been here."

"How did you know he wasn't here? If it comes to that, how did you know he was expected? I didn't tell anyone at the circus."

A quick shrug of the broad shoulders. He still looked very much the circus athlete. He had, of course, changed from his performer's outfit, but he was still wearing black—tight dark trousers and a black leather jacket which looked as supple and sleek with muscle as the skin of a wild animal. "You don't imagine I would come up and break into a place like this without finding all about it first, do you? Some of the servants live in the village. They were at the performance, and it was easy to talk to them afterwards and find out who the guests were. In this part of the world it is not customary for hotels to lock their doors at night, and I imagined that, short-handed as they were, there would be no night porter on duty . . . at any rate, not all night. So there was nothing to do but walk in and look at the register to find your room number—and make sure that he had not come after all." That grin again. "So don't try to frighten me, will you, madame, by persuading me your husband's going to come in and catch me here. And even if he did"—a brief gesture with the gun—"I could deal with him as easily as with you, no?"

"No, you stupid animal," I thought, but I didn't say it. I tried not to show the immediate relief I was feeling. Whatever he had come for, it was not Lewis, and it was apparent that he had not identified Lewis with Lee Elliott. He could hardly have found that 'Elliott' was expected, since I knew that Josef had only been told on his return from the circus, when the village contingent of servants had already left. So, though Balog didn't know it, Lewis was on his way, and, in place of the bewildered and frightened tourist he presumably imagined my husband to be, he would find himself tangling with a professional at least twice as tough as himself.

I said: "All right. You've made your point. You've frightened me and you've hurt me and you've made it very clear that I've got to do what you tell me. Supposing you tell me what it is? What have you come here for? What do you want?"

"The saddle," he said.

I stared at him. "The what?"

"The saddle. When I saw that brooch affair on you, I never guessed . . . but then Elemer told me about the horse, and said you'd brought the saddle up here, too. Where is it?"

"I don't understand. What can you possibly want?"

"You're not asked to understand. Just answer me. Where did you put it?"

I kept my eyes on his face. Suddenly I thought I understood only too well, and it took all my self-control not to let them flicker towards the dressing-table drawer where, wrapped in a handkerchief, lay the little pile of 'jewels' that I had cut off the harness tonight.

"It's in the stable, of course," I said, in a tone of what I hoped was surprise. "Where else do you think?"

He made a quick movement of impatience, a slight gesture, but one containing so much suppressed violence that I felt myself flinch back against the pillows. "That's not true. I went there first, naturally. Do you think I'm a fool? One of the servants told me the old man still kept a place for horses here, so I went straight there to look. I saw you'd put the horse to graze on the hill, and I thought the tack would be in the stable, but there was no sign of it. Did you bring it up here to tamper with it? Where is it?"

"Why should I tamper with it? It is in the stable, it's in the corn bin."

"The corn bin? What sort of story's that? Don't lie to me, you little fool, or —"

"Why should I lie to you? All I want is to get you out of here as soon as possible. I don't know what you want with the saddle and I don't care, and I'm not stupid enough to fight you over it when it's quite obvious I can't win. It's perfectly true I put the thing in the corn bin. There are rats in that stable—I saw traces of them, and I didn't want the saddle left out and damaged in the night. In case you didn't know, corn bins are usually made of metal, simply to keep the rats away from the grain. You'll find the saddle in the bin beside the door to the coach-house." I had been holding the bedclothes up above my breast, and now I pulled them closer round me with what I hoped was a gesture of dismissive dignity. "And now will you please get the hell out of here?"

But he didn't move. There was the now familiar gesture with the pistol. "Get up and get dressed."

"*What?*"

"You heard me. Hurry up."

"Why should I? What are you talking about? What are you going to do?"

"You're coming with me."

I was still clutching the bedclothes tightly under my chin, but I could feel the dignity slipping from me. I felt myself begin to tremble again. "But I—I've told you the truth. What reason would I have to lie? I tell you, you'll find the thing in the corn bin. Why can't you just go down there and take it and go away?"

Again that impatient movement that was a threat. "Do you think I'm going to walk out and leave you here to raise the place? Now come along, don't argue with me. Do as I say and get out of that bed." He gestured with the gun again towards the side of the bed away from the telephone and away from the door.

There seemed to be nothing for it. Slowly I pushed back the bedclothes and got out on to the floor. My nightdress was double nylon, but I felt naked. I remember that the feeling was not so much one of shame, as of sheer helplessness, the feeling that must have driven the first naked man to fashion weapons for himself. It is possible that if it had been I who held the gun I should have felt fully clothed.

I picked up my clothes. "I'll dress in the bathroom."

"You'll dress here."

"But I wouldn't be able to —"

"Damn you, don't argue. Get dressed. I'm in a hurry."

Despising myself for the pleading note in my voice, I said: "All right, if you'll please look the other way —"

"Don't be a fool. I'm not going to rape you. All women are the same, they think you've got nothing else to think about. Now get on with it and hurry up."

I did the best I could on the principle that what we don't see isn't there. I turned my back on him, so I couldn't see whether he watched me or not, but I knew that he did. If he had moved I'm not sure what I would have done, pistol or no pistol. But he didn't stir. He stood stone still, about three yards from me, and I could feel his eyes all over me as I got clumsily, fumblingly into my clothes, and tried to fasten them with shaking fingers. I didn't put on the dress I had worn for dinner; he let me take slacks and sweater and an anorak from the wardrobe. I dragged the things on and zipped them up. The warm hug of the woollen clothing was marvellously comforting, and as I pulled on my shoes I was brave enough to tackle him again.

"And when you've got the saddle, what then?"

"Then we shall see."

I stood up. My physical fear of him had been so immediate and overpowering that I had not been able to think clearly about the situation, but now, sharply faced with the prospect of leaving the lighted room that belonged to me, and going out with this brutal thug into the dark, my mind had begun to race, ticking the facts up and adding them as neatly as a cash register.

The stallion's saddle, covered with 'jewels': Sandor's solicitude for that saddle (I had been right in thinking he was not the type to run errands for Annalisa): the talk of 'loose stitching', yes, and the brooch which had hung loosely, and which Elemer had pulled off for me: Sandor's eye on it . . . he had presumably tackled Elemer immediately, only to hear that the whole harness, jewels and all, had gone up to the Schloss Zechstein. And now, Sandor asking me if I had 'tampered with it'. Yes, it all came together, with the other facts which (as yet) he didn't know— the Count's interest in my brooch, and the portrait of the Countess Maria wearing a sapphire that was in the museum at Munich . . .

Or was it? If Sandor Balog had, indeed, managed a theft of this magnitude where better could he hide such jewels than among the tawdry glitter of the normal circus trappings? If—as seemed more likely—he was just a courier for the thieves, how better get them out of the country?

So my innocent interest in the horse had pushed me firmly—and right against Lewis's orders—into the middle of this dangerous affair.

And that it was dangerous there could be no manner of doubt. If Sandor had taken my word for it and gone down again to the stable, I could have made my way to the servants' wing for help before he found that the jewels had gone and came back to get them—and me. But he was taking me with him; I should be in the stable with him—alone with him—when he took the saddle out from the bin and found it stripped of its treasure.

One more thing was certain: for Sandor there was a great deal at stake. Tonight he had shown how ruthless he could be, and I had no doubt that he was prepared to be worse than that. This, I was sure, was a man easily capable of murder.

Murder . . . On the thought, the last of the facts fell into place: the burnt-out wagon and the dying words of Franzl the horse-keeper; the insistent mumble (misinterpreted by Lewis and Annalisa) about 'Neopolitano Petra's saddle'. Franzl might (as Annalisa had imagined) have been trying to confess the theft of the horse; but the insistence on something as trivial as the saddle implied that, in the moment of dying, he had forgotten that the horse's name meant nothing to them, and was trying desperately to pass on the discovery for which he had been murdered, and Paul Denver with him. It seemed that the Piebald story had, after all, held a hotter clue than we had dreamed of, to Lewis's 'mystery'.

And what had been worth two deaths to Sandor Balog then, might be worth another now.

Well, no jewels were worth a death. And every minute of delay brought Lewis closer. I said quickly: "Just a minute. This saddle you're taking so much trouble for. I know why you want it."

That stopped him. "What do you know?"

"I know about the jewels you've stolen. That brooch that Elemer gave me that came off the saddle, that was one of them, wasn't it?" I would have liked to startle him further by telling him that I had recognised the jewels, but I had no wish to endanger the old Count by hinting that he had known the brooch. Nor was I going to risk my own neck by knowing too much about Franzl. I went on rapidly: "You gave it away when you tackled me tonight outside Annalisa's wagon; why should you care what happens to a piece of glass off a saddle? And now coming up here after it, it's obvious, I'd be a fool if I didn't see. Well, it's nothing to do with me, they're not my jewels, and I'm certainly not going to risk anything for them. If you do drag me down to that stable now and I show you the saddle, it won't do you much good. You don't think I wanted to take that saddle all covered with circus stuff, do you? I took the jewels off."

"Jewels," he said. "Jewels. You took the jewels off the saddle?"

"Yes, I did. I offered to put them in a box and send them back to Annalisa at Innsbruck but she said she didn't want them. You can take them; as far as I'm concerned, you can take the lot. Only just get out of this room and leave me alone. You'll be across the frontier in a few hours, so why should you worry? Just go away now and take them with you."

He was still staring as if I had taken leave of my senses. Then I saw the flicker of calculation behind the narrow dark eyes, and acted quickly, concerned not to let him begin thinking. If I could satisfy him by giving him the jewels, hustle him somehow out of the room, get that massive door locked on him . . . He might imagine himself safe, ready to cross the border within a matter of hours, with only me and Timothy—foreigners, and comparatively helpless—knowing something about him. It wasn't much of a hope, but it was all there was. It surprised me, in the fleeting moment I had to be surprised, that Lewis and the weight of his Service should be after a crime of this nature, but if this was indeed Lewis's quarry I wasn't fool enough to think that I could deal with him. I knew what Lewis himself would want me to do: stay safe, wait for him, and then help him to lock himself on to Sandor's wake.

I swung quickly round to the dressing-table, dragged open a drawer, and lifted out the glittering pile of stones which lay bundled in a clean handkerchief. I hoped he wouldn't notice that the sapphire brooch wasn't there.

For the first time, I approached him of my own will, and, ignoring the pistol, thrust the bundle at him. "Here you are. This was what was on the saddle. Now get out, and I hope it chokes you."

He made no move to take them. Then suddenly he laughed. It was the sound of quite spontaneous amusement.

I said, disconcerted: "What's the matter? Why don't you take them?"

He said contemptuously: "Jewels? Those are jewels only fit for a horse. Or perhaps a woman. Now, don't waste my time."

Then, as I stood with the things still cupped in my hands, gaping at him, he reached out one of those narrow calloused hands and scooped three or four of the stones from the bundle. He rolled them in his palm, so that they glittered and shone in the lamplight, green and red and something topaz yellow. He laughed again.

"An emerald, and a ruby, and – what, a yellow diamond? Oh yes, they are very fine, these crown jewels of yours." Then suddenly the smile was gone, and that white-toothed animal look was back. "These are glass. Fool. Do you think I would waste my time over such things as these? Even if they were real, what kind of market would there be for these things in my country? People over there don't want jewels, they want dreams, yes, dreams . . . beautiful dreams for the damned . . . You can always sell dreams." With a flick of the wrist he sent the stones flying. I heard them hit the floor and roll away behind the window curtain.

I said: "You're crazy."

"Perhaps. And now we go."

I backed away as far as I could, and came up against the

dressing-table. "And if I refuse?" My voice was breathless. "You really think you could get away with shooting me?"

"Oh, this." His glance down at the gun was almost casual. "I should not shoot you. That was just to frighten you." A twist of those strong fingers and the gun was reversed in his hand. "I should hit you with it, see, knock you out, and then . . ." A gesture towards the window . . . "It's a long drop, I believe." He smiled at me. "The only reason I don't do it now is because I still want that saddle, and I don't trust you, my pretty lady."

He had moved over to the door while he spoke, and his hand was on the knob, ready to ease it open. He slanted his head, listening. Then the narrow black eyes glinted at me, and he said softly: "Now, tidy the bed and pick up your nightdress. Don't go near the telephone . . . That's right. And pick up those jewels. We want the room to look as though you'd dressed and gone out of your own free will, don't we?"

I obeyed him; there seemed nothing else to do. After watching me for a moment, he pulled the door open quietly, and now was half through it, listening intently for any sound in the corridor. I could hear nothing. I stooped to pick up the red stone. The other two had rolled beyond the heavy curtains which masked the turret embrasure. For the moment, satisfied with my obedience, he wasn't watching me; all his attention was on the silent spaces of the corridor. My shoes were light and made no sound on the carpet. I reached casually through the curtains as if to pick up the other fallen stones . . .

He didn't turn. As silently as I could I slid between the curtains into the dark embrasure, and then like a flash I was fumbling at the catch of the little door that gave on the battlements.

Chapter Fifteen

. . . Blinkin' in the lift sae hie.
Robert Burns: *Willie Brewed a Peck o' Maut*

It opened without a sound, and I slipped out. I could hardly hope to have more than a few seconds' start—in fact, I think I hardly even hoped to escape this way, but my flight had been purely instinctive. There was nowhere else to go.

If I could get the key silently from the lock, and relock the door again on the outside, I could not imagine that he would risk making the noise necessary in forcing it or shooting it open. I had no idea what the time was, but if he had come up after the second house was over, most of the circus would be already on its way. He might well cut his losses, gamble on my having spoken the truth, go down for the saddle and hurry away with all speed.

But I didn't have time to put this lightning theory to the test. Even as I grasped the key to pull it from the lock, he realised what I was doing. I heard a quick exclamation from the room beyond the curtain, and the creak of the floor as he started after me.

I whipped out, slammed the door behind me and ran along the narrow walk behind the battlements.

The moonlight was hard, brilliant, merciless. It showed me my way clearly, but as clearly it showed my running form to Sandor. I was barely two-thirds of the way along between the battlements and the steep-pitched roof to my right, when I heard the door yanked open behind me and his urgent voice, "Stand still or I'll shoot!"

I don't know whether I believed the threat or not: I didn't take time to think about it. I could feel terror between my shoulder-blades, but I never paused. Like a bolting hare, I ran headlong for the little door that I had seen in the second tower

I heard him leap the steps, clear down to the stone walk. He landed lightly as a cat. Three more strides and I was at the tower. The door was the duplicate of the one in my own turret. I stumbled up the steps, seized the handle and pushed with all my strength. The door was locked.

I whirled, momentarily at bay, the palms of my hands pressed hard against the door behind me. He was coming. He was half way over. He had thrust the gun into his pocket and both his hands were free.

For one crazy moment I thought there was nowhere to go but straight up the steep slope of the tiles beside me. I suppose it might have been safe enough; they were dry and I was rubber shod, and if I had slipped I would only have fallen back to the walk. But Sandor was on the walk.

And below the battlements was darkness, and empty space, and the distant deep river . . .

Then I saw the steps, a little curved flight twisting up on the outside of the tower and round behind it; the stairway I had noticed earlier in the day, and had forgotten. It went up, not down, but it was the only way to go. I was flying up it, and round the curved wall of the turret and out of his sight, before he had reached the bottom step.

They talk about people being winged by fear. I suppose I was, and it must be remembered that Sandor, athlete though he was, had put in two strenuous performances that night. I know that I gained on him up that dreadful twisting spiral. On the moonlit side it was easy, and even when we twisted back into the black shadow of the side away from the moon, it seemed I couldn't put a foot wrong, though I heard him stumble and waste his breath in an ugly expletive, and once he paused, gasping, and called out another threat or command. And then the little stair-case whipped round the last curve of the turret and, it seemed, shot me out on to the open leads of the top of the castle.

I was past thinking. I didn't even dare pause to see where I was or what was ahead of me. I had a vague impression of moonlit leads broken by peaks and slopes of tiles tilted and shining in the moon, like icy steep-sided mountains shouldering their way up at random out of a plain; of gold-crowned pinnacles and turrets, of cowled chimney-pots and carvings like great chess-men set out round the edges of the roof, and here and there the great tubes of open chimneys, like ranked cannon blindly raking the sky. In the hard washed moonlight, it was like some night-mare world without plan or relevance.

I ran for the nearest cover, a great stack of chimney-pots, with beyond them the reassuring scarp of a steep-pitched roof.

The leads were ridged, trip-wire ridges, some two or three inches high, every six feet or so. I jumped one of them safely enough and swerved to avoid a broken chimney-pot which was lying lodged against the next.

He was near the head of the steps now. He'd seen me. He called something else in that furious breathless voice.

I could just see his head and shoulders; his feet must have still been five or six steps down. I don't remember thinking at all; it was pure instinct that made me check, turn, stoop for the piece of chimney-pot, and with both arms and all my strength, heave it over the ridged leads and send it rolling straight for the top of the steps.

It went true. It hit the head of the steps with a clatter, and hurtled straight over them and down. It must have caught his legs and swept his feet from under him, for his head and shoulders vanished with a crash, a slithering, and a flurry of breathless oaths, and I heard the flimsy iron railing creak as his body was thrown against it.

I didn't wait. As I dived for the shelter of the chimney-stack, I heard the pot in its turn hit the iron railing, then, seconds later, crash somewhere on the cliffs below, and later again, the dwindling crash and tinkle of the fragments falling piecemeal to the river.

Then I was past the chimney-stack and dodging quickly among the steep rooftop shadows.

I had gained time, but I certainly couldn't hope to dodge him for long, nor hide from him for any length of time in that exposed confusion. What I had to do, and fast, was to find a way down. He would—equally certainly—make sure I couldn't get down the way I had come, but where there was one outside stair, there might well be two . . .

Running still swiftly, but as softly as I could, I dodged past two enormous stacks, through the covering shadow thrown by a hexagonal roof, and ran for the battlements beyond. If there were any stair, I thought it would be on the outside. I had, in fact, some hazy memory of having seen such a stair, but where it was I couldn't in my confusion and terror remember.

The turret with the stairs up which we had come had been at the south-eastern corner of the castle, at the junction of the central hotel block and the south wing occupied by the Count and Countess. As soon as I had gained the shelter of the chimneys I had turned north, for it was in the north wing that the servants slept, and where I might expect to find help. Moreover, I hoped that the other corner turret, at the north-east, would have a stairway, the twin of the first, by which I might get down into the north wing.

I was now half way back along the centre block, about level with my own turret—I recognised the pointed roof and the winged dragon catching the moon. Deep in a shadowed corner I risked a pause to listen, fighting to control my breathing and hear above my thudding heart if there were still sounds of pursuit.

I heard him straight away. He wasn't coming fast; he was some distance away, at fault, casting about like a hound that has lost the scent. But a hound that knows its quarry's there ahead of it, and that it only has to go on to drive that quarry into a corner, will hardly give up and turn back for lack of scent. He came on.

But he cannot have been sure which way I had first run. Now, just as I tensed to bolt again, I heard him stop. He stood there for what must have been a full minute, listening (I supposed) as I was listening. I could imagine him, lithe and tough and black in his sleek animal's suit, peering among the angular shadows for a sight of me. I kept very still.

He took two slow steps forward, then stopped again. I was pressed back into my corner, my hands digging into a crevice of the stone, almost as if I would have burrowed my way into it, like a worm burrowing into a bank. Under my rigid fingers a piece of mortar broke away. It fell into my hand, silently, harmlessly, but the moment's imaginary sound that it might have made brought a spasm of terror so intense as to bring the sweat out on to my face.

Next second the feel of the rough mortar, a piece about the size of a pigeon's egg scoring my sweating palm, suggested something to me; an old trick, but worth trying—and I had very little to lose by trying it. Cautiously, I eased myself away from the stone, making no sound at all, then, still hidden, lobbed the piece of mortar as far as I could the way we had come, back towards the south wing of the castle.

The sound it made, falling with a crack and a slither a long way off, was satisfactorily loud; even more satisfactorily, it sounded very like a stone disloged accidentally by someone's foot. I heard the creak of rubber as he whipped round where he stood, and then the sounds, light but distinct, of his feet racing back the way he had come.

For a moment I thought of following quietly in his wake, and taking the chance of slipping down the same turret stair; but there was too much open roof to cross, and he might well be watching it.

I couldn't hear him now. It was to be assumed that he was hunting me along the southern wing. Turning the other way, I dodged along through the sharp lights and shadows, stumbling sometimes, both hands spread out in front of me, for so weird was this lunar landscape that, however brilliant the moonlight, one felt as if one was running blind.

In front of me loomed the turret at the north-east corner, the twin of the one up whose stairway I had come. Here, surely, must be the second stairway which I was so sure that I remembered . . . ?

There was indeed a stairway: the head of it lay in the shadow away from the moon. But as I ran up to it I saw that it was ruinous, its top railed stoutly off with timber, and the first half-dozen steps hanging, crumbling, over vacancy.

But beside it, in the wall of the tower, straight in front of me there was a door.

This was like all the other castle doors, heavy, and lavishly studded and hinged with wrought iron. There was no latch, only a big curved handle, which, as I seized it and pushed, felt under my hands as if it were the shape of some animal, a griffin or a winged lizard. The door was immovable. I pushed and pulled, hardly believing that this, which had loomed up in front of me as a sort of miracle of escape, was not, after all, going to work.

I think it was at this moment that it occurred to me seriously, for the first time, that perhaps I was not going to get away, that the thing which happened to other people might, now, soon, be going to happen to me. Possibly the very fairy-tale atmosphere of the castle—the lonely valley, the turrets, the moonlight, the battlements, this door with the griffin handle—the trappings of childhood's dreams and of romance, once become actual, were seen to be no longer dreams but nightmare. Caught up in one's own private world of fantasy, perhaps one would always trade it for an acre of barren heath under the grey light of day.

There was even, set in the stone beside the door, the familiar bellpush mounted in wrought iron. I pressed it. It seemed the perfectly normal thing to do in this crazy night. I believe it would have seemed perfectly normal if the door had opened silently and a wizard had bowed me in among the cobwebs and the alembics . . .

But nothing happened. The door was immovable, blank in the moonlight.

They say that every end is a beginning. Even as I stood there, with my hand on the silly bell, feeling the courage, and even the driving fear, spill out of me to leave me sprung and spent, I remembered where I had seen the other stair.

For me it couldn't have been better placed. It was a wide stone stairway leading down beside one of the gate towers—the twin turrets which flanked the main gateway at the bridge. Originally these towers had been joined by a stretch of machicolated curtain wall, a narrow catwalk above the gate, but this had fallen into disrepair and was a mere skeleton, simply an arched span of crumbling stone joining the two towers. The southern gate tower, similarly, had fallen into ruin, and had been left in its decay with its stairway fallen away and its roof sticking up like a jagged tooth. But the northerly one, I knew, was whole and perfectly negotiable, and it gave on the courtyard and the steps and the front door of the castle and the bridge and the road up which Lewis would be coming . . .

There was still no sign of Sandor. Chin on shoulder I slithered out of the shadow of the turret, round the curve, and then ran and dodged my crazy way along the rooftop towards the gate tower on the west front.

I was right. The stairway was there. And it was open. The head of it lay full in the moonlight, fifty yards ahead of me. As I burst out of shadow into the full glare of the moon, running, I saw Sandor again. He had done just as I had hoped. He had run right round the other wing of the castle, and was now heading for the opposite side of the gate—the side with the broken turret.

He had seen me. I saw the gun flash threateningly into his hand; but I knew that, here of all places, he wouldn't dare to shoot. In any case I couldn't go back; there was nowhere to go back to; he could reach the turret up which we had come before I could. And I could get down to the courtyard, down my stairway. He couldn't. His was broken, the turret itself just a jut of crumbling fangs. To get to me he would have to go all the way back. I ran forward.

I had run twenty yards, not looking at him, my whole being intent simply on the head of that stone staircase, when I suddenly saw what he was doing. I had forgotten who—or what—Sandor was. To a man who worked daily on the high wire, a nine-inch wall, in whatever state of repair, was as wide as a motorway. He never even hesitated. He went up that broken turret like a leaping cat, and then was on top of the arch and running—not walking, running—across it towards me.

As I stopped dead, I saw something else. Away below, down

the hillside, down among the dark trees away to the right, I thought I saw the lights of a moving car.

It was silly, it was futile, but I screamed his name. *"Lewis, Lewis!"* I doubt if the cry could have been heard from farther than ten yards away; it came out only as a sort of sobbing gasp, not even as loud as the cry of an owl. Sandor was three brisk strides from the end of the arch, straight above the stair head. I turned and ran back the way I had come.

He leapt down to the leads and came after me.

At least now I knew my way, and at least I now knew he didn't intend to shoot me. With a thirty-yard lead I might yet make the corner turret and the steps down to my own room. And now there would be someone to run to. Lewis.

Almost immediately I realised that, even with the lead I had, I couldn't hope to do it. My very fear had exhausted me, and Sandor's physical strength and fitness were far greater than my own . . . I didn't have my hands held in front of me now. Blind or not, I simply ran as hard as I could back the way I had come along the rooftop maze of the north wing, round the turret where that nightmare magic door stood in the shadows fast shut . . .

It was wide open.

I was almost past it when I saw, out of the corner of my eye, the blank, black oblong of the open door. Sandor was barely ten yards behind me. I could never reach my own turret now. This, whatever it was, was the only port in a storm. I jerked round like a doubling hare and almost fell through the open door.

He overran me. My sudden movement, as I seized the jamb of the door and swung myself round and back in through the gap, took him completely by surprise. I must have vanished almost literally from under his hands. I saw him shoot past me as I swung back into the shadow, and then I found myself sprawling breathless against a slippery wall on the inside of the tower.

I had not known what to expect inside the door – some kind of stairway, perhaps; but there was no such thing. As I swung round the door-jamb into the blackness, I found myself on a level slippery floor, and then, as I staggered and put my hands out to the wall to save myself, the door through which I had come slid fast shut behind me, and a light came on.

The floor, the shining steel walls, the light, dropped frighteningly downwards like a stone and I went with them. It was the lift.

Chapter Sixteen

O Lewis . . .!
Shakespeare: *King John*

There was barely time even to register this. It was only afterwards that I knew what had happened. When the lift had been installed they had made a thorough job of it and extended the shaft to the roof to give access to the rampart walks, and (I found later) a belvedere on the south side. My half crazy, wholly thoughtless action in pressing the bell-push had summoned it, and as I had swung myself into the small metal box one of my hands, outstretched and flailing for balance, must have caught the controls as I fell, and sent the lift earthwards.

I hardly realised when the dropping motion ceased. I was gasping and sobbing for breath, and still just picking myself up shakily from the floor, when the drop finished as smoothly as it had started, and with a click the doors opened. I caught a glimpse of some dimly lit passage outside, empty and silent. Dazedly, my hands slipping on the ribbed metal of the lift wall, I pulled myself to my feet, still barely aware of what was happening, and moved shakily towards the open doors.

They shut in my face. The metal cage moved again—this time, upwards. He had called it from the roof. He must have been standing with his thumb pressed on the button, and now, locked in my small metal trap, I was being hurtled straight back to the roof.

I flew at the controls. I had no idea what they were, and in any case all the labelling was in German. But one knob was red, and at this I shoved with all my strength. With a sickening sensation and a jar, the lift stopped in mid-flight. I jammed hard with my thumb at the lowermost of the rank of buttons, released the red, and after perhaps two seconds of intolerable pause I felt the lift drop once more . . .

This time I was pressed against the doors, waiting, one hand spread against the metal, ready to push, the other clutching the only movable object in the lift, a big oblong trough for cigarette butts, a foot long by nine inches wide, which had been standing in the corner underneath the control panel.

The doors slid open easily on to darkness. Before they were a foot apart I was through them and had turned to ram the metal trough between them as they slid shut. They closed smoothly on the metal, gripped it, held—and stayed open, nine inches apart.

It was enough. The lift didn't move. I turned in the shaft of light from its wedged door to see where I was.

I was standing on stone, rough stone flags, and I could tell somehow from the feel of the air around me that this was no corridor, but a large room or space. It was cold with the dank chill that one associates with cellars: and in a moment I saw that this was in fact where I must be. Back in the dimness, the faint glint from crowded ranks of bottles showed me that this was the wine cellar, neatly situated at the junction of the kitchen wing and the central block of the castle. They had certainly made a comprehensive job of the new lift, roof to dungeon. And, I reckoned, if they used the lift to come down for the wine there must surely be a light switch near it . . . ?

There was. My fingers, slithering and padding over the wall to either side of the lift, found the switch and pressed it, and a light, dim enough, but more than adequate, flicked into life just as the lift light (presumably on a time switch) went out.

If the lift had been an anachronism behind the panelling of the castle corridors, here it seemed like something from another world. I was in a great vaulted space, treed like a forest with squat massive pillars which supported the low ceiling on great branches of stone. Stacked here and there between the pillars were the racks for wine, themselves by no means new, but young compared with this Gothic dungeon, partly hewn, I suspected, out of the living rock of the crag. The shadowed spaces between the pillars seemed to stretch infinitely in every direction. From where I stood I could see neither door nor staircase, though patches of deeper darkness seemed to indicate where passages might lead off underneath the rest of the castle.

I swung back to face the lift and tried, remembering how it was situated on the upper floors, to imagine exactly where under the castle I stood now. Somewhere along to my right would be the main part of the castle with the central staircase. Off to my left the kitchen premises, and beyond them the stables and the gatehouse . . .

I bit my lip, hesitating. It was impossible to guess what Sandor's next move would be. I didn't know whether he had seen the lights of the approaching car; I thought not. But in any case it might be supposed that, with time slipping on, he would cut his losses, abandon the chase, and make straight for the stairway by the gate and the stable. Or he might go back by the way he had come, through my bedroom, in which case he would come down by the main staircase . . .

There was no way of guessing. Only one thing was certain, that I wasn't going to stay down here in this echoing vault. I had to get out somehow to the upper air, to the courtyard. And even if Sandor was there, there also any minute now would be my own safety, Lewis.

Only then did it occur to me that my safety was Lewis's danger. If by chance, as he entered the courtyard or the castle, he were to meet Sandor, then I no longer had any illusions about what the latter would do, and Lewis was unsuspecting, and for all I knew unarmed.

Foolishly or not, I was not going in the lift again. I turned to my left, and running between the pillars, began to search for a way out.

I was back in the world of fantasy, Red Riding Hood lost in the depths of the grey forest . . . on every side, it seemed, the vast stone trunks stretched away, ribbing the floor with shafts of darkness. Soon the dim electric light was lost behind the crowding pillars, and I was groping my way from stone to stone, stumbling on the uneven flags, heading apparently for deeper and ever deeper darkness.

At the very moment when I faltered, ready to turn back towards the light—even, perhaps, to use the lift and risk meeting Sandor in the upper corridors—I saw light ahead of me, and soon recognised this for a shaft of moonlight falling through some slit window in the outside wall. I ran towards this.

It was an old spearhead window deep in a stone embrasure, and it was unglazed. The sweet night air poured through it, and outside I got a glimpse of the moonlit, glinting tiers of pines, and heard faintly the sound of falling water. Inside, just beyond the window, and reasonably well lit by the edge of the moonlight, was a flight of stone steps leading upwards. At its top was the usual heavy door, liberally studded with iron. Praying that it wouldn't be locked, I half ran, half stumbled up the steps, and seizing the big round handle, lifted the massive latch and pushed.

The door opened smoothly and in silence. Cautiously I pushed it open a foot and peered out.

A corridor this time, flagged floor, rush matting, dim lights, probably somewhere near the kitchens. To my left it stretched between closed doors to a right-angled corner; but only twenty yards to my right it ended in another vaulted door. This was locked and bolted on the inside, but the bolts soon yielded, and quietly enough I was through. Outside was darkness and moonlit arches and a confusion of massive shapes. I shut the door softly and leaned back in the shadows, getting my bearings.

In a moment I had it. I had come out into the coach-house. The shape looming in front of me was the ancient closed carriage, its shaft sticking up like a mast and bisecting the moonlit archway that opened on the courtyard beyond. Beside it was the car, a big old-fashioned limousine. I tiptoed forward between the two vehicles, and, pausing at the edge of one of the arches, peered out into the courtyard.

This was empty. I could hear no sound. In the bright moonlight that edged the scene like silverpoint, nothing stirred, but at almost the same moment I heard the purr of a car's engine mount the last hill towards the castle, mount and grow and distort into a hollow echo as the car crossed the bridge. Then the lights speared through the archway, and a big car—a strange one—stole into the courtyard, swung round with its headlights probing the shadowed corners, and came to a quiet stop with its bonnet no more than a yard from the open archway of the coach-house.

The lights went off. The engine died, and Lewis got quietly out of the car and reached into the back seat for his bag.

As he straightened, bag in hand, I breathed: "Lewis."

He did not appear to have heard me, but just as I nerved myself, regardless of possible danger, either to call him more loudly, or to go out into the open towards him, he turned, threw his bag into the front of the car, got back into the driver's seat himself, and re-started the engine. As I still hesitated, tense and shaking, I heard the hand-brake lift, and the car, without lights, slid forward and into the open arch of the coach-house.

I remembered, then, his trained reaction to the news-reel cameras. When a whisper came from the dark, he was not likely to give anything away to a possible watcher. The car came to a stop a yard from me; he got out quietly with the engine still running, and said, very softly: "Vanessa?"

Next moment I was in his arms, holding him tightly enough to strangle him, and able to say nothing but "Oh love, oh love, oh love," over and over again.

He took it patiently enough, holding me close against him with one arm, and with his free hand patting me, comforting me rather as one does a frightened horse. At last he disengaged himself gently.

"Well, here's a welcome! What's the matter?" Then in a

suddenly edged whisper: "Your face. How did that happen? What's been going on? What's wrong?"

I had forgotten my bruised cheek. Now I realised how sore it was. I put a hand to it. "That man . . . it's that man from the circus . . . Sandor Balog, the Hungarian, you know who I mean. He's here, somewhere about, and oh, Lewis —"

My whisper cracked shamefully, half aloud, and I gasped and bit my lip and put my head down against him again.

He said: "Gently, my dear, it's all right. Do you mean the high-wire act from the circus? He did that to your face? Look, my dear, look, it's all right now . . . you're all right now. I'm here . . . Don't worry any more. Just tell me. Can you tell me about it? As quickly as you can?"

He had sounded startled and very angry, but somehow not surprised. I lifted my head. "You came back as Lee Elliott because you knew about him?"

"Not about him, no. But I was expecting the worst—having to get next to the circus again. Now it may not be necessary. If this is it breaking, pray heaven it does so this side of the frontier. Now, quickly, my darling. Tell me."

"Yes, yes, I'll try, but he's somewhere about, Lewis. He's somewhere here, and he's got a gun."

"So have I," said my husband matter-of-factly, "and we'll see him before he sees us. What's behind that door?"

"A back passage, somewhere near the kitchens, I think. I came up that way from the dungeon."

"My poor sweet. Come on, then, back here, behind the car . . . If he comes out that way now, we'll get him. And if he comes in through the arch we'll see him easily. Keep your voice down. Now, please, Van, if you can . . . ?"

"I'm all right now. Everything's all right now. Well, it started with Annalisa giving us the old piebald horse that belonged to Uncle Franzl, so we arranged to bring him up here tonight and his saddle and bridle along with him . . ."

As briefly and as quickly as I could I told him everything that had happened, even the business of the jewelled brooch and the portrait. "And I think he'll have gone back that way," I finished, "to my room. There was still the brooch, and the stones that were spilt on the floor. He said all that about their not being valuable, but I think he was only talking stupidly to put me off. 'Dreams for the damned', he said he was selling, 'you can always sell dreams.' He was still determined to get the saddle, and I don't see why, but it means he's bound to see if I was telling the truth about putting it in the corn bin, so whichever way he comes down, he'll be making for the stable, and he may have seen you arrive—and if not, he'll have heard you—and now he'll be waiting for you to go in, before he slips out and away. Lewis, if you don't go in the main door, he'll wonder why; and if you do, and he sees you, he'll recognize you, and then —"

But he hardly seemed to be listening. He was still holding me, but half absently, with his head bent, thinking.

"'Dreams for the damned'," he quoted softly. "I begin to see . . . And he still wants the saddle, does he?" He lifted his head, and his whisper sounded jubilant. "By God, I think you have broken it, at that, bust it wide open! No, I'll tell you later. Where are the stables? Next door?"

"Yes, that way. That's the connecting door, beside the carriage. And there's a door off the courtyard."

"Right. He won't have gone back to your room: I think you can take it he was telling the truth, and the 'jewels' really are only stage props. Why bother to lie, and throw them down like that, when he'd already had to give himself away to you, and was probably going to get rid of you anyway? No, the only reason he was interested in the brooch was because it meant you'd been meddling with the saddle . . . And he still wants that saddle, which means he'll be making for the stable. Do you reckon he's had time to get down off the roof, pick up the saddle, and get out over the bridge before I arrived?"

I tried to think back. "It's hard to judge, it seemed like years, but I suppose it's only been a few minutes . . . No. No, I'm sure he hasn't."

"Then either he's still above the gate waiting to come down, or he's already in the stable waiting for me to go. In either case he'll have seen or heard the car arrive. Stay there half a minute, while I think."

He drifted from my side like a shadow, then from the car came clearly audible movements, the creak of upholstery, a grunt, a sharp revving of the engine before he killed it, the sound of his feet on the cobbled floor, and finally the slam of the car door.

Then he was beside me again, with his case in one hand. His free arm went round me, pulling me close. I could feel the calm, unhurried beat of his heart, and his untroubled breathing stirred my hair. As my own body relaxed into this unruffled calm I reflected that it was something to be able to hand over to a professional. It was something that that sleek animal in black leather should find he had tangled, not with a stray English tourist and her bewildered husband, but with Our Man (Temporary) in Vienna.

"I'll have to go in by the front door," said Lewis. "He'll be waiting for that. I'll see he doesn't recognize me if he's watching, and he won't know the car. I've brought a Merc this time. Then I'll come straight back here, by that door of yours. The lay-out's simple, I'll find it in two minutes. Will you let me leave you here for two minutes?"

"Yes."

"That's my girl. Now, just on the off-chance he's inside, you'd better not go back in there. Stay out here. Not in the car . . . what about that old carriage? Yes, the door's open. In you go, then, and keep still. I'll be back."

"What are you going to do?"

"As far as you're concerned, I suspect he'll cut his losses, and he won't know how fast to get out of it. But I also think he'll get in touch with his bosses straight away, and when he does I want to be there. So I think we'll let him take what he wants."

"You mean you're just going to let him go? Now? Tonight? Not do anything to him?"

His hand touched my bruised cheek very gently. He said: "When I do lay hands on him, I promise you he'll never walk a high wire again, or anything else for that matter. But this is a job."

"I know."

I couldn't see him smile, but I heard it in his voice. "We both know a bruise on your cheek is worth more than a cartload of Top Secret papers, but the fact remains, I'm afraid, that I'm still on the pay-roll."

"All right, Lewis. It's all right."

"Get in there, then, and stay still. I won't be long."

"Lewis . . ."

"Yes?"

"Be—careful, won't you? He's dangerous."

Lewis laughed.

.   .   .

The inside of the old carriage enclosed me like a small safe box, smelling fusty and close, of old mouldering leather and straw. There were curtains at the windows, thick and dampish; they felt like brocade. With fingers fumbling in the dark I found the loop that held them, and loosened it, and the curtains fell across the window, shutting out what little light there was. Then I crouched back on the burst and prickly squabs to wait.

Though I could see nothing, shut safely away in the darkness of my little box, I found that I could hear. The top sections of the carriage doors were of glass, rather like those of a railway compartment, and on the side nearest to the stable either the glass was broken, or the window had been lowered and was standing wide. I could feel a draught of air from it, and almost immediately I heard the sound of stealthy footsteps in the courtyard, and then the quiet click of the stable latch.

Now, the old carriage was parked within two yards of the wall dividing stable and coach-house, beside the connecting door. This was shut, but, peering out avidly between the folds of damp brocade, I saw a wide bar of light at the foot of the door wavering a little, but growing as Sandor, flashlight in hand, approached the end of the stable nearest me, where the corn bin stood.

He was being quiet, but not especially so; he must have watched Lewis, the late-coming guest, go into the house; he would guess it was the delayed husband, but might count himself safe enough for the time it would take for Lewis to reach his room, find his wife gone, and start to look for her. All he wanted now was to get what he had come for, and escape as quickly as possible.

There was a soft metallic clink as the corn bin lid was lifted. A shuffling sound followed, and a falling rustle as the saddle was lifted clear of the corn, then it was dumped on the floor, and the lid closed.

He didn't hurry away as I had expected. I strained my ears to hear what he was doing, but couldn't guess . . . I heard more shuffling sounds, even the noise of his rapid breathing, and presently I could have sworn that I heard the sound of ripping cloth. Since there were no more 'jewels' left for him to tear away, he must be opening the thing up. Lewis was right; the 'jewels' were worthless after all; there must be something else contained in the saddle, and, sooner than carry away the whole clumsy burden, Sandor was taking the time to remove whatever he had so carefully stitched into the padding. I remembered his offer to stitch the thing, and its much-mended look.

Two minutes, Lewis had said. With no light to see the time, there was no judging it at all. It might have been two minutes, or four, or forty, but it was probably not much more than Lewis's two, before quite suddenly, near me, the sounds ceased.

In the silence that followed, I heard again the click of the stable latch, and steps approaching, quiet but unconcealed.

Unbelievingly, horrified, I heard Timothy's voice.

"Who's that—why, Herr Balog! What are you doing here?" And then, sharply: "What on earth are you doing with that saddle? Look, just what is going on around here? And where's Vanessa? Ah, you —"

The rush of feet; the brief sound of a scuffle; a cry from Timothy, bitten off. A thud, and then the racing sound of retreating footsteps. They made for the stable door, and out, then I heard them cross the corner of the courtyard, to be lost as he reached the archway and the bridge.

"Timothy!" Somehow I got the carriage door open. I stumbled out, missing the single step and almost falling. The light had gone with Sandor, but my hands found the door handle and the massive key of their own volition, and in a matter of seconds I had the big door open and was in the stable.

Moonlight spilled mistily through the cobwebbed window opposite Grane's box. Beside the corn bin, huddled on the floor near the wreck of the saddle, lay Timothy.

I flew to kneel beside him, and almost choked on a cry of thankfulness as he moved. He put a hand to his head, and struggled strongly enough up on to one elbow.

"Vanessa? What happened?"

"Are you all right, Tim? Where did he hit you?"

"My head . . . no, he missed . . . my neck . . . blast, it's sore, but I think it's all right. It was that swine Sandor, you know, the —"

"Yes, I know. Don't worry about that now. Are you sure you're all right? You went with the most awful crack, I heard you clear through the door, I thought you'd hit your head on the corn bin."

"I think that must have been my elbow. Hell, yes, it was, the funny bone." He was sitting up now and rubbing his elbow vigorously. "I think it's paralysed, probably for life, the stinking swine. I suppose he's made off? I say, he was ripping the saddle open. What in the world —?"

"What in the world —?" The echo came from the shadows just behind us, and we both jumped like guilty things upon a fearful summons. We'd have made very bad agents, Timothy and I. It could easily have been Sandor returning: but it was Lewis, looking for one fantastic second not like Lewis at all, but like something as dangerous as Sandor himself, and straight from Sandor's world.

But almost before we had seen the gun in his hand it had vanished from sight again, and he said: "Timothy, it's you. I suppose you caught him at it. What the devil brought you down? No, never mind, he's gone and I've got to get after him. Did you see what he took?"

"Packets of some kind, flat packets . . . about the size of those detergent samples they shove through your door." Timothy abandoned the elbow, and began to scramble to his feet. "He's left one, anyway. I fell on it."

Almost before the boy's body had left the ground, Lewis had pounced on the thing. It was an oblong flat package, not much bigger than a manilla envelope, made apparently of polythene. Lewis whipped a knife out and slit a corner of it, gingerly. He sniffed, then shook a few grains of powder into the palm of his hand, and tasted them.

"What is it?" asked Timothy.

Lewis didn't answer. He folded the cut corner down, and thrust the package back into Timothy's hands, saying abruptly: "Keep that safely for me, don't let anyone see it. Are you all right?"

"Yes, quite."

"Then stay with Vanessa."

"But I —"

But Lewis had already gone. I heard the door of his car open and then slam behind him as he got in. The engine raced to life.

As the Mercedes swung backwards out of the coach-house I jumped up and ran out into the courtyard. The car swept back in a tight arc and paused. I jumped at the offside door and dragged at the handle. Lewis leaned across and flicked the lock open and I pulled it wide.

"Yes?"

"I'm coming with you. Don't ask me not to, please. I won't get in your way, I promise. But don't ask me to stay away."

He hesitated only fractionally. Then he jerked his head. "All right, get in." As I scrambled in beside him, Timothy reached in over my shoulder and pulled open the lock of the back door.

"Me, too. Please, Mr March. I could help, I honestly could. I'd like to."

Lewis laughed suddenly. "Come one, come all," he said

cheerfully. "It's just as well I've handed in my cards, isn't it? All right, get in, only for God's sake hurry."

Before Timothy's door was shut the Mercedes had leapt forward from a standing start, swept round with a whine of tyres, and was shooting for the narrow archway like a bullet from a gun. Her headlights flicked on momentarily, the archway lighted, leapt at us, echoed past us with a slam like the smack of a sail. The bridge boomed for a second beneath us, and then, lights out, engine silken and quiet, we were running downhill under the tunnel of the dark pines.

Chapter Seventeen

If Lewis by your assistance win the day . . .
Shakespeare: *King John*

"I don't suppose he's using lights either," said Lewis. His voice was rather less excited than if he had been driving to meet a train. "But take a look and see if either of you can see where he is, will you?"

"Did he have a car?" asked Timothy.

"A jeep. At least, I saw a jeep parked to one side among the trees when I was on my way up. I had a look at it. I'll bet it was his. See if you can see anything."

The Mercedes swung left-handed into the first arm of the zigzag and Timothy and I peered out and down, through the black stems of the trees. At first I could see nothing, but then, just as Lewis swung wide to take the next bend, I saw a flash of bright light, momentarily, it seemed a long way below.

Timothy and I both exclaimed together: "There! There he is!" I added quickly: "There was just a flash a fair way down. It's gone again."

Timothy said: "Wasn't there a sort of woodman's hut away down there? I seem to remember noticing it before. When his lights flashed on, I thought I saw it in the beam."

"Yes, there was," said Lewis. "Damnation."

"Why?"

"I think I know why he put his lights on. Just beside that hut there's a forest track going off. I can't imagine why he should flash his lights unless he wanted to see his way into it. He'd manage it easily enough with a jeep, but whether we can with this car's another matter. We'll see. Well, supposing you tell us what happened, Tim. What were you doing down in the stable?"

"Something woke me, I'm not sure what it was. A cry or something. Did you call out, Vanessa?"

"Yes."

"That must have been it, then . . . But I wasn't sure. You know how you lie awake and wonder what it was that wakened you? Well, I lay and listened for a bit, and I didn't hear anything else, and I thought I must have been mistaken. Then—I don't know . . . I felt sort of uneasy; so after a bit I got up out of bed and went to the door. I thought I heard a door open somewhere, so I opened my own door and looked out into the corridor. But there was nobody there, and then I definitely heard a sound. I thought it was from Vanessa's room."

"That would be when he had my inner door open," I said. "You might have heard something."

"Yes? Well, anyway . . . It occurred to me then that you might have come, Mr March, and you might have been going to Vanessa's room, so I thought I'd just made a fool of myself, and I went back into my own room and shut the door. I was wide awake by that time, so I went across to the window, and just stood looking out. The moonlight was marvellous, and I just stood looking, and—well, thinking . . . and then I thought I saw someone dodging about among the battlements, over by the gate tower. I couldn't see at all clearly, because of the trees beyond, and the shadows, and at first I thought I was just being imaginative, but after a bit I was certain there was someone there. So I shoved some clothes on and ran along to tell Vanessa. I mean, enough odd things have been happening to make me wonder, if you know what I mean."

"We know what you mean," said Lewis.

"I opened the outside door of Vanessa's room to knock on the inner one, but that was wide open, and then I saw the room was empty and the curtains were pulled back all anyhow, and the little door was open. So of course I went out on the roof. I was a bit uneasy now—I mean, you and Vanessa might just have gone for a moonlight walk or something, but I didn't think you'd have left the door open, or the curtain dragged back like that . . . In any case, I kept pretty quiet, and I'd got a fair way round the roof when I saw the car arrive. Everything was dead quiet, so I just stood and waited where I couldn't be seen. Then you went into the castle, and you hadn't been gone two seconds when I saw him move. I couldn't see who it was, but it was Sandor, of course. He was on the roof beside the gate tower. He ran down those steps into the courtyard. I looked over, and saw him go into the stable."

"So," said Lewis, rather dryly, "naturally, you followed him."

"Yes. Well, naturally." Timothy sounded faintly surprised. "I mean, there was the cry I thought I'd heard, and all the mystery and everything. I don't know what I thought about it, I thought it might have something to do with old Piebald. After all, he was a stolen horse, and I suppose he's valuable. But I tell you I didn't think about it at all, I just went in very quietly, and there he was on the floor, ripping the saddle to pieces. I think I asked him what he was up to, and then he went for me. I'm sorry if I've done anything wrong and spoilt things."

"You jumped the gun a bit, but probably not much. He hadn't much time to spare, and I still hope we're not going to lose him. In any case, I'm grateful to you for your care of my wife."

"Oh . . ." Timothy swallowed, then managed, negligently enough, and man to man: "Well, naturally, anything I can do . . ."

"Believe me, you've done plenty. Whether you meant it or not, it was a master-stroke getting that package. Now we know exactly where we are. I really am grateful to you for that."

"Single-minded swine," I said, without rancour.

I saw him grin. Timothy cut in again from behind us. "What was it? Something must be pretty valuable."

"It is. Hang on to your package, Mr Lacy. It's several hundred pounds' worth of cocaine, unless I'm much mistaken."

"Cocaine! Drugs? Dope rings, and all that jazz? Gosh!" Timothy sounded neither shocked nor alarmed, but only excited and vastly pleased. "Gosh! I say, Vanessa, did you get that? Sandor Balog, eh? I knew he was a stinker! And I'm sure there were at least half a dozen packets, maybe more. Big deal."

"As you say," said Lewis calmly, "big deal. And likely to be bigger. It is indeed dope rings and all that jazz. I've a feeling that you two little do-gooders with your long-lost Lipizzaner have got a lead on a ring the police have been trying to break for quite some time, but leave that great thought for later: here's the hut. Hang on."

The Mercedes rocked to a stop. Just by the offside door was a break in the thick trees, where a rutted woodland ride led off, twisting upwards and out of sight through the forest.

"Wait," said Lewis, and swung out of the car. I saw him stoop over the verge, examining it closely in the moonlight which struck brightly down the open ride.

A moment later he was back in his seat and the car was moving again.

"Not that way?" I asked.

"No sign of it. He's making for the main road, thank God."

"I gather you don't think he'll be heading back for the circus?"

"I doubt it. He knows your husband's arrived, and that he—the husband—will certainly raise an alarm as soon as possible. Balog can't possibly go over now with the circus . . . not carrying the stuff, that is . . . He'll reckon that that will be the first call the police will make after we alert them, and obviously the circus will be stopped at the frontier and searched from stem to stern . . . if that's the right idiom for a circus?"

"It does seem to be the only one you know," I said.

"Are you a Navy type?" asked Timothy.

"I once owned half of a twelve-foot dinghy, and I've fallen in twice on the Norfolk Broads. If you think that qualifies me— hold it, he's throwing out the anchors."

Below us the red lights blazed suddenly. The Mercedes slowed sharply to a crawl. Beside the road the trees were sparse, and we could see over and down the next slope. We were half way down the hill. The jeep's brake lights vanished, but flashed again as he turned out on to the bridge.

Lewis said: "We'll wait and see which way he turns. Left, for a bet . . . I don't think he'll risk going back through Zechstein . . . Can you see him?"

"Just," said Tim, craning. "There . . . he touched the brakes again. Yes, he's turning left, away from the village. What d'you reckon he'll do?"

The Mercedes surged forward smoothly. "What would you do, mate?" asked Lewis.

"Telephone the boss," said Tim promptly. "You can't tell me that blighter's anything but a second-class citizen. He'll not be able to make his own decisions."

"That's just what I'm hoping for—that our second-class citizen may give us a lead to higher things; if not to the boss in Vienna, then to the local contact. It could be the best thing that happened, your bolting him like that." I wondered if he was thinking, as I was, of the trip across the frontier which he might not now have to make. "He's got the stuff on him now—he may think he's got it all—and he's been startled by you two into running for it. He won't be in a panic hurry yet, because he won't have any idea we're after him so quickly, and he's certainly not worried that the police can have taken him up yet. The evidence is, from the way he blazed his lights, that he thinks he's still on his own. So we follow and watch."

"If I were him," said Timothy, "I'd ditch the stuff, and fast."

"He well may. If he does, we may see him, with luck."

"Yes, but we've got him anyway, haven't we? Oh, I see, someone else would have to come and pick it up, and you could have it watched?"

It had occurred to me that Timothy was taking with remarkable ease Lewis's change from P.E.C. salesman to armed investigator. But then, I supposed, it was to be expected. Timothy was not unintelligent, and I had offered no explanation of Lewis's original disguise as Lee Elliott; and now Lee Elliott had turned up once more, armed, remarkably well informed, and fully prepared to launch himself without hesitation or question into the wake of a drug smuggler. Timothy must have made some more or less dramatic guess long since.

I was proved right next moment. He leaned forward between the two front seats as the Mercedes swam down the last arm of the zigzag and turned on to the bridge:

"What sort of gun is it?"

"Beretta ·32," said Lewis, and I heard Timothy give a long sigh of pure happiness.

The car swept silently across the narrow bridge, and turned north into the main valley road. Lewis said: "Here we go. We'll move up. Thank God for the moonlight."

The Mercedes seemed to leap forward. Timothy said: "If he does telephone his bosses, surely one can't trace calls from an automatic telephone? Or can the police do that kind of thing?"

"No. But there's a good chance we can find some contact. You mayn't realise," added Lewis, "that in Austria the public telephones are only for local calls. If Balog wants to get Vienna —or anyone outside this *Bezirk* or district—he'll have to do so from a private telephone . . . and private calls can still be traced."

"You mean, if he wants a private phone at this time of night he'll have to ask a friend of his, and so —?"

"Exactly. Any friend of Sandor Balog's who lives so near the border, and who lends his telephone at three in the morning, will bear watching."

"Especially," said Timothy, "if the Hungarian Rhapsody ditches the dope there, too?"

I saw Lewis grin again. "You have the makings," he said, and then fell silent, watching the road.

He was driving fast now, and for a time none of us spoke.

The road followed the line of the river, twisting between river and cliff, now and again running under trees whose black shadow would sweep blindingly over the car like clouds across the moon, then out again into the bright glare of moonlight which seemed to expose us, lightless though we were, like a fly crawling up a window. Once, I glanced back. High, pale, glinting in the moonlight, glimmered the Schloss Zechstein, tipped with gold. Then the car snarled under a railway bridge, swept round a badly cambered corner, and the tyres were whirring over a stretch of bumpy *pavé*.

"There!" said Timothy.

"Yes," said Lewis. In the same moment that Timothy spoke, I had seen it too; a small black fleeing shape, the square shape of the jeep, mounting the long hill ahead of us, barely three hundred yards away. For a moment, as he mounted the crest of the hill, he was exposed against the moonlit sky beyond, and then he vanished.

"As far as I remember there's a stretch of wood a bit farther on," said Lewis. "He should be well into that before we have to expose ourselves on the hilltop, even supposing he's watching for us. And I think there's a village some way beyond the wood. Get the map out, will you, Van? There's a torch in there. Tell me how far the village is."

I obeyed him. "There's a village called St Johann, just beyond the wood. What's the scale?"

"An inch."

"About two kilometres from here, then. No more."

"Good. That may be it. There'll be a phone-box there."

Next moment we in our turn were sweeping over the crest of the hill, and there in front of us, as Lewis had said, was the sprawled darkness of the wood, an avalanche of thick trees spilled down from the mountainside above, and flooding the valley right to the river bank. Beyond this, clear in the moonlight, shone a cluster of white painted houses, and the spire of a village church with its glinting weathercock. Only a glimpse we had of it, and then the car dropped quietly down the hill with a rush like that of the castle lift, and we were whispering through the dark tunnel of the pines. The road slashed through the forest as straight as a footrule, and at the far end of the wooded tunnel we could see yellow points of light which must be the lamps in the village street.

The end of the tunnel hurtled towards us. I think I half expected that Lewis would leave the car in the shelter of the wood, and reconnoitre the village telephone on foot, but when we were two-thirds of the way through the wood, he suddenly switched on the headlights, slowed, and took the village street at a reasonably decorous speed.

It was very short. I saw a little Gasthof with painted walls; a low-browed house brilliantly white for a fleeting second with a great fruit tree throwing shadows against the wall; a well; a row of cypresses against the church wall; a big barn with wood stacked up along its side, and just near it a little café set back from the road, and the glint of glass from the corner where the telephone-box stood . . .

And, in the shadow of the cypresses, the jeep parked.

With a whirl of light and the snarl of our engine we were round the corner, up the hill past the barn, and running over the hollow boards of a wooden bridge.

"He was there," said Timothy, excitedly, "he was there. I saw him."

"I saw the jeep," I said.

"He was in the phone-booth, just as you said," said Timothy.

Lewis didn't answer. Just beyond the village, the woods began again. As the car ran under their shadow, he switched the lights off, stopped, backed off the road, and turned back the way we had come.

He switched off the engine then, and the big car coasted silently down the gentle slope back towards the village. Any noise we might have made crossing the wooden bridge was drowned effectively by the noise of the tributary stream as it rushed down to meet the river. Then we were off the road, and on to the rough grass in the lee of the barn, where fruit trees crowded to make a thicker shade. The big car drifted round through these in a quiet circle, and was brought to a halt into the lee of the barn, facing the road, but hidden from it.

Lewis spoke softly. "Keep down, both of you. If he sees this he'll think it's just something parked here for the night. If he's at all worried about the car he saw, going at a reasonable speed and with its lights on, he'll think it's lost ahead of him. This way, we can see which way he heads when he's finished, and get after him with no time lost. Now, I'm going out to see what he's up to. Don't make a sound, please."

He slid out of the car, shut his door very gently behind him, and all in a moment was lost in the shadows of the building.

I wound down my window silently to listen. I could hear nothing but the sounds of the night. Somewhere near by cattle moved in a byre, and I heard the sweet, deep tone of a bell, stirring as it were in sleep. In the distance a dog rattled a chain and barked once, and then was silent. Nearer at hand, suddenly, a cock crew, and I realised that the brightness of the moonlight was fading and blurring towards the dawn.

Neither Timothy nor I spoke, but as he followed my example and wound down the rear window of the car to listen, I glanced back and caught his eye, and he smiled at me, a brilliant smile of pure, uncomplicated excitement.

Then, shockingly loud in the still air, came the sound of the jeep's engine. It revved up sharply, and we heard the tyres whine forward on gravel and then meet the metal road.

I made a swift gesture to Timothy, but it wasn't necessary. His head had already vanished before I myself ducked down below the dashboard of the Mercedes. I heard the jeep's engine roar up through its gears. For a moment it was impossible to tell, crouched down as I was under the dashboard of the car, which way the jeep was heading. But then the sound burst past the end of the barn, and went by within a few yards of us.

He was still travelling north. As the bridge boomed hollowly under him, I risked a look. The jeep was already invisible in the thick shadow of the trees. He was using no lights.

Next moment the car door was pulled silently open and Lewis slid in beside me. Our engine sprang to life, and we were away on the track of the jeep before he had even shut the door behind him.

"He was going at a terrific lick," I said.

"Wasn't he?" said Lewis. The speedometer swung to the right and held steady.

Timothy's head came between us again. "I suppose you didn't see him hide the drugs in the shadow of the old barn?"

"No. Nor did he hand them to a one-eyed Chinaman with a limp. But the negative result's as good. He still has them on him, and he has his orders. So you might say we have ours."

"Orders?" It was the nearest Tim had come to a direct query about Lewis's activities, and Lewis answered him with a calm assumption of frankness that sounded—at the time—not only convincing but adequate.

"I was speaking figuratively. I'm not a policeman, Tim. I'm a private citizen who's walked into this while engaged in a private—a very private—inquiry for my own firm. The common denominator of the two affairs is Paul Denver, who must have come across some clue to this business in Czechoslovakia (where the circus was recently) and decided to follow it up in his own time. His death could have been an accident, but in the light of what's happened now, I'll take an even bet it wasn't. We can take it that Franz Wagner found out about the stuff in the saddle, and talked in his cups, as they say . . . He must have said just enough in front of Sandor to frighten him, and then Sandor may have found him with Paul, and decided to stop him talking then and there. He may have joined the pair of them, waited till Franzl was pretty well incapable, then tackled Paul, pulled the lamp down, and set the place alight. The fact that Franzl had had a fire before may have suggested ways and means to him. How he caught Paul out, I've no idea . . . but God willing, we'll get it all out of him before the night's out. Sorry."

This as he swerved, with no diminution of speed, to avoid a fallen bough protruding into the road. "So don't go thinking we've any official standing; we haven't. We were merely first on the scene, thanks to you and your horse-rescue act. And you might say I've got my own urgent private reasons now for an interview with Herr Balog . . . But I've done my best to legitimate us—I rang up Vienna from the Schloss Zechstein."

"Vienna?" I said cautiously.

"A man I know," said Lewis. The easy voice was convincing in its very casualness. "This is Interpol's territory, the Narcotics Branch. I don't know any of the Narcotics boys themselves, but I do know a couple of men in Interpol. I once"—this was thrown quickly over his shoulder for Tim's benefit—"I once got involved in Vienna over a client I'd come to see who turned out to have a forged import licence. I rang up this chap from the castle. It was a lightning call, and all I could tell him was that I thought we might be on to the edge of the drug ring. Incidentally, I asked just for the record if there'd been a jewel robbery of any size, and there hasn't, in Munich or anywhere else. So there's that red herring disposed of, and you can keep your sapphire, Van . . . But Interpol seemed to think that Sandor and the circus might well be the set-up they're looking for—and Tim's package proves that it is—so I'm to go right ahead. They obviously can't give us any immediate help, since we don't know ourselves where this chase is going to lead us, but there'll be patrol cars out any minute now looking for the jeep, and the circus will be stopped at the frontier, and the Graz police alerted to be ready for a call from me."

"Then we'd better not lose him, had we?" Tim's voice was a touchingly faithful imitation of Lewis's cool tone, but the excitement came through, and I saw Lewis smile to himself. A sudden affection for them both caught at me irrelevantly, chokingly.

Lewis said: "Officially or unofficially, God help us if we do. Have you got the map, Vanessa?"

"Yes."

"I want to get up as close as I dare behind him without frightening him. I think I know this part of the world fairly well, but keep me posted as we go, will you? When's the next turn-off?"

I crouched over the map, straining my eyes. The light of the pocket torch slid and jerked over it as the Mercedes raced along the winding, badly surfaced road. "We should be out of the trees in a minute. Then there's a stretch of about half a mile along the river. It's clear there; you might be able to pick him up. Then we turn away from the river, and there's a curly bit, back in trees again, I think . . . Yes. Then a bridge, not across the river, but across another stream coming down. Then the valley takes a turn to the left, the west. That's about three miles ahead. There's nothing going off except tracks."

"Tracks? How are they marked? Double lines?"

"Just a minute . . . Single dotted lines, most of them. That means they're just country tracks, doesn't it? Half a second, there's one with double lines. It's very short; it leads down, yes, it just leads down to a farm. We must have passed that already, Lewis. It was just the other side of that wood. I'm sorry. I didn't see it in time."

"Never mind. It's very unlikely that he was making for that."

"Why?" asked Timothy.

"Because then he wouldn't have stopped to telephone, he'd have gone straight on. It was only another mile. Go on, Vanessa."

"The next proper turn-off's about four miles ahead, in a village. It's called Zweibrunn am See, and it looks very small, just a hotel or two and a few houses at the edge of a little lake. This road, the one we're on, goes straight through it along the lake; but there's another branching off to the left in the middle of the village. I can't see clearly enough to see the contours, but the road's terribly twisty, and it must be going uphill. Yes. Yes, it seems to be a dead end, just going off up into the mountain. The main road goes straight on, and after the village —"

"Zweibrunn am See?" said Timothy. "Josef told us about that, remember? He said it was a little tourist place, where the rack railways started."

"Oh, yes, I remember that. Then this must be a mountain

road. Half a minute, I think I can see the railway marked. Would it be a line like a fish's backbone? It goes up to nowhere, as far as I can see."

"The rack railway?" said Lewis. "I know where you mean, then. There's a restaurant place, a Gasthaus, on top of the mountain. It's a fair way up, two or three thousand feet anyway from the floor of the valley. I expect your road goes up to the same place. Ah, thank God we're off that bit of road. If anything should be marked like a fish's backbone, that should."

We shot out of the deep shadow of the woods into the open valley. Under the racing wheels the road seemed to smooth itself and straighten, and the Mercedes went forward like a horse suddenly given the spur.

"And there he is," added Lewis.

And there indeed he was, a tiny, racing shadow, barely a quarter of a mile ahead. To our right the river, smooth here, gleamed like silver, and the road lay in a sort of blurred brightness in the light of the dying moon. Along the water-meadows the faint white haze of early morning was rising from the grass. The cattle stood knee-deep in it. The air pouring through my half open window was pure and cold and sharp with the scent of pines.

"Won't he see us?" Tim's voice was quick with apprehension.

"I doubt it," said Lewis. "We're not in his mirror yet, and he'd have to turn right round and take a good look to see us at all, and he's not going to do that, not at that speed. If he's expecting to be chased at all, he's expecting the police, and they'd be after him with all lights blazing, I have no doubt."

"He must have had a fright when we came after him through the village."

"I'm sure he did, but if we'd been police we'd have stopped then and there. We couldn't help seeing the jeep, and he knew it. He wasn't expecting them to be after him as quickly as that. No, I don't think he has any reason to be apprehensive. I'll try to close up a little, when we get near the turning. We don't want to overshoot him."

"What are you going to do?"

"Heaven knows," said Lewis cheerfully, "play it as it comes, and keep our powder dry."

"With a Beretta —" began Timothy.

"There's the village," I said quickly, "just beyond that curve. I can see the church spire over the trees."

Next moment the fleeing jeep had vanished round the curve.

"Then hold on to your hats," said Lewis. "This is where we close up."

Chapter Eighteen

What! will the line stretch out to the crack of doom?
Shakespeare: *Macbeth*

Lewis had been right. It seemed that Sandor was not worried about the possibility of being followed. As the jeep reached the outskirts of the cluster of houses on the edge of the lake, we were barely two hundred yards behind him. But he gave no sign that he was aware of the following car. He slowed down for the village street, and when he reached the turn-off by the big hotel, he swung left without a pause.

A matter of seconds later we took the turn after him.

The road was narrow and very steep, almost immediately beginning its twisting course up the hillside. As we turned into it our quarry was already invisible, but even above the sound of our own engine the roar of the jeep's engine echoed back as it tore its way up the narrow canyon between the houses.

Lewis made a sound of satisfaction. "This is a push-over. We've only to keep a couple of bends behind him and he hasn't a chance of knowing he's followed . . . though heaven knows it may be a different matter when we get up above the tree line."

"Can you see?" I asked. To me the road was barely visible,

its gravel surface pitted, and streaked with the shadows of the houses, and here and there lost deep in blackness under looming trees.

"Well enough." And indeed the Mercedes was climbing at a fair speed. He added: "I suppose, Tim, that the biter isn't being bit. Anything behind us?"

"Good lord." Timothy sounded thoroughly startled. There was a pause. "No. No, I'm sure there isn't. Should there be?"

"Not that I'm aware of," said Lewis tranquilly, "but it's as well to know. He made a telephone call, after all, and it needn't necessarily have been to warn the people ahead of him. My God, what a road! Van, I suppose it's not the slightest use asking you to look at the map under these conditions?"

"Not the slightest, I'm sorry, I can't see a thing."

"Well, at least there's no need to look for turnings," said Lewis. "There'll be nothing going off this but a chamois track. All we have to avoid is running slap into his rear bumper."

We were clear of the few houses now, and the road, though not quite so steep, was aiming along the flank of the mountain, and had deteriorated into something little more than a track with a gravel surface here and there badly broken. Below us lay the little cluster of houses and the church and the gleaming waters of the small lake. Above us, to the left of the road, the mountain pines were already crowding. The road ran under a dense and overhanging wall of them, like a river under a breakwater. Then at the next upward bend it twisted back and was into them, burrowing immediately through deep forest, only here and there shaking itself clear of trees so that for a few yards the fading moonlight, coupled with the growing light of dawn, could show us the way. Lewis drove with no noticeable hesitation and certainly with no diminution of speed. But I thought it was not a road I would have cared to drive myself even in broad daylight.

As we raced and lurched upwards, bend after bend, I could hear above us the intermittent splutter of the jeep's engine, the sound coming in sharp echoing gusts as trees and rocks flashed between to cut it off. Above the sound of our own motor it came as little more than a recurrent echo for which one had to listen, and to Sandor in the jeep it was to be hoped that the noise of our climb, less audible by far than his, came merely like a periodic echo of his own.

The trees were thinning. The road twisted again under us, and the Mercedes lurched across ruts and swung round another hairpin, running momentarily clear of forest, so that down to our right we got a sudden dawnlit view of the valley bottom tucked between its dark hills. The lake was polished pewter wisping with silver mist. The stars had gone, and the moon hung in the morning air, rubbed and faded like a thin old coin.

The Mercedes came to a rocking halt, and the engine died. Lewis wound down his window and in with the cold damp air came the mountain silence, broken only by the stuttering roar of the jeep's engine somewhere above us.

"The map, please."

I handed it over, folded open at the place. He studied it for a moment, peering close in the light of the probing torch.

"As I remembered. This doesn't go the whole way up. There's some building marked . . . I don't know what, it doesn't look much, but there's a halt for the rack railway, and the road doesn't go any farther. That's about two-thirds of the way up. The remaining third is only traversed by the railway. The rocks up there look pretty sheer; there are crags marked. The railway goes right to the restaurant on the summit; I suppose it tunnels some of the way. Thanks." He dropped the map and torch back on to my knee and started the car again. "I reckon we're almost there now. Wherever he's making for, he'll have to leave the jeep at the end of the road, and that can't be more than about three bends above us. We'll stop while we're still under cover of his engine. Here's a good place."

A matter of seconds later the Mercedes was berthed deep in the shadow of the trees with her nose to the road, and Lewis was giving us our orders in an urgent undertone.

"You'd better both come with me, only for God's sake keep quiet and keep under cover. Stay about twenty yards back and don't break cover until I give you the sign. I may need you, even if it's only as messengers. Here's the spare car key. I'm leaving it here."

At the foot of a tree a clump of toadstools showed sharply in the misty dusk. They had long pallid stems and scarlet caps spotted with white—the traditional toadstools of fairy-tale. A small flat stone lay beside them. As Lewis stooped to lift this and thrust the spare key underneath, Timothy said sharply:

"He's stopped."

"Then come on," said Lewis, and swinging himself up the bank, vanished at a run up through the trees towards the next branch of the road.

We followed him. The going was very steep; smooth enough, clay and rock covered with pine needles, but here and there the rock was loose and there were brambles, so we went carefully, glad of the now steadily growing light.

The next arm of the track was some seventy feet above where the Mercedes was parked. Lewis, above us, was edging his way cautiously out among the thinning trees, to stand there motionless for a moment, hardly visible even to us. The light was in that curious shifting phase between the clear brilliance of moonlight and the brightening day; where it fell most strongly it was a pearled and misty grey, but everything lacked definition; the trees, the track, the grey rock, the hanging woods still above us, looked as insubstantial and vague as those in a badly focused and fading film.

It was even difficult to be sure when Lewis gestured us to follow him, but suddenly the place where he had been standing was empty. Panting a little, I laid hold of a sapling and pulled myself, in my turn, up to the edge of the road. This was empty. But a faint movement in the trees to the other side of it showed where he was heading up towards the last curve before the building. As we followed, I was thankful to realise that our progress was covered by the splash and fall of a small rivulet tumbling down from some spring and losing itself in a stone-faced gully by the roadside.

Lewis was pausing above us once more, but this time after he had beckoned us up he stayed where he was, and as we scrambled to his level he reached an arm down, pulled me up and held me.

The first thing I saw was the building. This was not a house, but simply a small square chimneyless block with a pitched roof of corrugated iron, set at a passing place of the railway—one of those short stretches of double track where trains can pass—and acting perhaps as a shelter for railwaymen or a place for storing materials. Whatever it was, it marked the end of the road. Outside it the track petered out in a cleared space of beaten earth and gravel which looked like a disused quarry, overhung with bushes and ragged saplings. Just at present the place was a tangle of misty shadows, but backed well into it under some hanging creeper that dangled from the rock above, I could dimly see what I took to be the jeep.

There was no light or movement anywhere.

Lewis said softly: "There's the jeep, do you see? But he's not there. I've just seen him a little farther up the hill. He's still alone, and it's pretty clear he has no idea there's anybody after him. I'd bet my last penny he's going up to the restaurant—there's nowhere else to go—and he's going up by the railway. I'm going straight after him. Tim, I want you to take a look at that jeep. Do you think you could immobilise it? Good man. Do so, and have a quick look at the building—I don't suppose for a moment that the stuff's there, he hasn't had time, but you know what to look for. Then come on up after us. You can't get lost if you stick to the railway. Vanessa, you'll stay with me."

We ran across the open piece of road, dodged past the quarry in the shelter of the overhang, and were soon picking our way round the side of the building. Behind us came the faint metallic noises of Timothy tackling the jeep. As we slid past the door of the shed, Lewis tried it quickly. It was locked.

"Well, that saves a bit of trouble," he said. "Not that it'd be there, but no stone unturned is the motto of the P.E.C. Sales Department."

"You've got yourself quite a job, then, considering the terrain," I said dryly.

"You're telling me. I'm praying to all the gods at once that he'll double straight up to the restaurant and dump it there. Here's the railway, and it looks as if there's a path of a sort running beside it . . . Just as well, railways are hellish to walk along. Can you manage it?"

He was already leading the way at a good pace. The question, I gathered, had been no more than one of those charming concessions which make a woman's life so much more interesting (I've always thought) than a man's. In actual fact, Lewis invariably took it serenely for granted that I could and would do exactly what he expected of me, but it helps occasionally to be made to feel that it is little short of marvellous for anything so rare, so precious, and so fragile to compete with the tough world of men.

"Wither thou goest, I will go. Excelsior." I said heroically, going after him up the perfectly easy path beside the track of the railway.

This was a narrow-gauge affair, cutting its way up through rocks and trees in what was, for a railway, a series of frightening slopes. Some of its climbs would, indeed, have been steep even for a motor road. I had not before seen how a rack railway worked. Between the rails, which gleamed like steel ribbons with the constant daily use, was the rack, like nothing more or less than a heavy cog-wheel unrolled and laid flat, a fierce-looking toothed rail standing well above the other two. I supposed that some answering pinion wheel on the engine engaged with the teeth of the rack line and held the train, whether climbing or descending the steepest gradient, at the same controlled and regular speed.

We were still making our way through trees, but these were now more sparsely scattered, and soon gave way to the barer slopes of the higher reaches of the mountain. Visibility was still poor. The only movement I could see was that of the mist which shifted and clung between the scattered pines, and once a big black bird—a jackdaw—which flew clumsily down past us with a startled "Tchack!"

"Where did you see him?" I asked.

Lewis pointed above and ahead to where the line swooped in a lifting curve round a shoulder of white rock. "Just a glimpse of him there. He was going at a hell of a speed."

He himself was setting no mean pace. By the time he had reached the same corner I was beginning to feel a little more genuinely precious and fragile myself, but I was able to get my breath while he left me to reconnoitre the stretch ahead of us. Apparently the line was clear, for he beckoned me up beside him again, and on we toiled. At least, I toiled. Lewis seemed as fresh as a daisy. In fairness to myself I thought that anyone would have been feeling fragile after what I had already been through that night. All Lewis had had to do was to drive two hundred kilometres or so since he had left Vienna . . .

We got along at a fair speed, prospecting carefully at the bends, and making very little sound. Fortunately my shoes were rubber-soled, and Lewis, though not wearing what I had dubbed to myself his spy kit, seemed able to move as quietly as he had done in my bedroom at Oberhausen. And presently there was no need of cover at all, because the mist came down.

I suppose this would in normal circumstances have made the going much more difficult, but it lifted just then the worst of our responsibilities, that of being seen by our quarry; and there was certainly no danger of our losing the way with visibility varying from ten to twenty-five yards. The railway led us as surely as a pillar of fire into the dim heights of the mountain.

But by no means as straight. If we had to keep to its track we had to go the long way round. It was to be assumed that the permanent way would double back on itself to take the easiest course up the mountain, as a road zigzags its way up the steepest slopes. If we had been able to see, we could have short-circuited the curves; as it was, not knowing the terrain, and afraid of where a false step or a false trail might lead us, we were forced to stay beside the rails. There was only one comfort in this, that, unless he knew the mountainside very well indeed, Sandor Balog would have to do the same thing. With any luck we should be following closely on his exact trail, and in his turn, Timothy would be able to trace us.

Lewis said: "It'd be interesting to know what time the first train comes up."

"I do know. The first one's at seven. The porter told us, and there was a sort of time-table in the hall at the hotel, and we checked with that, because we thought that if we were here a few days, we might take the trip." I added, grimly: "It seems funny, doesn't it, to think of coming up here for pleasure?"

He grinned. "You never know your luck."

Then he put his arm out quickly, barring my path, and we stood still. Ahead of us the mist had thinned, smoking momentarily aside to show us a long empty stretch of the mountain ahead. I saw long reaches of pale rock, strewn with dwarfed bushes and drifts of thick tough grass, and here and there a solitary tree, warped and broken by frost, and reaching long fingers down the wind. What bushes there were were low growing, thin-leaved mountain varieties, that seemed to cling against grey rock where nothing should have been able to survive.

But I hardly took this in, except as a quick impression. I was looking at Lewis. That last response of his had been casual, even ironic, but—it came to me like a blinding light out of the thin mist—he had meant it. I knew every tone of his voice, and he had meant it. For me the night had held terror, relief, joy, and then a sort of keyed-up excitement; and drugged with this and sleeplessness, and buoyed up by the intense relief and pleasure of Lewis's company, I had been floating along in a kind of dream—apprehensive, yes, but no longer scared; nothing could happen to me when he was there. But with him, I now realised, it was more than this; more positive than this. It was not simply that as a man he wasn't prey to my kind of physical weakness and fear, nor just that he had the end of an exacting job in sight. He was, quite positively, enjoying himself.

"Lewis," I said accusingly, "can you possibly be *wanting* some rough stuff?"

"Good heavens, no!" He said it very lightly, and it was a lie —a lie he didn't even trouble to follow up, but gave it away with the next sentence. "Is your face still sore?"

217

"My face? I—yes, I suppose it is." I put a hand to the swollen cheek, realising how stiff my bruised mouth was. "I was too busy to think about it, but it must look awful, does it?"

"Not from this side, beautiful. Praise be, this blessed mist's clearing just in time. There's a tunnel ahead."

"A tunnel?"

"Yes. See? It looks like a cave mouth. Heaven knows how long it is. I wish to God we could see a little farther, and take a short cut straight up. Too bad if we had to—ah!"

Even as he spoke there came another of those queer freak currents of air, lifting the mist away. He pointed straight up the mountainside away from the rail track. "There, you can see where the track goes, cutting along above this again. Come on, we'll take a chance on this. Let's by-pass this tunnel."

Luck was still with us. A few minutes' scramble brought us to the place he had seen, with only a few stray trails of damp mist to blur our way, though the crest of the mountain remained lodged in cloud, mercifully blinding our quarry to the pursuit. We had seen no more sign of him and heard no sound, except here and there the trickle and splash of little springs that threaded the rock, and once the bells of sheep still tingling in some small agitation from Sandor's passage ahead of us.

Just before the mist of the upper track swallowed us in our turn, we saw Timothy away below. He waved, then spread his hands in the time-honoured gesture which means 'I found nothing'. Lewis lifted a hand in acknowledgement, then pointed higher up the mountain. The gesture said as clearly, 'Follow us', and the distant figure, wasting no time, turned aside from the railway and began the steep scramble after us.

"Are we going to wait for him?" I asked.

"We can't afford to, but he can't get lost. There's always the railway. That's a good lad, Vanessa. From what you tell me, his father must be a fool. What's he going to do?"

"He's talking of a job with the Spanish Riding School. I don't know what Carmel would say, but I think she'll find he's a bit over her fighting weight now—and of course if she's marrying again she may be too wrapped up in that to bother.

I don't know what the regulations are about getting work here, Lewis? He's hoping his father can help."

"I could probably help him there myself. I know a man — Watch that stone, it's loose."

"You know, I'm beginning to think you're quite handy to have around."

"Time alone will tell," he said, with a glance up ahead through the mist. "We'll see what Tim says, anyway. But if I'd a son like that . . . Managing all right?"

"I'm with you, literally all along the line."

"Meaning we can give it some thought, as soon as this job's over?"

"Why not? I dare say supply can meet demand, as the P.E.C. Sales Department would put it."

He reached a hand back and helped me up a steep patch. "How my other Department would put this I hate to think; but thank God it's turned out to be a police job after all."

"And Tim and I have a perfect right to be here and help as ordinary citizens?"

"Indeed you have. What's more, so have I, in as private a capacity as you like. Mark you, I'm certain there'll turn out to be a Security tie-up, simply because Paul sent for me in the first place; but that's another story, as they say, and by the time we're through with this the Department may well decide to let someone else cope with it. I have a feeling that Lee Elliott has just about exhausted his cover with the Circus Wagner. As for your part in this, even if I weren't quitting, I doubt if my Department could raise much hell over it now."

"A man'll do anything when he's under notice," I said.

"How right you are."

At something in his tone I said quickly: "What d'you mean?"

"What I have to discuss with Sandor," said Lewis, "isn't exactly in the book."

"You mean your 'private reasons' for wanting to catch up with him?"

"Exactly that. Any objections?"

"I can hardly wait."

"I always did say you weren't a nice girl. Damn this mist, it's a mixed blessing. From what I can see of this blessed mountain, they couldn't be better placed. I seem to remember that the place has what's called a 'panorama' . . . that is, it's got a clear signalling-line across at least two borders."

"What are you going to do?"

"Go straight in, if I can, and pick up Balog, his contact, and the dope. The police might have got more information by just watching the Gasthaus, but Balog knows his cover's been blown, so we might as well muscle straight in and pick up the two of them before they clear out of it. Something'll turn up if they take the place apart—and two birds can be made to sing faster than one."

"What do you want me to do?"

"When we get there, stay under cover till I give the word. I may need you to do the telephoning, if I have my hands too full . . . Or, if anything goes wrong, you're to get straight downhill with Tim, get to the car, drive down to the hotel and get them to telephone the police at Graz. Then get the local bobby and a few solid citizens and send them up here. Don't come back yourself." He smiled down at me. "Don't look like that; that's only if things go wrong, but they won't . . . I'm only doing what they call covering all contingencies. Got it?"

"Yes."

"Now we'd better stop talking. Sound carries in mist the way it does over water, and I don't think it can be far now."

"Look," I said.

Away above us, and slightly to the left, nebulous and faint through the fog, like a strangled star, a light suddenly pricked out and hung steady.

"Journey's end," said Lewis.

"Or the start of the fun?" I asked.

"As you say," he agreed, smoothly.

Chapter Nineteen

Heat not a furnace for your foe so hot
That it do singe yourself.

Shakespeare: *King Henry VIII*

The Gasthaus was not a big building. As far as one could see in that misty half-light, it was solid, long, white-washed, with the roof of grey wooden shingles so common in the valleys, and to one side a sheltered veranda made of pine where tables were laid in summer. It lay some twenty yards beyond the final halt of the rack railway. At the other side of the Gasthaus lay a terrace edged with a low wall, a belvedere, beyond which the cliff dropped sheer away for some two or three hundred feet, but on the railway side, from which we approached, it was just an ordinary long low building with shuttered windows and a heavy door, to the side of which were the refuse bins and crates of empty bottles.

It was from one of these windows—the only one unshuttered —that the light came which Lewis and I had followed. Half the outside shutter had been pushed open, and the window with it, back against the wall. It was possible that this had been done deliberately after Sandor's telephone call in order to guide him up the mountain in the mist. There was no other light.

There was a shed at the terminus of the rack railway, a squat oblong building which did duty as a station. We ran forward under cover of this, and dodged through the crush barriers to the misty window at the rear. Between the window and the Gasthaus there was no cover except the stacked boxes and dustbins near the wall. We could see clean in through the open window, and what was going on in the room was as obvious and well lighted as something on a picture stage.

The room was the kitchen. To the left as I looked I could see the gleam of the big cooking stove and above it a row of copper pans and a blue dish hanging. Against the wall opposite the window could be seen the top of a kitchen dresser, shelves of some sort with more of the blue dishes, and some cardboard boxes stacked. The wall to the right, where presumably the door was, I couldn't see. The end of a big scrubbed table jutted out near the window. More important than anything, on the wall beside the dresser, at shoulder height, was an old-fashioned telephone, and near this Sandor Balog stood, talking hard to another man, obviously his host, who stood by the stove with his back to the window. From what I could see of him this was a stocky, heavily built man, with thinnish, greying hair. He had an old overcoat huddled on anyhow, over what I assumed were pyjamas or whatever he wore at night. He was in the act of lifting what looked like a coffee-pot off the top of the stove, and had paused to say something over his shoulder to Sandor.

All this I got in one swift impression, for in that moment Lewis, with a breathed "Stay here", had left my side and was running lightly across the intervening space between the shed and the kitchen wall.

He ran in a curve, keeping out of the direct line of vision, and in a few seconds, unnoticed, was backed up against the wall to the side of the open window, from where, presumably, he could hear what was being said.

I don't know to this day whether the light in that room was electric or whether it came from a lamp, but in the uncertain dawn it seemed very strong, and lit the scene in the kitchen with startling clarity, in spite of the veils and fingers of mist that still drifted between; whereas Lewis, crouched beyond the direct beam of the light, was less than half visible. All the same, I saw the gun in his hand . . .

But at the same moment a movement within the room caught my eye. The second man carried the coffee-pot across to the table, still talking, and proceeded to pour coffee into a couple of mugs. I saw the steam of it rising, and I still remember—overlaying even the excited apprehension of the moment—the glorious sudden pang of hunger caused by the sight of that coffee. I seem to remember that I could even smell it; but that of course was ridiculous. There were still twenty yards of damp grey air between us.

Next moment I forgot the coffee completely. I saw Lewis drift away from the window, along the wall, to try the door.

It was locked; they must have shut it again after Sandor had been admitted. Lewis drifted, ghost-like, back towards the window. I was surprised that they had left that, but perhaps they hadn't noticed, and Sandor, after all, had shown no suspicions of being followed.

Even as the thought crossed my mind, he did notice it. He said something, pointing, then put his mug down on the table, and turned towards the telephone. His host glanced, shrugged, then stepped towards the window. He was going to shut it. Sandor had lifted the receiver, and was waiting. And Lewis— I could see it now— Lewis, incredibly, had put out a hand to hold the window and shutter tightly back against the outside wall.

The man thrust out an arm and yanked at the window. It jerked, and stuck. He pulled it again, and even from where I stood I could hear his irritable exclamation as it still stayed fast open. Sandor gave a half glance over his shoulder, then turned back to the telephone, and said something brief into it, a number, perhaps. The man at the window leaned right out over the sill and reached to one side to pull it to.

Lewis hit him hard over the head. The heavy body slumped across the sill, then slowly slipped back into the lighted room. It had hardly begun to slide before Lewis had gone with it, and was astride the sill, silhouetted sharply against the light, with the gun in his hand.

At the same moment, an upstairs light came on.

I left my hiding-place, and ran like a hare across the intervening space towards the kitchen window.

All hell had broken loose in the kitchen. Lewis, of course, had had to jump blind for the window and, though he must have heard Sandor at the telephone, he could only guess at the situation inside. Quick though he had been, Sandor had had a moment's warning, for even as Lewis jumped for the sill,

Sandor slammed the receiver back and whirled round, reaching for his hip.

But he never got his gun levelled. Lewis shot. He didn't shoot to kill: it seemed he was content with shattering one of the blue dishes on the dresser; but the shot had its effect. It managed to freeze Sandor where he stood, and then at a barked command he sent his gun skidding across the floor to Lewis's feet.

I heard Sandor say incredulously: "Lee Elliott! What in hell's name?"

Lewis cut across him. "Who is this man?"

"Why, Johann Becker, but what in the devil's name—?"

I said breathlessly, from the window: "A light went on upstairs. Someone's awake."

Sandor's face, as he saw me, changed almost ludicrously. It held amazement, then calculation, then a kind of wary fury. "You? So it's you who are responsible for this crazy nonsense? What's she been telling you?"

Lewis had neither moved nor turned at the sound of my voice. He said: "Come on in. Pick up that gun. Don't get between me and Balog." Then to Sandor, curtly: "Who else is in the house?"

"Well, Frau Becker, of course. Look, are you crazy, Elliott, or what? If you'll listen to me, I can —"

"Keep back!" snapped Lewis. "I mean this. It won't be a plate next time." As Sandor subsided, I slid quickly in through the window and stooped for the gun. "That's my girl," said Lewis, still with eyes and gun fixed on Sandor. "Have you ever handled one of those things before?"

"No," I said.

"Then just keep it pointing away from me, will you? It doesn't much matter what happens to Balog, but I want you to keep Frau Becker quiet with that, so —"

Sandor said furiously: "Look, will you tell me what this is about? That girl—the gun—what the hell's she been telling you? You must be crazy! She thinks —"

Lewis said impatiently: "Cut that out. You know as well as I do why I'm here. I've heard pretty well all I want to know, but you'll save yourself a lot of trouble if you'll tell me just where Becker and his wife come in —"

He got no further. The door of the room was flung open, and in surged one of the most enormous women I have ever seen.

She had on a vast pink flannel nightgown with a blue woollen wrapper over it, and her hair was in tight plaits down her back. She may have been roused by Sandor's arrival, but it was the sounds of the first scuffle that had lit her window, and now the pistol shot had brought her downstairs. It hadn't apparently occurred to her that a pistol shot in the night was anything to be afraid of; what she had apparently come to investigate was the sound of broken crockery. I can only assume that she thought her husband and his visitor were indulging in some kind of drunken orgy, for she swept into that room like Hurricane Chloe, unhesitating and unafraid—and poker in hand.

I jumped to intercept her, thrusting the pistol at her much as David must have waved his little sling at Goliath.

She took no notice of it at all. She lifted an arm the size of a York ham to sweep me aside, and bore down on the men. And I'm sure it wasn't the sight of her unconscious husband, or the raging Sandor, or even Lewis's pistol, that brought her up all standing for one magnificent moment in front of the dresser.

"My dish! My dish!" It was only later that Lewis translated for me, but the source of her emotion was unmistakable. "My beautiful dish! You destroy my house! Burglar! Assassin!"

And, poker raised high, she bore down on Lewis.

I'm still not particularly clear about what happened next. I jumped for the woman's upraised arm, and caught it, but in her attempt to wrench herself free of me she sent us both staggering across the room, and for a moment we reeled between Lewis and Sandor.

Lewis leaped to one side to keep Sandor within range, but it was too late.

Sandor went for Lewis's gun hand like a tiger to its kill, and the fight was on.

I didn't see the first stages of that fight; I was too busy with

Frau Becker. If Lewis was not literally to be weighted clean out of the battle, it was up to me to keep the lady out of it. Even he, I supposed, could hardly shoot the woman.

It was all I could do not to shoot her myself. For two or three sizzling minutes all I could hope for was to hold on madly to the hand which held the poker, and prevent my own gun from going off, as I was shaken about that room like a terrier hanging on to a maddened cow.

Then suddenly she collapsed. She folded up like a leaking grain sack, and went down as if I had indeed shot her. By the mercy of heaven a chair was in the way, and into this we went together, me on her ample lap, still hugging her like an avid nursling. I thought at first that the chair had smashed under our combined weights, but it was a rocking-chair, and, tossing like a ship at sea, it shot screeching backwards to fetch up against the door just as Timothy, white-faced and bright-eyed, came hurtling through the window, tripped over the prostrate Becker, swept a mug off the table in falling, and landed on the floor in a pool of coffee.

Whether the sight of a third assassin was too much even for Frau Becker, or whether (as I suspect) the smashing of the mug had finally broken her spirit, she was finished. She opted out of the fight, sitting slumped there in the rocking-chair, massive, immobile, wailing in German, while I picked myself up off her and took the poker from her, and Tim rolled off her husband and took the poker from me, and then together we turned to watch the other hurricane that was sweeping that hapless kitchen.

The two men were evenly matched, Sandor's strength and sheer athletic skill against Lewis's toughness and training. Sandor was still hanging on to Lewis's gun hand, while Lewis fought grimly to free himself and regain control with the gun. At the moment when we turned they were both, tightly locked, hurtling back against the hot front of the stove. It was Lewis who was jammed there, for two horrible seconds; I was too distraught to hear what he said, but Timothy told me afterwards with unmixed admiration that he had learned more in that two seconds than he had in six years at public school—which, I gathered, was saying a lot. I know that as Lewis cursed, I screamed, and Tim jumped forward, and then Lewis's wrist was brought with a crack across the edge of the stove and his gun flew wide, to go skittering under the table, and then he kneed Sandor viciously in the groin and the locked bodies reeled aside and came with a back-breaking slam against the table's edge, while Tim's poker, missing them by inches, smashed down on the stove top to send the kettle flying.

"My kettle!" moaned Frau Becker, galvanised afresh.

"Tim! The other man!" I shrieked, holding her down.

Becker was moving—was even on his feet. Sandor saw him, gasped something, and the man lurched forward.

But not to help. He was making for the telephone. He was at it.

Lewis said, quite clearly, "Stop him!" and somehow swung Sandor away from the table. One of Sandor's hands, those terrible steel hands, was at Lewis's throat. I could see the flesh bulge and darken under the fingers. The sweat was pouring off both men, and Sandor breathed as if his lungs were ruptured. Then instead of pulling away I saw Lewis close in. He had Sandor round the body; he heaved him up and across, somehow twisting his own body . . . then suddenly brought him slamming down across his knee in a back-breaker. Before Sandor could roll painfully free, Lewis had dragged him up again, and I heard the sickening sound of bone on flesh as he hit him hard across the throat.

Becker wasn't lifting the receiver. He was yanking at the wires with all his strength.

I yelled: "Put that down!" and swung the useless gun away from the struggling men, towards Becker. He ignored me. I didn't know if I had a mandate to shoot him, and I doubt anyway if I could have hit him even at that range. I reversed the gun and jumped for him.

I was just too late. Tim had whirled, jumped, and struck, just as the telephone wires came away with a scatter of plaster and a splintering of wood, and poor Becker went down once more, and lay still.

"My dish!" wailed Frau Becker. "My beautiful cups! Johann!"

"It's all right," I said feebly, desperately. "We won't hurt you, we're police. Oh, Tim —"

But there was no more need of Tim and his poker. The fight was over.

Lewis was getting to his feet, and dragging Sandor up with him. The latter's breathing was terrible, and though he still struggled, it seemed to be without much hope of breaking the cruel grip that held him.

I think I started forward, but Tim caught at me and held me back. He had seen before I had what was happening.

Sandor was being forced, step by sweating step, towards the stove.

It was all over in seconds. I still hadn't grasped what Lewis was doing. I heard Sandor say, in a voice I didn't recognise:

"What do you want to know?" And then, quickly, on a sickening note of panic: "I'll tell you anything! What do you want?"

"It can wait," said Lewis.

And with the other's wrist in his grip, he dragged the arm forward, and began to force it out towards the stove where the kettle had stood.

Sandor made no sound. It was Timothy who gasped, and I think I said: "Lewis! No!"

But we might as well not have been there.

It happened in slow motion. Slowly, sweating every inch of the way, Lewis forced the hand downwards. "It was this hand, I believe?" he said, and held it for a fraction of a second, no more, on the hot plate.

Sandor screamed. Lewis pulled him away, dumped him unresisting into the nearest chair, and reached for the gun I was still holding.

But there was no need for it. The man stayed slumped in the chair, nursing his burned hand.

"Keep your hands to yourself after this," said my husband, thinly.

He stood there for a moment or two, getting his breath, and surveying the results of the hurricane: the unconscious Becker, the wrecked telephone, the woman snuffling in the rocking-chair, Tim with his poker, and myself probably as pale as he, shaken and staring.

Timothy recovered himself first. He went scrambling under the table, and emerged with the gun—the precious Beretta—held carefully in his hand.

"Good man," said Lewis. He smiled at us both, pushing the hair back out of his eyes, and seeming suddenly quite human again. "Van, my darling, do you suppose there's any coffee left? Pour it out, will you, while Tim and I get these thugs tied up. Then they can tell us all the other things I want to know."

Chapter Twenty

Emprison'd in black, purgatorial rails.
Keats: *The Eve of St. Agnes*

As Timothy and I emerged from the Gasthaus, it came somehow as a surprise to realise that it was full light. Cloud or mist still hung around the summit of the mountain, so that it was impossible to see into the distance, but the visibility was now two or three hundred yards, and clearing every moment. The air seemed thin, grey and chill, but the coffee had worked wonders for us.

I said: "Have you the foggiest idea what time it is? I didn't put my watch on."

"Nor did I, but I noticed the time by the kitchen clock. It's about half-past four."

"It's a mercy that didn't get smashed, too. Poor Frau Becker.

Lewis seems pretty sure she knows nothing about it, so the worst she'll suffer is being deprived of her husband's company for a bit."

"I'd have said the worst was the bust dishes."

"You've got something there. Oh gosh, and the grass is wet. It's beastly cold, isn't it?"

"What's that to us?" said Timothy buoyantly. "Intrepid, that's us. Archie Goodwin also ran."

I said, a little sourly: "You got some sleep, I didn't."

"There's that," he admitted. "And then you've had a pretty rough time, belting about like that on the roof."

"I suppose you don't reckon you had it rough, being hit on the head by Sandor in the stable? Or do you take that kind of thing in your stride? Look, for goodness' sake, don't try to go at such a speed. This grass is beastly slippery, and there's a lot of loose rock about. And you're carrying that thing."

'That thing' was Sandor's automatic, which Timothy handled with what was to me a terrifying and admirable casualness.

"I hope you do know all about those things?"

He grinned. "Well, yes, it's dead easy. As a matter of fact this is rather a neat little thing. My grandfather had an old Luger left over from the war. The first war. I used to go potting rabbits with it."

"You loathsome boy. I wouldn't have thought it of you."

"Oh," he said cheerfully, "I never got one. Have you any idea how difficult it is to pot at rabbits with a Luger?"

"I can't say that I have."

"As a matter of fact, it's impossible. My hands so far are pretty clean of blood, but at this rate whether they'll stay so or not I just have no idea. I say, that was some scrap up there in the kitchen, wasn't it? Why did he burn Sandor's hand? To frighten him and make him talk?"

"I don't think so. It was a private thing."

"Oh? Yes, I remember, he said so. You mean they got across one another in the circus or something?"

I shook my head. "Sandor hit me."

His eyes flew to my bruised face. "Oh . . . oh, I see." I could see myself that his admiration for Lewis had soared to the edge of idolatry. I thought with resignation that men seemed in some ways to pass their lives on an unregenerately primitive level. Well, I could hardly cavil. I had had a fairly primitive reaction myself to my husband's eye-for-an-eye violence in the kitchen. That I was coldly ashamed of it now proved nothing.

"Well, whatever it was for," said Timothy, "it did the trick. He didn't know how fast to spill the beans. Did you understand any of it?"

"No," I said. Lewis's quick interrogation—since it included the Beckers—had been in German. "Suppose you tell me now."

So, as we hurried down through the damp greyness, he passed the main items across to me. The important thing from our point of view I knew already; that (as Lewis had overheard before he had even entered the room) Sandor had managed to cache the drugs on his way up the mountain, in a tree on a section of railway that Lewis and I had short-circuited. He had in fact got to the Gasthaus only a very few minutes before we did, and had still been telling Becker about his flight with the drugs when Lewis had arrived under the window to listen. This bit of information Lewis could probably have got out of them later: where the luck had come in was in the timing of his own attack through the window. He had managed to delay it just long enough to hear the Vienna number that Sandor had given over the telephone.

So there had not been much difficulty with Sandor. Tim had been right; I had seen for myself that he hadn't known how fast to talk. I supposed that, as well as his immediate fear of Lewis, there was some hope of leniency if he turned State Evidence. And Becker had followed suit. At first he had tried to shout Sandor into silence, but soon changed his tune when he realised how much Lewis knew. And presently the facts—and the names—began to emerge . . .

"Not everything by a long chalk," said Tim, "but then they're only messengers. But Lewis says there'll be plenty to find when the police start to take the Gasthaus apart, and he did get the Vienna number just before Sandor had to slam the phone down.

Of course, the exchange may have put the call through before they knew he'd rung off, and the Vienna end may have got the wind up; but Lewis says they'll hardly fold their tents like the Arabs when it might just be a wrong number, and even if they tried, they couldn't clean up before Interpol starts moving. In any case there'll be more than enough for Interpol to get a wedge in here and there, and crack the ring open. I suppose if Sandor was passing the stuff along through Yugoslavia into Hungary, Interpol could fix a trap up to catch the people at the other end. Or so Lewis seems to think."

Something about his voice as he spoke made me shoot a glance at him. Not quite authority, not quite patronage, certainly not self-importance; but just the unmistakable echo of that man-to-woman way that even the nicest men adopt when they are letting a woman catch a glimpse of the edges of the Man's World. Timothy had joined the club.

I said, not quite irrelevantly: "He thinks a lot of you, too. Now, for heaven's sake, I hope we can find this blighted tree where Sandor said he'd put the stuff."

"The stretch between the tunnels. A lonely, blasted pine. It's just as good," he said joyously, "as a one-eyed Chinaman with a limp. Oh, we'll find it, don't you worry! There's the railway again now."

We had gone at a fair speed down the first long slope of rock-strewn grass, cutting across one of the arms of the rack railway. This went in a wide sweep for some quarter of a mile to the right but curved back again to pass about two hundred and fifty yards below us. We could just see the pale-coloured cutting in the rock where the line lay, and beyond it, the grey distances of morning with one or two darker shapes of bushes looming like ghosts. The grass was soaking. The thick turfs squelched under our feet like sponges, and the longer fronds swung heavy with drops like dimmed crystals which drenched us to the knee. Everywhere among the grey rocks there were clumps of some large violet gentian, just unfurling, a sight which would have stopped me in my tracks at any time but this. As it was, I don't think I even took particular trouble not to tread on them, but hurried on down the hill, intent only on one thing, speed.

We reached the shallow cutting where the railway ran and I jumped down into it with a thump. Behind me Timothy slithered with a rattle of stones and a sharp lamentable phrase as he slipped on the wet grass and almost lost his balance.

"Watch it. Are you O.K.?"

"Yes. Sorry. I wish I'd my boots here. These shoes are murder on wet grass. Can you see the next bit of line below this?"

"Not from here. The slope's more gradual, but we'll go straight on." Once again we ran forward and down over the tufted alpine grass. Timothy was ahead of me now. Visibility was getting better, and the colours even seemed to be growing warmer towards sunrise. On this part of the mountain there were more bushes, thick clumps of juniper and mountain rhododendrons, and sometimes we had to make longish detours round hollows where rocks had fallen in long since, and which were treacherously overgrown with thistles and long grass.

In front of me Timothy faltered, seemed to cast round like a hound at fault, and then stopped. I came up to him.

"What is it?"

"There's no sign of the railway. Surely it should be there?" He turned a dismayed face to me. "Supposing we've lost it? When it went back there to the left it must have been going round the other side of the mountain. We're probably on the wrong bit altogether now . . . It all looks so much alike. I wish to goodness we could see farther . . . If only we could see right down, we'd probably be able to see the lake and the village and everything, then we'd know where we were. D'you think we'd better go back to find the railway and follow it down?"

"Surely not. I don't see how we can have missed it. Wait a minute, Tim, stand still. It's getting clearer every minute . . . Look down there . . . No, farther to the right. That tree, that dead one, with the divided trunk. It's just the way he described it. What d'you bet that's the very one? Straight bang on the target, who'd have thought it? Come on!"

He caught at my arm as I ran past him. "But where's the railway? Between two tunnels, he said."

"Don't you see?" I threw it at him over my shoulder. "That's why we can't see the line . . . We're probably crossing the upper tunnel now. Between the tunnels, the line'll be in a cutting. I'll bet you it's lying down there, just below that little cliff where the pine is. Come on, let's look."

And sure enough, it was. The dead pine stood, split and hollow, clinging to the face of a low cliff, and there, some fifteen feet below its exposed roots, ran the railway. Seventy yards down the track yawned the black exit of the first tunnel, and about the same distance the other way was the entrance to the second. It was the place.

"Bang on," I said. "This is it. How's that for radar?"

"Do you home on to drink as well as drugs?" asked Timothy. "Vanessa March, dope-hound. This is terrific! Let's have a look!"

When, from the top of the little cliff, we examined the tree, we realised that it was not quite as easy to get at as it looked. A six-inch wide track, presumably made by rather athletic goats, twisted its way down towards the permanent way. One had to step off this track, and, hanging tightly to the trunk of the dead tree, reach up to the obvious hiding-place, a hole in the main trunk some five feet from ground level.

"Airs above the flaming ground," said Timothy. "I suppose it would be dead easy for Sandor. Well, you'd better let me have a go. You go on down to the bottom, and I'll chuck the packages to you."

"If they're there."

"If they're there," he agreed, and set his foot gingerly on one of the exposed roots of the tree, while equally gingerly I slithered past him and edged my way down the goat track on to the permanent way.

And they were there. As Tim, clinging like a monkey, managed to shove a hand into the hollow of the tree, I heard him give a barely suppressed whoop of triumph. "I can feel them! I can't get high enough up to see, but there's the corner of one, two . . . yes, three . . ."

"He said there were eight. With the one you've got, that makes seven in the tree."

"There's another, that makes four. I wish I dared stand up. If I hitch myself a bit higher, I may be able to reach down and feel to the bottom of the hollow. Yes . . . five, six . . . and seven. Gosh, if there's one thing I hate it's putting a hand into a hollow tree. You always feel as if a squirrel's going to latch on with all its teeth."

"If Lewis is right it's a wonder that stuff isn't biting. Can you just chuck them down to me one by one?"

"Can do," said Tim, and the first one came flying. It was solidly packed, a nice oblong package with what felt like several smaller packets inside it, flat and neat and wrapped in water-proof and sealed down. A few hundred pounds' worth of dreams and death. I shoved it in my anorak pocket. "O.K., next, please." The others came dropping down in turn and I stowed half away and left the others out for Tim.

"There," he said from above, "I think that's the lot. Was that seven?"

"Yes, seven, don't bother any more, I'm sure he was telling the truth. Watch yourself."

"It's all right, I'm hanging on like a Bandar-log. No, I can feel, there's nothing more. Right, I'm coming down."

It was as he eased his way off the tree roots back on to the goat track that it happened. Either he trod on something loose, or else those treacherous soles slid on the damp rock, for he missed his footing, and came hurtling down to the railway track in a sort of slithering feet-first fall which would have landed him in an unpleasant little drainage gully at the edge of the track which was filled with broken stones, but that in a frantic effort to save himself he managed a wide sprawling leap which carried him clear of it and on to the railway itself.

He landed completely out of control, his feet skidding on the wet gravel, his left foot coming hard up against the metal line, his right just missing this, but being driven against the raised central rail, the rack; and next moment, with a sharp cry of pain, he was sprawling right there at my feet, among the scattered packets which I had laid aside for him.

"Tim, Tim, are you all right? Are you hurt?"

I went down on my knees beside him. He had made no attempt to pick himself up, but seemed to be bunched all anyhow, ungainly over the rails. His head was down. He was making gasping sounds of pain, his body hunched tightly over the right foot.

"I . . . I think it's stuck . . . my foot . . . Oh, God . . . it's broken or something."

"Here, let me see. Oh, Tim!"

It was the right foot. By the force of his slithering, feet-first fall, it had been driven hard forward in to the little space underneath the centre rail where this was lifted clear of the gravel, and the solid sole of his shoe had jammed there, with the foot twisted at a horrible angle.

"Hold on, I'll try to get it out." But wrestle as I would with the shoe, it was fixed tight, and though Tim had now got control of himself and was making no sound, I was afraid how much I might hurt him if I persisted.

"We'll get the shoe undone, then you can try to slip your foot out of it."

The laces, of course, were soaked, and knotted tightly. I said: "We'll have to cut them. Have you a knife?"

"What?" He was very white and there was sweat on his face. He looked as if he might faint. I had once sprained an ankle badly myself, and could distinctly remember the feeling of nausea that came through the pain.

"A knife. Have you a pen-knife?"

He shook his head. "Sorry."

I bit my lip, and tackled the laces. I had nothing with me either, not even a nail file, and Tim's foot was swelling rapidly. After minutes, it seemed, of frantic wrestling, and a broken finger-nail, I gave up. In a very short time it would be impossible to get the shoe off at all without cutting the leather. Scrabbling, searching desperately among the gravel, I found a sharp-edged stone, but after only a few moments' experiment with that I had to give up. It wasn't possible to saw downwards on to the swollen foot.

"I'll try and scrape out some of the gravel under your foot. Perhaps we can loosen the shoe that way." But when I attacked the ground underneath the rail, I found that for this short space, the rail was running over solid rock. There was nothing to be done. And indeed, I dared do no more. For all I knew the foot was broken, and the bitten-down pain in the boy's face terrified me.

All the same it was Timothy who made the only possible suggestion.

"You'll have to leave it. You can't do it yourself. Go and get help. I'll be all right. It's not so bad when we're not hacking at it, and if I turn myself like this . . . yes, that's better. I'll be O.K. Honestly. I—I'll give it time and then try again. And anyway, it's Lewis who matters just now. You'd better do as he said, and send help. Even if you did get me out, you certainly couldn't get me down the hill. Go on, you'll have to leave me."

"Tim, I hate to, but —"

"It's the only thing to do." He was, understandably, curt. "You get down there to the telephone. Take the gun. I dropped it over there."

I picked the pistol up from where it had skidded, and pushed it into his hand. "I don't want it. I'd rather leave it with you. Here. All right, I'll go. I'll be as quick as I can."

"Don't forget the dope. You'd better take the lot. I don't exactly fancy being left stuck here with all that strewn round me, even if I do have a gun." He managed a smile. "Good luck."

"And to you."

And I turned and ran.

As I reached the first scattered trees at the edge of the wood, the sun came up.

.   .   .

It was almost a surprise to find the shed, the jeep, and the quarry exactly as we had left them, except that now the early

237

sun, streaming between the pines, took away some of the ghostly loneliness of the place and made it a picture of golden lights and sharp blue shadows. Thankful for this at least, I ran on past the quarry and down the road into the wood.

The Mercedes was there. And there, under the little stone beside the red and white elfin toadstools, was the key. I let myself into the car, stripped off my anorak with the clumsily bulging pockets and threw it into the back seat, then started the engine. It lit at a touch. The tyres tore at the gravel as it lurched forward, and I turned it gently on to the rutted surface of the track and headed it downhill.

It was a heavy car, far heavier than I had been used to driving, and the bends were sharp. I had to make a severe effort to suppress in myself the feeling of hurry, to crush any feelings of urgency or danger right out of mind, and just concentrate on getting this powerful car down this very unpleasant and difficult little bit of road. What would happen if we met anything coming up, I couldn't even begin to imagine . . .

But at least it was daylight. Already the sun was brilliant, laying great palisades of light between the pines all the way along the road. I wound my window down and let in the sharp sweet air. Birds were singing wildly, almost as if it were spring. I thought I heard a cock crow not far off, and somewhere, nearer still, a train whistled. In spite of myself, my spirits lifted. It was morning, the sun was up, and soon now all this would be over.

The road rounded a thick knot of pines, and below me, now, were the green rolling foothills, with beyond them the glitter of a spire and the glint of the lake. Smoke was rising from a farm chimney, and a little beyond that, behind a thick belt of pines, another column of smoke, black this time, spoke of some factory or other already at work. Seen in the morning light this peaceful pastoral scene couldn't possibly hold any terrors. All I had to do was to go down into the pretty village and go to the hotel. They would be awake there, and moving, and they would speak English, and there was a telephone . . .

I drove carefully round the last bend and headed the Mercedes down the straight slope, past the railway station and towards the village. I remember that the only thing which made me brake and pause as I passed the station was that the gate was open and a man in blue dungarees was sweeping the little stretch of platform between the miniature ticket office and the siding where the train stood with its curious little tilted engine and its three carriages waiting for the day. There would certainly be a telephone here.

He had seen me. He paused in his sweeping and looked up. I stopped the car, and hung out of the window.

"Excuse me, do you speak English?"

He put a hand up to his ear, and then with a sort of maddening deliberation, turned to lay aside his broom before he approached the car.

Torn between the desire to drive straight away and waste no more time, and the desire to get to the first available telephone as quickly as possible, I shoved open the car door, jumped out, and ran in through the station gate to meet him.

"Excuse me, do you speak English?"

I think he said no, and I think, too, that undaunted he started on a flood of totally unintelligible German, but I was no longer listening.

There were two sidings in the tiny station. In one of them stood the train, with its little down-tilted engine ready to push the three carriages up the long mountain track; the other siding was empty. From it, a long shining section of track led up into the pine woods and vanished. And away up in the same direction beyond the first tree-clad foothill, I saw that towering column of thick black smoke that I had taken to be the smoke from some factory chimney; and I remembered two things. I remembered the column of smoke that Josef had called the 'fire-engine', or 'Fiery Elijah'; and I remembered the engine's whistle I had heard three minutes ago.

I whirled on the man, and pointed up the track.

"There! That! A train? A train?" He was elderly, with a drooping moustache, and watery blue eyes which would normally be rayed with laughter lines, but which now were puckered and puzzled and a little rheumy with the early morning. He stared at me with complete non-comprehension. I waved again frantically at the standing train, at the smoke above the trees, at the track, in a sort of desperate pantomime; and then pointed to my wrist.

"The time . . . the first train . . . seven o'clock . . . *Sieben Uhr* . . . train . . . gone?"

He gestured towards the wall behind him where I now saw a station clock marked half-past five, and then, pointing like me up towards the smoke on the mountain, he poured out another flood of German.

But it wasn't necessary. I had seen that the black smoke was indeed marching slowly, but steadily, inexorably, up through the trees, and now, clear above them, over a lovely rounded slope of sunny green, I saw the engine moving, an engine exactly like the one standing here in the station, but pushing only one carriage. Not even a carriage, something that looked like a truck . . .

Beside me, the old man said: "Gasthaus . . . Café," and then proceeded with some pantomime involving the train standing at the platform. If he had been speaking in purest English it couldn't have been more clear. I understood quite well now. The time-table that I had studied had of course only put down the trains scheduled for the tourists, and the first one did indeed run at seven o'clock. No one had seen fit to mention that an engine took supplies up for the restaurant at half-past five.

German or no German, the telephone was not a blind bit of use in this. The old man was still talking, volubly, kindly, and rather pleased to have an audience at this ungodly hour of the day. I believe I said "Thank you", as I turned and left him still talking to the empty air.

By the mercy of heaven there was room to turn. The Mercedes swept round like a boomerang, and I put her at that ghastly little road again with something of the fine careless rapture that I might have indulged in on the Strada Del Sol.

Chapter Twenty-One

The best of all our actions tend
To the preposterousest end.
Samuel Butler: *Satire upon the Weakness and Misery of Man*

At least going up was a little easier than coming down.

I had been too preoccupied during my recent descent to notice much more than the surface of the road, and of course on our way up in the early hours it had been dark and I had been wrestling with the flashlight and the map. Now as I drove the big car like a bomb up that horrible little road I was trying desperately to recall the relationship between road and railway.

As far as I could remember, there were only two places where they conjoined. A few bends above the station the road met the track, and ran along with it for perhaps a hundred yards before a rough escarpment carried the train away to the left along the edge of the mountain, while the road doubled back to the right on the long sweep below the edge of the forest proper. The second place was at the quarry—the end of the road. And that would be my last chance to catch him.

In cold blood, I doubt if I could have hoped to do it in the time, but I was past thinking, past reckoning what might happen if I miscalculated with this heavy car on these violent hairpin bends. She was so heavy and the road was so bad that I could hardly spare a hand for the gears, so I kept her in second and hauled her round the corners with no regard at all for either tyres or paintwork. Afterwards we found a dented hub cap, and a long scrape in the enamel on the offside, but I have no recollection of how they happened. I just drove the big car on and up as fast as I dared, and tried to remember how soon it was that we came to the railway.

The fifth or sixth bend, slightly easier than the others, brought us round facing a long straightish sweep between trees through which the sunlight blazed, strong now, barring the rutted road across and across, like a railway track barred with sleepers. Away at the end of this a cloud of black smoke hung, puffed, trundled deliberately by.

I put my foot down. The bars of shadow accelerated across us in one long flickering blur. And then suddenly the shining rails swooped in from our left to join the road.

For perhaps a hundred and thirty yards track and road ran side by side. The stretch of rail-track was empty, but there was black smoke still hanging in the boughs of the trees. I steadied the car on the narrow road and leaned as far out of my window as I could, straining to see forward up the railway before it curved away into the darkness of the forest, where the cliffs hid it from the sun.

It was there. I saw the square black tail of the little engine with its hanging lamp, lit for the mountain mists, swinging a small vanishing red eye into the tunnel of trees. Above it the appalling black cloud of smoke puffed furiously.

It was going slowly, the gradient so steep there that I could see the roof of the truck beyond the engine, and beyond that again the fretted curve of the rack up which it was hauling itself, cog by cog and puff by puff. There were two men in the cabin, one leaning out to look forward up the track, the other absorbed in up-tilting what looked like a bottle of beer. I shoved my hand down on the horn and held it there.

I'll say this for the Mercedes; she had a horn like the crack of doom. Fiery Elijah must have been making a fair amount of noise, but the horn positively tore the forest apart.

Both men looked round, startled. I leaned out of my window and waved frantically, shouting—futile though it was—the most appropriate German word I could think of: "*Achtung! Achtung!*" After a couple of seconds' agonising pause I saw one of them—the driver—reach out a hand as if for the brake.

Another few yards and my road would bear me away from the railway again. I trod on my own brake and hung out, waving more frantically than ever.

The driver found what he had been reaching for, and pulled. It was the steam whistle. The engine gave a long, friendly *toot-toot*. The other man lifted his beer-bottle in a happy wave. The engine gave a third and last toot, then the forest closed in behind it and it was gone.

Why I didn't run the Mercedes off the track I shall never know. I just managed to wrench her nose round in time, as the road bore away from the railway, and along under the skirts of the forest. I still had the one chance, and through my exasperated fury I realised that it was a fairly strong one. Even with the extra distance she had to travel the Mercedes would surely be more than capable of reaching the railwaymen's hut in time for me to stop the train . . .

She had certainly better be. All that this last little effort had done was to make the train announce its coming to Timothy, and, however the boy had felt before, he would certainly be sweating it out now, trapped up there with the approaching engine mounting the hill puff by puff towards him.

Mercifully with every yard, with every curve, I was more used to the car, and with every curve the gradient eased and the bends grew wider. I have no idea at what speed we took the last six or seven stretches of that road, but it seemed to me as if the whole hillside was reeling past me and down in a long flickering blur of sun and shadow, and then suddenly we were up round the last bend, and in front of us was the space with the railwaymen's hut, and the shining stretch of track beside it.

I couldn't see the train.

The Mercedes zoomed along the last straight stretch like a homing bee, and fetched up with shrieking tyres and rocking springs within a yard of the railwaymen's hut. I jumped out of her and ran forward on to the line.

I had done it. Below where I stood I saw the smoke, perhaps a quarter of a mile away, where the engine chugged its stolid, unexcited way up the rack. They could not, of course, yet see me; would not see me until the engine broke from the cover of the trees some fifty yards away. I hoped they would, even at that early hour, keep a sharp look out forward. If I sounded the horn again, perhaps, or waved something . . . if I had had anything red . . .

But I had seen how they had reacted to that horn before. And to my waving. In my mind's eye I saw it all again, repeated here with horrible finality: the horn, my waving, the cheerful responsive waves of the two men, and then the engine going past me and the red swinging lamp disappearing round the far curve . . .

The red rear lamp. There was at least the Mercedes.

I ran back to the car. As I jumped in and slammed the door, the cloud of black smoke burst above the trees to my left and I saw the blunt nose of the truck. I switched the car's lights full on, shoved her into gear, and drove her as hard as I could for the railway lines.

As her front wheel hit the rail, I thought at first she was going to be deflected, but the tyre bit, clung, climbed, and then lurched over, the rear tyre after it, and the Mercedes stopped once more, her two near wheels over the offside track, her rear lights, brake lights and all blazing what message they could towards the approaching train. For good measure I jammed my hand down hard over the horn as well, while I leaned across and with my free hand shoved open the offside door. I would give them till twenty-five yards, and then I would be out of the car like a bolting rabbit. If they didn't see the car I could do nothing to save her, but I didn't imagine that the train could come to very much harm; locked on its cogs it would probably weather the collision.

Why had I thought the engine slow? It seemed to be roaring up the hill all of a sudden with the speed of a crack express train. The black smoke burst and spread. I could hear the heavy panting of the little engine, great beats of it, above the blare of my horn. Thirty-five yards. Thirty. And I thought I heard a shout. I let go the horn and started my dive towards the open door. There was the clang of a bell, and a shrill furious whistle from the engine. I flung myself out of the door and ran clear.

With a horrible shriek of brakes, another toot and a flurry of angry shouts, 'Fiery Elijah' came to a standstill about seven yards behind the Mercedes.

The two men leaped down out of the cabin, and advanced on me. A third—there had been a guard after all—swung down from the truck. The co-driver was still holding the beer-bottle, but this time as if it were a lethal weapon, which, from his face, he looked fully prepared to use. They both started to talk at once, or rather to shout, in furious German—and I can think of no better language to be furious in. For a full half-minute, even had I been Austrian myself, I couldn't have got a word in edgeways, but stood there helpless before the storm, my hands out in front of me almost as if to ward off a blow from the beer-bottle.

At last there was a pause, on a fusillade of shouted questions, not one word of which I understood, but of which the gist was naturally very plain.

I said desperately: "I'm sorry. I'm sorry, but I had to do it. There's a boy on the line, on the line higher up, farther along, a boy, a young man . . . A—a *Junge*, on the *Eisenbahn*. I had to stop you. He's hurt. Please, I'm sorry."

The man with the beer-bottle turned to the one beside him. This was a big man in dark grey shirt, old grey trousers, and a soft peaked cap; the driver. "*Was meint sie?*"

The driver snapped a couple of sentences back at him and then said to me, in a ghastly guttural, which at that moment I wouldn't have exchanged even for a Gielgud rendering of Shakespeare: "Is that you crazy are? There is no young on the line. There is on the line an auto. And why? I ask why?"

"Oh, you speak English! Thank God! Listen, *mein Herr*, I'm sorry, I regret I had to do this, but I had to stop the train —"

"*Ach* yes, you have the train stopped, but this is a danger. This is what I will to the police tell. My brother, he is the police, he will of this to you speak. For this you must pay. The Herr Direktor —"

"Yes . . . yes . . . I know. Of course I'll pay. But listen, please, listen. It's important, I need help."

All of a sudden, he was with me. The first reaction of his own shock and anger had ebbed momentarily and let him see what must be showing clearly in my face, not only the swollen bruises, but the strain of the night and my terror for Timothy. Suddenly, in place of an angry beefy bully, I found myself confronted by a large man with kindly blue eyes who regarded me straightly, and then said: "There is trouble, yes? What trouble? Why do you my train stop? Say."

"There is a young man, my friend, he fell on the line up there. His leg is hurt." I pantomimed it as best I could. "He is on the railway line. He can't move. I was afraid. I had to stop you. Do you understand? Please say you understand!"

"Yes, I understand. This young man, is he wide?"

"Not very. As a matter of fact, he's quite thin." I caught at myself. "Is he *what*?"

"Wide." He waved towards the upper track. "This is not right, no? In German, *weit*. Is he wide from here?"

"Oh, *far* . . . Is he *far*! Not very, only a little farther—more far—beyond the tunnel, the first tunnel." How the devil did one pantomime a tunnel? Frantically I tried, and somehow he seemed to understand even this—or else perhaps he by-passed the explanation and was content to act on what he certainly had understood.

"You will show us. We shall now the auto off bring."

It didn't seem to take those three burly men long to shift the Mercedes. I made no attempt to help them. Reaction was hitting me, and I simply sat down on a pile of sleepers and watched without seeing them as they strained and rocked at Lewis's poor car until at last she came clear and was shoved away from the rails. Then between them, almost as if I were a parcel, they heaved me up into the cab of the engine, and with a positively horrifying eruption of vile black smoke and a straining shriek of cog-wheels 'Fiery Elijah' resumed his slow ascent.

I suppose there is something in every one of us, boy or girl, which at some level, or at some age, makes us want to drive an engine. Now that my apprehension had lifted, I almost enjoyed the ride, and indeed, of all the engines that I have ever seen, this one, though certainly not the most exciting, was the most entertaining, being a nineteenth-century relic and possessing all the almost forgotten charm of the nursery trains of childhood. Its steep tilt, so absurd and pathetic on the flat, meant that on the upward climb the floor of the cabin was level. The tank was squat and black, the smoke stack enormous and funnel-shaped, and every available inch of the engine, it seemed, was festooned with tubes, wires, and gadgets of unimaginable uses. The paint was black, the wheels scarlet, and the whole thing was smelly, dirty, diabolically noisy and entirely charming. If the baroque age had produced a railway engine, this would certainly have been it.

We were soon clear of the trees, and ahead of us in the morning sunlight the line lay like a deeply clawed triple scratch through the white limestone. We threaded our way along a naked curve of hill clothed with the tufted turf thick with gentians, and then the line ran into a cutting, and rough perpendicular walls of rock crowded us from either side to a height well above the roof of the truck; so closely indeed that I shrank back into the cabin, but not before I had seen, some hundred yards ahead of us, the black mouth of the first tunnel.

I shouted as much, quite unnecessarily, to the driver, who grinned and nodded and made signs that I should keep back in the cabin and under the cover of the roof. He could have spared himself the pains. I had ducked already. The tunnel looked singularly uninviting and not nearly big enough, but through it we went, with what I'll swear was not more than a foot to spare.

It was quite a long tunnel, and if I had been digging it myself I would certainly not have dug it any bigger than need be, but going through it was like being threaded like cotton through a narrow bead. In the tight, heavy blackness the din was horrifying. The enormous beating bursts of smoke from the engine, magnified a thousand times, volleyed and echoed back from the sides of the rocky tube. And there was the steam. Within twenty seconds of our entering the tunnel the place was like a steam bath, and a dirty one at that. It was enough to beat the wits out of anybody, and when the driver put his hand on the throttle and reduced speed I could—Tim or no Tim—almost have screamed at him to go on as fast as he could out of this inferno of heat and blackness and shattering noise. I am certain that no guard—even if his eyes would have adjusted to the sudden light after this utter blackness—could have kept a look-out forward and been in time to see Timothy on the line.

Light was running now through the filthy clouds of smoke that lined the tunnel. One could see the fissures and bulges of the rock. It grew stronger. The air cleared. As I pulled myself up to look, sunlight struck suddenly straight ahead of us, and then our front, the nose of the truck, was out in it, and the sharp edge of black shadow was sliding back over the shining roof towards the engine.

A bell clanged, sharply. Again I heard the sliding screech of brakes, and the scream of steel on steel. The train stopped with a great puffing sigh, then a long hiss of escaping steam which shut off sharply, leaving the engine simmering gently in the still mountain air like a steam kettle.

I put a hand to the rail and vaulted down to the gravel.

"Tim, Tim, it's me! Are you all right?"

He was still there, his foot still wedged under the rack. When I ran up to him he was slowly uncurling himself from what looked like some desperately cramped position, and I realised that, hearing the train, he had tried to cram his long body down between the rack and the rail, hoping that if the worst happened and the train ran over him unseeing he might escape one or other of the wheels. That he could not have done so was quite obvious, and this he must have known. If he had been white before, he now looked like death itself, but he pulled himself back into a sitting position and even managed, lit by relief as he was, some sort of a smile.

I knelt beside him. "I'm sorry, you must have heard it coming for miles. It was the best I could do."

"A bit . . . over-dramatic, I'd say." He was making a magnificent effort to take it undramatically, but his voice was very shaky indeed. "I felt like Pearl White or somebody. I'll never laugh at a thriller again." He straightened up. "Actually, I'd

248

say it was a pretty good best. Transport and reinforcements for Lewis, all at one go. Did they let you drive?"

"I never thought to ask. Maybe they'll let you, on the way down."

I put an arm round him and helped to prop him up. The men had run up the track with me, and, though I could see Timothy was trying to pull himself together still more and dig out his fund of German for explanations, there was no need. The driver and guard lost no time in starting efficient work on his shoe, and in a matter of seconds had the laces cut from the now badly swollen foot and were beginning, very gingerly and gently, to cut the leather of the shoe. The co-driver was also a man with a fine grasp of situation. As the others started work he vanished back in the direction of the truck, and now appeared with a flat green bottle which he uncorked and presented to Timothy with a phrase in German.

"The flask, she was for the Gasthaus," explained the driver, "but Johann Becker he will not speak no."

"I'm dead sure he won't," said Tim. "What is it?"

I said: "Brandy. Go on, it's what you need, and for pity's sake don't drink it all. I could do with half a pint myself."

And presently, as the brandy went round—the railwaymen had evidently felt the strain of the recent excitement quite as much as Timothy or I—Tim's foot was drawn gently out of the wreck of his shoe, and willing hands were half carrying, half supporting him back towards the waiting train.

The truck, where they deposited us, was stacked high with stores, but there was just room to sit on the floor, and the doors (I noticed) could be locked.

"We will now," said the driver to Timothy, "take you straight up to the Gasthaus. No doubt Frau Becker will attend to your foot, and Johann Becker will give you breakfast."

"If you have the money," said the guard sourly.

"That is no matter, I shall pay," said the driver.

"What are they saying?" I asked, and Tim told me.

"Well, I wouldn't guarantee the breakfast," I said, "but actually, we could hardly do better than go straight up with them. I can't think of a better way to bring those thugs down to the village than in this truck. And we've even provided the escort of solid citizens Lewis asked for—the driver's the police-man's brother, and they're none of them great friends of Becker's, from the sound of it. Do you suppose you could explain to them before we start, that when we get up there, they're going to find my husband with the Beckers and another man at the other end of an automatic pistol, and that they, as solid citizens, must render him every assistance and take the whole boiling down and hang on to them till the police come?"

"Well, I could try. Now?"

"If you don't tell them before we start you'll never make yourself heard. 'Fiery Elijah' rather makes his presence felt. Go on, have a bash—that is, if you've got the German to tell them with?"

"O.K., I can but try. I wish I knew the German for cocaine . . . What's the matter?"

"The cocaine," I said blankly. "I'd forgotten all about it. I left it in my pockets in the back of the car."

"*You what?* Well, if the car's locked —"

"It isn't. In fact, the key's still in it," I said.

We stared at one another for a long moment of horror, then suddenly and with one consent began to laugh, a weak, silly sort of laughter that turned to helpless giggles, while our three friends stood over us looking sympathetic and filling in time on the bottle of brandy.

"Well, I only hope," said Timothy at length, dabbing his eyes, "that you've got the English to explain to Lewis in."

And so it was that Lewis, sitting on the edge of Frau Becker's kitchen table drinking Frau Becker's coffee and holding Frau Becker, her husband, and her husband's friend at the business end of the Beretta, was relieved of his vigil, not by the cold-eyed, tight-jawed professional men he must have been expecting, but by a peculiarly assorted gang of amateurs, two of whom were slightly hilarious, not to say light-headed, and all of whom smelt quite distinctly of Herr Becker's brandy.

·　　·　　·

It was some four hours later.

The cocaine had been recovered, our prisoners had been delivered to the correctly tight-jawed, cold-eyed professionals, and the battered Mercedes had somehow brought us all home to the Schloss Zechstein where Timothy's foot had been fixed up by a doctor who had talked soothingly about sprains and a day in bed; and I had had a bath and (feeling genuinely fragile now) was floating in a happy dream of relief and reaction towards the bed, while Lewis dragged off his wrecked clothes and fished in his case for a razor.

Then I remembered something, and stopped short.

"Lee Elliott!" I said. "That's who they'll think you are! Did you register as Lee Elliott?"

"I didn't register as anything. There was a female in the hall who bleated something at me, but I just said 'Later' and pressed the lift button." He threw his sweater into a corner and started on his shirt buttons. "Come to think of it, the porter did start in the other direction with my case, but I took it from him and came along here."

"Lewis—no, just a minute, darling . . . *Hadn't* you better go down straight away and get it cleared up?"

"I've done all the clearing up I'm doing for one day. It can wait till morning."

"It's morning now."

"Tomorrow morning, then."

"But—oh, darling, be serious, it's after ten. If anyone came in —"

"They can't. The door's locked." He grinned at me, and sent the shirt flying after the sweater. "If we need to reopen communications, we can do so later—by telephone. But for the present, I think it can come off the hook . . . There. First things first, my girl. I want a bath and a shave, and—didn't you hear what the doctor said? A day in bed's what we all need."

"You could be right," I said.

Epilogue

His neigh is like the bidding of a monarch, and his countenance enforces homage.

Shakespeare: *Henry V*

The hall was white and gold, like a ballroom. The huge crystal chandeliers, fully lit, glowed as ornaments in themselves rather than as light, for the September sunshine streamed in through the great windows. Where there should have been a polished dance floor there was a wide space of sawdust and tanbark. To begin with it had been cleanly raked into a pattern of fine lines, but the hoofs had beaten it into surfy shapes as the white stallions paced and danced and performed their grave beautiful patterns to the music.

And now the floor was empty. The five white horses had filed out through the archway at the far end of the hall and vanished down the corridor towards their stable. The Boccherini minuet faded into a pause of silence.

The packed alcoves of people craned forward. Every seat was full, and in the gallery people were standing, trying to see past one another's shoulders, the movement and the whispering and the crackling of programmes filling the sunlit pause. Beside me Timothy leaned forward, taut with excitement, and on my other side sat Lewis, relaxed and sunburned, reading the programme as if nothing else mattered in the world but the fact that on this Sunday morning in September the great Neapolitano Petra was back at the Spanish Riding School, and the Director himself was going to ride him, and all Vienna had come to see.

Beyond the archway the lights grew to brightness. The half-door opened. A horse appeared, his rider sitting still as a statue. He paced forward slowly into the hall, ears alert, nostrils flared, his movements proud and cool and soberly controlled, and yet somehow filled with delight.

There was no hint of stiffness now. Round he came, the dancing steps made even more beautiful by their silence: the beat of the music hid even the muffled thudding in the sand, so the high floating movements of the hoofs seemed to take the stallion skimming as effortlessly as a swan in full sail. The light poured and splashed on the white skin where the last shadows of black had been polished and bleached away, and his mane and tail tossed in thick fine silk like a flurry of snow.

The music changed: the Director sat still: the old stallion snorted, mouthed the bit, and lifted himself, rider and all, into the first of the 'airs above the ground'.

Then it was over, and he came soberly forward to the salute, ears moving to the applause. The crowd was getting to its feet. The rider took off his hat in the traditional salute to the Emperor's portrait, but somehow effacing himself and his skill, and presenting only the horse.

Old Piebald bent his head. He was facing us full on, six feet away, looking (you would have thought) straight at us; but this time there was no welcoming whicker, not even a gleam in the big dark eye that one could call recognition. The eyes, like the stallion's whole bearing, were absorbed, concentrated, inward, his entire being caught up again and contained in the old disciplines that fitted him as inevitably as his own skin.

He backed, turned, and went out on the ebb-tide of applause. The grey half-door shut. The lights dimmed, and the white horse dwindled down the corridor beyond the arch, to where his name was still above his stall, and fresh straw waiting.

MARY STEWART

WILDFIRE AT MIDNIGHT

It was midnight on Skye when a young crofter's daughter was ritually murdered on the bleak mountainside. Very soon Gianetta Brooke finds herself enmeshed in a web of rising fear and suspicion on the beautiful island . . .

CORONET BOOKS

MORE BESTSELLING TITLES BY MARY STEWART
FROM CORONET BOOKS

All these books are available at your local bookshop or newsagent, or can be ordered direct from the publisher. Just tick the titles you want and fill in the form below.

Prices and availability subject to change without notice.

CORONET BOOKS, P.O. Box 11, Falmouth, Cornwall.

Please send cheque or postal order, and allow the following for postage and packing:

U.K. – 55p for one book, plus 22p for the second book, and 14p for each additional book ordered up to a £1.75 maximum.

B.F.P.O. and EIRE – 55p for the first book, plus 22p for the second book, and 14p per copy for the next 7 books, 8p per book thereafter.

OTHER OVERSEAS CUSTOMERS – £1.00 for the first book, plus 25p per copy for each additional book.

Name ....

Address ....

....